KING OF NONE

BOOKS BY KATHRYN ANN KINGSLEY

The Masks of Under series
King of Flames
King of Shadows
Queen of Dreams
King of Blood
Queen of All

The Iron Crystal series
To Charm a Dark Prince
To Bind a Dark Heart
To Break a Dark Cage
To Love a Dark Lord

For a full list, visit www.kathrynkingsley.com

KATHRYN ANN KINGSLEY

KING OF NONE

SECOND SKY

Published by Second Sky in 2024

An imprint of Storyfire Ltd.
Carmelite House
50 Victoria Embankment
London EC4Y 0DZ
United Kingdom

www.secondskybooks.com

Storyfire Ltd's authorised representative in the EEA is Hachette Ireland
8 Castlecourt Centre
Castleknock Road
Castleknock
Dublin 15 D15 YF6A
Ireland

ISBN: 978-1-83618-352-5
eBook ISBN: 978-1-83618-351-8

ONE

The sun was rising in Under for the first time in five thousand years.

The chirping insects in the trees had gone silent.

The world itself was holding its breath and waiting to see what might happen next.

Turning, Lydia squinted against the light, raising her hand to shield her eyes as she watched the horizon turn ruddy amber. She had become so used to the dark. She never thought she'd see sunlight again. It was beautiful, and it was horrifying for what it represented.

The Ancients were free. All bets were off.

Aon turned her back around to face him, clutching her to him in desperation. "Forgive me, *please*, forgive me. I could not let you remain at the bottom of that cursed lake. I could not let you be taken from me a second time. I could not live in this world without you. I—I burned it all down."

Reaching up, she cradled his head in her hands and kissed him. Tears still slipping down his cheeks, his lips were salty with them. He leaned into her touch like a man who felt this was goodbye.

She had no platitudes to give him. There was nothing she could say to make this better. She had no idea what was going to happen. Saying it was okay would be a bold-faced lie.

"There's nothing to forgive. I love you." That was all she could do. All she could say. "No matter what happens, Aon. I love you." She tilted his head down to rest his forehead against hers. He was still holding her to him like a vise as if something was about to tear her away.

Maybe something was.

His shoulders caved in toward her, as he seemed to be pressed by some heavy emotional weight. "For those words, I would destroy all of creation again and again. I will cherish them until the day they finally allow me to die. I thank you for that gift, Lydia, my dragonfly. But I know it shall not last. Your heart will change."

"What?" She tilted his face back to look at her. His spilled-ink eyes were searching hers, flicking back and forth.

"They are coming for me, my love. And when they do—" He cringed, his face contorting in a painful memory. He turned away from her as if ashamed.

"What? What'll happen?" She turned him back to her. He was trying to hide from her. The light from behind them—of the rising sun—was growing bright as it peeked up over the horizon. She felt as though it was a ticking clock. The sands of an hourglass were running low.

"I am not human."

"None of us are."

"*No.*" He held on to her, his fingers twisting in the fabric of her wet coat. "I was *never* human, Lydia. They... they made me. I am their Adam. I am their golem. I am—I never was—like *you.*"

"What?"

"All of you—all the rest of you, even Edu and the others, were taken from Earth. They were all once human. I... never was. I am their only son. They made me. They will come for me. They will never let me be free." With a half-hearted laugh, he sighed. "I buried that memory deep. But now, with the rising sun, it seems it's returned to ruin me."

Like ice, a shiver ran down her spine. That was what they had called him—their only son. Numbly, she shook her head. "I don't care. I don't care what you are."

His laugh that time was cruel. "You will. You will when you see what they made. I never wished to rule this world, Lydia. I never wished to be the King of All. I never wanted the throne. I never desired anyone to kneel at my feet." He was becoming frantic, terrified. She had never seen him like this. Not once.

"Aon, you're scaring me."

"Good. You need to run."

"I—no, Aon—"

He interrupted her, trying to say as much as he could in the little time they had left. "The royals all hate me and suspect me for good reason. They all despise my very nature and have done so long before the Great War. Their passionate hatred runs deeper than any of my misdeeds. Their mistrust was intrinsic. You noticed, surely you did."

Yes. She had. Everyone hated Aon, and she couldn't ever figure out why everyone who came out of the lake of blood had a deep aversion to him. She could only nod.

"But they could not remember *why* they despised me. They could not remember why they would rail against me at every turn. They could not remember the old days. I do not blame them—I chose not to remember either."

Lydia swallowed the lump in her throat. "Why, Aon?"

A weary kind of acceptance came over him as he looked up at the sunlight behind her. All fear faded away from him. A man on the gallows, accepting the noose even as it slid around his neck. "I do not want the throne, for that is what I gave up so long ago."

There was an odd sound behind her. It was like a weird, quiet roar. She turned her head, and her eyes went wide.

There on the horizon, creeping closer, was a cloud. Or a wave. It took her a long moment to realize what she was looking at. The shifting gray and beige mass seemed pushed forward or rolling over itself as it moved closer. It didn't look like it was moving that fast, but it was far away. It was a sandstorm.

"Aon, we have to go." She twisted in his grasp and reached out to take his hand. He slipped away from her and backed up a step. She turned to look at him, confused and afraid. "Aon?"

"They have already come for me." His voice was a horrified whisper. He winced as if something had stabbed him. "Of course, they have. You must run." His face warped in pain again, and he shuddered. He put his hand to his face as if an icepick had been driven home through his temple. "They speak to me, even now."

Lydia took a step toward him, reaching out. No, they couldn't take him too. He growled and with both hands snatched her by the shoulders. His eyes met hers, and she watched as he changed. Nothing about him warped. His face was the same. But like an actor playing a role...

Aon was gone.

The fear drained from his face, and he was smiling down at her. Faint and gentle. Like a slow cloud passing over the moon, she watched another man take his place. There was no wicked glee in his eyes. No twisted smirk. This man was looking at her, awed and amazed, as if he had never seen her before.

He lifted his metal hand to touch her face, and he recoiled from the sight of his own clawed gauntlet as if it were foreign to him. His face suddenly drew up in agony, and he grabbed his head with both hands. "No! No! Do not touch her! She is not *yours!*"

"Aon, please—what's happening?"

"Run, my dragonfly. Run. You must go!"

Lydia took another step toward him, and this time, he pushed her away with both hands. She staggered and nearly fell to the ground.

He was looking at her with such twisted agony and fear, her heart shattered in her chest. "You have come to love a broken thing. A mirror with so many pieces missing—so many shards that I thought I had lost. But now, I remember... they were never there. They could not make me whole. They tried. But even they cannot make a *soul*. So instead, they hold me together. They plug the pieces. They will possess me to make me whole, Lydia. You must run to the farthest, darkest corner of this world!"

"Hide from the Ancients? This is their world. There's nowhere I can go!"

Aon took another step away from her, toward the oncoming sandstorm. Even as she watched, it was as though he were struggling to keep hold of himself. That someone else was surging forward to take control. He placed his hands over his face, let out a low moan of pain, curled in on himself, and then stilled. As he straightened, he let his hands calmly fall to his sides.

The look on his face was unlike any she had ever seen from him. It was not just dark, but... regal. *Noble.* A small smile decorated him as he watched her with a calm fascination.

This man had a face of stone, free of the fast and vivid expressions she had known from Aon.

Whoever he was... this was not the warlock she knew. Power came from him in waves—a feeling that made her skin crawl. But this wasn't the velvet knife in the darkness. This was cold iron.

He took a step toward her slowly, and she found herself rooted to the spot. She felt so small in front of this man, whoever he was, whatever had become of him. The feeling that filled the air around him and left her stunned like a deer in the headlights.

"No, you must not run from them." His voice was a low rumble. He closed the distance between them and lifted his flesh-and-blood hand to run the backs of his fingers down her cheek. She shuddered at the touch. "You must run and hide from *me*. For once I have you, I fear I will never wish to let you go."

"Aon—" His lips against hers silenced her. Her stomach fell off a mountain at the embrace. She had kissed him a hundred times, but he felt like a stranger. Aon was passionate, a fiend with an insatiable hunger. What she felt now was... control. Cold and hard and demanding. Bending her to his will, even as she felt her stomach twist in an excitement and fear she knew quite well.

Aon took in a blaze of black fire. This man took in the crush of unyielding force.

He slowly broke the kiss, his lips still curled into a smile as his warm breath washed against her. He drifted his face slowly to her ear to whisper to her. She was shivering, trembling, and overwrought.

His voice was like cold water down her spine.

"So... run and let me chase you..."

With that, he stepped away, pacing backward. She had been so frozen, so afraid, so caught up in what had happened to him, that she hadn't noticed that the storm was on top of them now. She looked up at the wall of sand as it threatened to break over them like a wave.

Aon—or whoever he was now—lifted his arms at his sides as if to accept it. As if calling her to him. Lydia didn't even have the time to scream before the storm hit her.

Bits and pieces of tiny rocks sliced at her skin as she did her best to hide her face. She threw her arm over her eyes and felt the wind and sand whipping at her. Lydia had never experienced anything like this. It was painful—it was disorienting. She felt tossed around in a washing machine, the sudden blast instantly removing any sense she had of left and right, up or down. It felt like a cheese grater was running against every piece of exposed skin she had.

"Q, help!" she screamed into the roar of the wind, burying her face in the collar of her coat to try to keep the sand out of her mouth. It didn't work. The grit was instant, and she tried not to cough and inhale more.

There was no answer.

The storm knocked her off her feet, sending her tumbling to the ground. It wasn't grass that she met; it was more sand. It was already inches deep, judging by how far her hands sank into the surface as she tried to push herself back up to standing.

Lydia was forced to close her eyes. There was nothing to see in the raging sandstorm anyway. She got back up to her feet. *Q, help me!* she shouted silently into her mind. There was still no response.

For a second time, the wind and the sand knocked her back down to her knees. The pieces of stone in the air were cutting at her. She knew she was bleeding. This had to stop. She dug her hands into the sand near her knees and did the first thing she could think of.

Lydia was a dreamer.

She was the Mother of Monsters.

Time to make it count for something.

There was a roar and a rumble from next to her, and she felt the biting sand lessen and then stop. Something had burst up from the ground and moved around her. Rather, it moved over her. It was the size of a school bus and had been the first thing she could think of to summon from her mind.

As it reared up over her, she watched as it shifted its body. It was a huge, armadillo-esque creature with large panels that covered it like a suit of armor. It dropped the plates to the ground, warping its limbs to create a shield around them both. It was now a giant... armadillo dome, igloo, thing. *Armadigloo?* It had made a protective cave around her, with its vulnerable body now inside the shelter of its exoskeleton. The sound of the storm was blotted out as the creature shuffled into the sand a bit further. Its head was over her, and it peered at her curiously, barely visible in the darkness.

The giant creature had appeared in the blink of an eye. She had willed it into existence in a moment of need. She'd be in awe of that revelation when she wasn't bleeding from a thousand tiny scratches along her face and anywhere that hadn't been protected from the storm.

"Thanks." She patted the creature's leg nearest to her.

It merely yawned broadly in response. It was hunkered down to ride out the storm already, and she knew it couldn't speak anyway. These things were just beasts, like that creature with the lantern she had made. Light that was leaking in through the gaps in the panels of its armor provided her only ability to see. It was incredibly bright outside, even through the darkness of the sandstorm.

Lydia stripped off her coat. It had been soaked, and now it was covered in wet sand. She tossed it to the ground and—oh.

Oh. Fuck.

There was writing on her arms.

Turquoise marks traced down from her shoulders in square, jagged spirals. They created an almost Aztec-looking pattern out of the esoteric, occult writing. She had worn a low-cut dress to the celebration that had ended so poorly, and she could see a line of the same turquoise writing running straight down the middle of her chest. She peeked, and sure enough, it ran all the way down to her navel. There were two other lines on her torso, running down her sides.

Through the slices and rips in her leggings put there by the storm, she could see more writing on her legs. Where had the ink come from? *Why're these things here now?*

The realization hit her like a brick.

She sank down to the sand as she felt as though her heart had been ripped out of her chest.

Q hadn't answered her cry for help. In fact, she hadn't heard from the snake at all since she had gone into the pool that third time because of Rxa.

She hadn't had any time to think about it. Everything was happening too damn fast.

Looking down at the marks on her arms, she ran her fingers along a line of them. Q had only ever been inside her head. He was her manifestation of her power, keeping it separate from her own mind. He was an imaginary friend made to help her cope with what had happened after Edu had killed her. A traumatized mind, seeking the only shelter it could.

Something about her visit with the Ancients had changed all that. Rxa had been right. She had been forced to her knees before those horrible creatures, and now...

Q was gone.

Putting her head in her hands, she felt the tears start to form.

Ever since coming to Under, she had always had someone there to help her. Nick, Lyon, Evie, Aon, Q—they had all been there to support her, to offer her solace, assistance, or friendship. But they were all gone now.

Aon. What she had just seen hadn't been the warlock she knew. Hadn't been the man she loved. He was cold. Austere. Dangerous, yes. But in a very different way. What had the Ancients done to him? What was he now?

He had told her to run so that he could chase her. He wanted her to be his prey. The thought made her shudder. As terrifying as Aon had always been, it had never been like this before. Even when she had first met him, something told her he had only ever been playing games.

This man, whoever he was, whether her Aon was buried somewhere deep inside or not—something told her that this was no longer just a *game*.

Now, even Q was gone. Her imaginary companion. Her voice of reason, her guiding cynical snake. Even if he was just a manifestation of herself—some part of her with the volume turned up—he had become precious to her.

Tears ran down her cheeks, and she let herself cry. She let herself sit there in the sand, with this giant armadillo-gone-cave around her to protect them both from the raging sandstorm outside. The weather aptly reflected how she felt.

She was alone.

TWO

The city of Yej was gone, swallowed into the dirt and rock as though Under itself was feeding upon it. How many were lost, he could not say. He had taken as many as he could to safety before he had been forced to retreat.

Edu slammed the wooden door shut behind him against the raging storm outside. Sand had replaced the normal snow of his home. The Ancients had risen. True terror filled his heart for the first time that he could remember. He knew not what was going to happen. Worse yet, he thought he might now recall what this world once *was*.

A sickening, burning feeling began to creep at the edges of his mind like bile.

"Edu?" he heard from behind him as he dropped the thick wood bar over the door that may keep the storm from smashing it inward. The rest of the windows were already being barricaded. It did not matter. The sand was like an acid, chipping away at his home—tearing away at the very rock.

This storm was corrosive. It was erasing all that had been done in the past five thousand years.

Edu turned to the voice and opened his arms as Evie ran to

him. She wrapped her own around his neck and hugged him as tightly as she was able. She was scared. They all were. Edu held her tight and let out a weary, wavering sigh.

"The Ancients have been released," Ylena said for him from nearby. "Rxa must have chained Lydia with them, and Aon was forced to kill Rxa to save her. With one chain went all the rest."

"Poor bunny!" Evie cried.

Edu had to laugh. It was a weak, tired laugh.

"What's funny?" Evie glared up at him.

"Our world is ending, and that is how you respond?" Ylena said. Her sense of self was caving underneath Edu's own storm of emotions.

"I can't stop the world from ending." Evie shrugged. "I can't worry about everyone. But I can worry about bunny. And I can worry about you." Evie hugged him again. "What'll happen to us now?"

"Master Edu does not know."

"As long as I stay with you, I don't care." Evie nuzzled into him with a faint smile on her beautiful, freckled features.

Edu looked down at the young girl. His heart felt full at her words, and he realized... he loved her. He truly did. Come what may, he knew he would die to keep her safe if it came to that. He would die to keep her at his side. With a tired exhale, he felt the ache of his years for the first time in a very long while. He was so very old. Yet he always seemed to fall into this same predicament.

He always seemed to come to realize how he felt the moment it was about to be taken away. *Isn't that the nature of life? Not to know what you have until the moment it is gone?*

It was for that reason he did not begrudge what Aon had done. The warlock had torched this world to free Lydia. Edu would have done the same in his case, without a shadow of a doubt.

Edu reached up to his face and pulled his mask off, feeling

glad for the removal of the hardened leather. It wasn't until he removed it that he realized how stifling it really was. Evie gasped as she looked up at him, wide-eyed and surprised, her lips parted in shock at the sight of his features.

It was for those lips he had done it. He scooped her up to lift her to his height and kissed her.

Even if it was the only time he would do so, he would greet the end of their days with the memory of her.

* * *

Lyon awoke.

Or, perhaps more accurately, he assumed he did.

He did not know where he was or how he had come to be here. His head was pounding, a deep and immense headache that seemed to come from the very base of his skull. He had to reach back to ensure that nothing was protruding from him.

The memory of chains came over him, a vision of seeing the thin links protruding from his own face. He felt himself overcome by a shudder, his whole body remembering the agony—sharp and brief as it may have been. After the visceral image had passed and he could see once more, he tried, as best he could, to take stock of where he now found himself.

He was lying on a stone floor, but it was not the polished stone of the cathedral. It was sandstone, hewn into massive blocks that seemed impossible for any number of men to move. The ceilings were high and arched overhead, built out of more of the massive block construction. Most of the stones were larger than he was tall. Columns—hewn of black stone—supported the walls and were adorned with figures and creatures that looked like nothing he had ever seen.

It looked... ancient. And to him, at his age, that was quite a feat. Nowhere he knew on Under, even before the press of the void, had looked anything like this. The only place he had ever known that resembled this were the ruins of Egypt or Babylon, long designated to antiquity even when he was a mortal man so long ago.

The sun was high in the sky outside. The glare made him hiss and turn his face away. The sunlight did not burn him, but it was extremely painful and unpleasant. Even though he was in the shadow of its light, it was uncomfortable. Standing, he found himself barely in control of his body. He collapsed to the stone twice before he was able to find a darker shadow in which to wedge himself.

There were no windows or doors to this place. It was open to the world outside, with only the columns on two sides. Solid walls were on opposite ends, one of which where he found himself now, sheltering from the light that made him squint. His eyes were having difficulty adjusting to the bright glow, which he did not find surprising. But he thought perhaps he could see palm trees and an arid landscape in the distance. The air was hot and dry.

Sinking to the ground, he pressed his hands to the side of his face.

He remembered dying.

Remembered once more the feeling of chains piercing his skull. Rxa had betrayed Aon's friendship, had imprisoned Lydia, and then betrayed Lyon himself in turn.

It was his own fault he had died, Lyon scolded himself. He should have known Rxa would react violently to such a show of insubordination on his part. But to let Lydia suffer that fate without lifting a finger to stop it? That was beyond his capabilities.

Where was he now? Some kind of afterlife? He had never considered the possibility that their souls went anywhere else but to return to the lake of blood after they met their end.

"No, High Priest.

Our King of Blood.
You live now to serve Us.
You live because Our Dreamer bade it so.
She who could not let you die.
She chose well.
She sacrificed herself for you."

The voices he heard made him bury his head in his hands and groan in pain. It was deafening and silent all at once. The sound of so many speaking at the same time, hissing and shouting, whispering and roaring. He shivered and felt cold and overly warm at the same time.

He did not need to ask who they were. He knew them and knew them well. The voices called to him, pulled at something buried deep within his soul. It was like they tugged on his very spine, they were so intrinsic within him.

They were the Ancients.

This was Under. There was only one option left for what had transpired. Rxa had imprisoned Lydia in the pool of blood... and Aon had killed Rxa to free her. If what they said was true, the Ancients had offered Lydia her freedom, and yet she had chosen to resurrect his sorry soul instead.

Lydia had spared him. If she had chosen differently, she could have avoided pitching the whole of Under into chaos. Lyon cringed in pain and lowered his head. In his mind, she had chosen quite poorly. But he could not blame her. Of course, she would decide to spare him his death—she was as empathetic a creature as he was. Though how many had she sent to the grave in his place instead?

A vision struck his mind, nearly blinding him. Rxa, lying dead in a halo of blood. Aon, standing upon the platform as the chamber that was once known as the Pool of the Ancients crumbled apart around him.

When the imagery left, what came after was a strange kind

of calm. A bizarre... peace. It was what he knew, each time he set foot within the lake of blood and witnessed the Ceremony of the Fall. But now, it filled him entirely. Any pain or strife he had just had a moment prior was swept away within it like the wash of a tide, and all worry over this new world was simply... gone. It should have alarmed him, but that emotion, too, seemed so small and not worth his time.

Lyon rose from the ground and brushed some of the dust from his clothing. The sun was still painfully bright. Such was his nature, after all. Vampires were not meant for the light, for he hunted in the shadows.

He saw a corridor nearby, now that he could focus his gaze on the world around him. It went down deeper into the building, and the darkness there was calling him. It was promising to be a balm against the glare. He felt pulled in that direction and did not fight it.

The stone staircase was cool and dark, and it felt like bliss compared to the brightness of the sun above. The passageway wound down into the structure, which must be enormous, he judged. Massive stair after massive stair, he marveled at the beauty and the horror of all he saw around him.

He traced his fingers along the artwork that covered every square inch of the walls, colorful depictions of battles and monsters and of the Ancients he recognized from the statues that had lined the halls of his cathedral.

Lyon paused before the depiction of one scene. A man with long black hair, bare-chested and swathed in ebony fabric. Lines of black ink adorned him. He stood on a battlefield, the proud conqueror over all that lay dead and scorched about him on a field soaked in blood.

The King of All.

He should feel horrified. He should be terrified of what he saw. But still, the sense of calm overrode his logic. Seemed to shush him, soothe him, and lure him deeper into the building.

These are not concerns to be had in this moment. These are not concerns to be had at all. He is your King.

Finally, he reached the bottom. There he found a chamber with statues on one end that looked familiar to him. They were depictions of the Ancients, with their twisted and horrifying forms. They towered overhead, some thirty or forty feet in height. They loomed over an altar at their feet.

Candles burned there, ringed with offerings of every kind. Fire burning in cauldrons along the center path lit the room, casting stark and dramatic shadows on the walls that looked like monsters and demons in their own right.

Even as he watched, the shadows seemed to flicker and warp, twisting in shape, revealing that there was more in the darkness here than met the eye. The Ancients were free. And this was where they dwelled.

The statues seemed to be calling to him. He walked up to them slowly, in awe of what he saw, of where he stood. The chamber was surrounded on three sides with water that glowed a familiar shade of red.

This was the *true* Altar of the Ancients. Not the abomination he had maintained for so long.

Serve.

The thought was a demand. It was a call that struck him like a bolt of lightning. It was not their voices in his mind—it had been his own.

Serve. It is only right. It is the true nature of this world.

It was not a command. It was deeper and far more intrinsic than a simple missive. Yes. He served them. Rxa was dead, and Lyon was their High Priest. Now, he was their King of Blood.

Lyon slowly fell to his knees at the foot of the statues and bowed his head.

"What would you have me do?"

THREE

Lydia had cried until no more tears would come—until she just couldn't do it anymore. The storm was still raging outside the weird giant armadillo monster she had blinked into existence to protect her from the whipping sand. She was exhausted and worn out mentally and physically.

Too much had happened in too short a time. That was becoming the norm for her, ever since she woke up with that mark on her arm. She took her wet, sandy coat, folded it inside-out, balled it under her head, and tried to fall asleep.

That was a mistake.

She had no idea what it felt to be "curb stomped." She had wound up with more than one gang violence victim on her slab in Boston. Her day job felt like it had been a lifetime ago now. One of those poor souls had suffered that fate and had their teeth placed on the edge of the stone and their head stepped on until their face caved in. It had been one of the worst cases she had ever had to work on. She wondered if this wasn't just a little bit like how that must have felt.

Her mind felt torn apart. Literally ripped away at the seams.

It was like someone was stuffing too much into her head like a bad Thanksgiving turkey and causing it to split.

Lydia had made Q out of self-defense to protect her from *this exact moment.*

She had created him to save her from the enormity of power that had come along with being a dreamer. Not just any dreamer, though—she was *the* dreamer, after all. And now, Q was gone. There was no more shelter. The moment she had let down her guard and as soon as she was no longer struggling to keep the world at bay, the floodgates opened.

She thought she might have been screaming. Or maybe she wasn't making any noise at all. It was impossible to tell. She lost all sense of where she was, the pain was so driving.

Everything she had held at bay since she had died was now all there, tearing through her like battery acid. Images ripped through her at a million miles an hour, flashes of creatures and monsters, rising from nothing, hunting their world and Earth alike.

Power tore at her like she was licking a car battery. Knowledge did the same. As though it had always been there, it all clicked into place. Like a sheet had been pulled off a piece of furniture that had always been in the room, she had just never noticed it somehow. The Houses, the marks, the laws of the world. The reason why things were as they were. It was what she had been missing, all this time.

It was too much. It was all just *too much.*

Arms circled her. The familiar contour of his body. The press of a cheek against hers. "Breathe it in..."

"I—I can't—"

"You fight it still. It will break you if you do." His voice a low, baritone sound that she felt roll through her. "You have held your breath under the waves for too long. Fight it, and you will die, and I cannot stop it. *Breathe it in.*"

She imagined herself sinking in that red water. Feeling that horrible glowing liquid punch its way into her body. She'd fought it both times.

Now, the whole *world was them.*

Clinging to him, she didn't even know if he was real. But the feeling of him there was the only thing keeping her from losing her mind. Giving her the strength to hold on.

With an exhale, she did as he said. She let the power in. And the licking, the live wire turned into being struck by lightning. But now, she might just be a lightning rod and not a hapless victim.

Everything just made sense. She felt as though she was connected to the world around her. That this place was hers just as much as anyone else's. It was a deep-rooted feeling of belonging. Was this what she had been fighting against this whole time?

Monsters, of men and beasts alike, trading blood and flesh to continue into eternity. Hunting the humans of Earth when the two worlds came into alignment was a sport and a release of tension, of pent-up aggression between hungry dogs snapping at each other in a kennel. It was a world consumed by the thrill of the hunt, of dark devouring. Of feeling a body cave underneath hers and taking what she wanted from them. Of needs and desires of every kind being fed.

She had been told as much. But now, she *knew* it. And now, more importantly, she understood her place within it. She understood it all. Men and women, and those who no longer resembled the humans they once were, ruled this world. But in truth, her creations were just as powerful and just as dangerous as the others. Hers were the true animals who did not care to protect the marks that kept them all alive after death. For that reason, they were a far more vicious threat than those who had once been human. For her creatures did not care for whose lives they took.

Pride welled within her, even through the pain. The desire to sink her teeth into flesh, to kill and be killed, to taste blood. This was who she was now. The Mother of Monsters. She felt so stupid, now that she really understood. At any point she could have summoned an army from the depths of her mind to fight for her. Power burned away under her skin, and she knew that far more than merely a few parlor tricks or crackles of lightning would be at her disposal now.

But she learned the rules just in time for the game to change.

Her thoughts felt muddled and jumbled, jumping around from one thing to another, one thought to the next, back and forth, tossed about like rocks in a cement mixer. She couldn't focus. It felt like she had a fever dream as she tumbled about in her own mind. No matter how hard she tried to grab hold, her thoughts slipped through her fingers like the sand that now surrounded her.

Images of a world devoured by sand suddenly overtook her, forced into her with the rest of it all. Visions of a burning sun, searing away all that it touched. Of a cruelty that the royals had managed to temper in their own destructive reign. Truly the lesser of two evils. For five thousand years, that madness had been suppressed. That kingdom of death over which the Ancients would rule had been erased. Now, they had risen, and everything was overturned.

The Ancients. They had chosen her. They had brought her here. They had planned it all from the very beginning. Now, she danced on the end of their strings. As miserable as she might be about her state of being, there was nothing she could do to break the ties. But like a horse on the end of a lead, she felt the urge to kick and fight against being broken.

But their power was etched onto her skin. She wore their marks. They had made her something more—or less—than human. If she tried to go back to Earth and the portals closed behind her, she would die without them. Why should she bother fighting?

It all hurt so very badly. She clung to the figure there above her. She didn't even know if he was real or just a ghost of a memory. And she was afraid to find out.

She needed Aon to hold her, to soothe her, to explain what was happening to her. To talk her through what felt like someone cramming a watermelon into her skull.

Aon. The name brought sudden loathing that tightened her throat. A strange, inexplicable disgust and wariness welled up within her. He wasn't the King of Shadows—he was the King of Lies.

No! She shoved those thoughts away. They weren't hers. They couldn't be. Growling, she dug her hands into the sand beneath her. The Ancients were trying to make her hate him, just like all the others. They could do whatever else they wanted to her, but that was something she would never let them touch.

She loved Aon, and she would not let them take that away.

She tried to draw a line in the proverbial sand and circle herself away from all the things that were there inside her mind.

She was still herself.

She was still the forensic autopsy technician who had fallen into a world of monsters.

She was the ex-EMT.

She was *Lydia*.

She was the Queen of Dreams, fine. But both could be true at the same time.

There was one thing she knew, more than any of the rest. One thing that pulled her from the rising waters of her mind like a life preserver. Her love for Aon.

The Ancients said they had done all this to test her. When she had been at the bottom of that godforsaken lake, they said they wanted her to prove to them that she was worthy of their "only son." She didn't know if this was another part of their stupid games, but she wasn't going to let them warp her into hating him. *You can take the rest of me. But you can't have that.*

The faint ghost of a kiss against her cheek had her reaching for him, but her hands passed through empty air.

Slowly, like the tide, the agony of the presence in her mind began to recede. But with it, went the feeling of the figure above her. Blinking her eyes open, she saw that she was alone.

He hadn't been there, after all. Not really. Or, if he had, he had done so because he was *like them.*

The confessions Aon had made to her before the storm hit them still chilled her to the bone. The very possible reality occurred to her that she loved Aon... and he may not exist anymore. The man who had stood there before the oncoming storm and kissed her was a stranger wearing the face of the man she knew.

Who was he now?

His words echoed in her mind. *"Run and let me chase you."*

Everything in Under was both predator and prey. Now, it was clear he meant for her to be his quarry. Now, she needed to run from him, or else... she didn't even know what to expect. It was possible she had only known the "nicer" version of the man. Whatever he was now, the coldness in him had terrified her.

The exhaustion of it all caught up with her. Finally, the pain receded enough that the darkness could come for her. And finally, once and for all... she slept.

Once again, her dreams weren't her own.

Lydia found herself standing in a dark void. She recognized it... or she almost did. Instead of the hard glass surface beneath her feet like the times Aon had invaded her dreams, she was standing on a sea of black sand. It stretched on in all directions, mottled and rippled by a wind that wasn't there. But she could only see for so far before it disappeared into the nothingness that was this place. She dug her feet into the sand curiously. It moved like it should, it felt like it should, even if it was utterly the wrong color.

Isn't sand the raw form of glass?

She knew who had brought her here. Or at least... she knew his face.

Power filled the air like the weight of an anvil suddenly falling on her. She could feel it now, tingling on her skin like the feeling before a thunderstorm. She knew he was standing there, even without having to look. "This routine again? I thought we were done with this bullshit."

Silence.

Clenching her fists, she fought the urge to turn around. Once she turned, he would be real. She'd have to face him and what he'd become. Or, rather, what he had reverted into. This was debatably the "real" him, after all, wasn't it? The man who might have existed long before human civilizations had graced the Earth?

If he had never really been human, if he really was the only creature ever made by the Ancients, he could be as old as time. Maybe that would explain the disgust and the hatred everyone felt toward him. He was an imposter, an outsider, and they could feel it. Sense it.

But it seemed to go further than that. The Ancients seemed to force people to hate and fear him. But why? Why the implanted mistrust? "One thing I don't get," she commented idly, still avoiding having to face him, "is why the Ancients make everyone hate you, Aon. If you're their favorite and only son, what good does that serve?"

Silence.

"And—seriously? This dream stuff again? I need to buy you a phone. If you want to just talk to me randomly, there are better ways to do it than invading my dreams. You could call.

Text. Maybe we could FaceTime." Her cynicism and sardonic humor were a poor shelter from what she felt surrounding her like a dark cloud. But damn it all, it was the only one she had, so she was going to freaking use it.

It was as though the dark tendrils of power he used were curling around her, readying to snap. She felt him there, filling her with a sense of dread and awe. She felt in the grasp of a massive claw, just as she had as she drifted to the bottom of that godforsaken lake. He made her feel so... very small, now.

Still, nothing but silence.

Aon had always loved the sound of his own voice. From the very first moment she met him, he had never been *quiet*. He had goaded and tormented her, teased and pushed her.

But he had never just let her hang like that.

It scared her more than anything else that had happened so far.

Finally, she couldn't take it anymore. She turned to find him standing behind her like she suspected he was. As she turned, he stepped in closer, narrowing the distance between them down to a few inches. He was silently daring her to step back and calling that her angry and dismissive tone with him had been a bluff.

And it worked. She couldn't help it. She retreated a step away from him. Not only because he was scaring the hell out of her—but because his appearance was so different from what she was used to. Like an actor disappearing perfectly into another role, he had changed.

His clothing was bizarre. It looked like the robes of an ancient king or god from mythology. He was bare-chested, and around his waist were long wraps of black fabric that reached down to the sand. Etched into them in black thread were the eldritch symbols she had come to recognize. They were only visible when he moved, the light catching the texture on the otherwise invisible black-on-black pattern.

The fabric was belted to his waist with a thick, black metal collection of circular disks and medals, each etched with a symbol. He wore a matching necklace. It resembled the jewelry of an Egyptian pharaoh but morbid and warped like everything else in this place.

But it was the expression he wore that worried her the most. Gone was the dark mischief, the curl to his lips that promised danger and devilish excitement. Aon, for all his age, felt far younger than the man who stood before her.

He looked ancient. He *felt* ancient. He was watching her with a hardness that remained untouched by the faint smile on his thin lips. There was a flat expression of aloof *superiority* on him that terrified her worse than any wickedness she had ever seen from Aon.

He was breathtakingly beautiful. He was unearthly. He made her stomach twist into knots of panic and a familiar kind of nervousness she had come to recognize around him. He was as foreign as he was achingly familiar. But that coldness in his eyes made her want to shrink away.

"Aon...?" She took another step away from him and was about to take a third before she stopped herself and sighed. It was pointless. She was inside her head—or his head, she never really did figure out which it was—and she couldn't run from him here.

Silence. But he wasn't a statue.

Slowly, he reached out his hand to her. He moved carefully as if worried he would frighten her, before brushing his fingers over her cheek. It was so tender, it almost made her want to cry.

Maybe he's still in there somewhere. Maybe he's the same man, deep down.

Or maybe this is a better version. Aon was never that gentle with her. Never so tender as *that*. His touch felt so wonderful. So warm and so safe. She wanted to lean into his hand and pray it never left her. He stepped into her slowly.

Maybe this is just him, healed of his madness. Maybe he's whole now. Maybe the man I knew was a lie, and this man's the truth.

He slipped his hand slowly along her features, tracing the lines of ink on her one by one. It was captivating, and she wanted to let him hold her. To press herself into his embrace and beg him to never let her go.

Wouldn't that be better? If he wasn't insane anymore?

He slipped his hand to the back of her neck, cradling her head, as he leaned down to kiss her. She felt her eyes slip shut and let it happen. It was slow, and it stole her breath away just as badly as it ever had before. There was so much power in that embrace. So much *control.* She wanted to surrender to it.

This feels right. This is how it should be.

Aon had been a rabid animal. This man was a force of nature.

Whenever Aon had kissed her before, he seemed like a man dying of hunger seated at a banquet. He was expressive, emotive, and felt no need to hide the pleasure he felt. She felt worshiped and devoured all in the same embrace.

This felt like she was in the palms of his hands. That she was at his mercy. That he could do with her whatever he wished. This was a kiss of a man who was taking what was owed to him and would pull her along inch by inch, piece by piece, luring her into the darkness. But there was safety in it all the same. It was patient, careful, but just as inarguable. This man controlled the world. He could protect her.

He really is the King of All.

Finally, his metal hand curled around her back and pulled her flush against him. The kiss deepened, became more demanding. His tongue slipped past her lips to claim her as his.

It was his right, and she didn't even think to fight him.

There was no stopping him. More importantly, she didn't want to. Pleasure jolted through her, and she felt as though electricity was coursing through her body. Everything in her felt on fire at his touch. Pulling away was the very last thing on her mind as she let herself sink against him and slid her hands up his bare chest. He was so warm beneath her hands. This felt familiar. This felt like him. This was bliss.

He is all I will ever have, and he is all I will ever need.

He loves me. He is my King.

I must kneel to him.

That last thought that came to her jarred her.

It was like a slap to the face.

She would never—*ever*—think anything of the sort.

It snapped her out of the reverie that had come over her, shattering it like a wine glass on concrete. She hadn't even realized she had fallen into the trap until it was almost slammed shut around her. She'd only noticed because he had pushed it too far. He had gotten greedy.

"Damn you!" Shoving him as hard as she could, she staggered backward. She was shaking, trembling from what he had done. It was like going from a hot tub to a frozen lake all in the snap of a finger. "What the *fuck* was that? Hypnotism?" *How dare he!* Anger rose to take the place of the shock. "Really, asshole? You're going to resort to that? Fuck you!"

He laughed quietly and shrugged unapologetically as if to say, *"Whatever works."* She had to go off her presumptions, because he still didn't speak. Just watched her with an icy smile that still felt like a man ten times older than the one she had known.

Shaking her head, she tried to clear the rest of the fog that was the haze he had placed over her. He had tried to paint himself as the safe harbor in the raging storm, calling her home like the flash of the lighthouse. And maybe he was right, but this felt *wrong*. "Aon. Please, you're scaring me." She tried to sound as firm as she could. "Stop this."

He tutted her and stepped in to close the distance she had put between them.

When she moved a matching distance back, he growled low in his throat. His hand snapped around her wrist, and he yanked her toward him, his metal hand twisting in her hair, wrenching her head to look up at him. With her captured wrist, he folded her arm behind her back and used it to trap her against him once more.

With her free hand, she pounded her fist into his bare chest, but it did no good. He merely watched her with that same knowing and smug smile. All her struggling was useless, but she still had to try. Patiently, he waited for her to tire. It was inevitable, after all. With a disgruntled sigh, she gave up and stilled her attempts to push him away. Not only was he stronger than she was, this was a dream he controlled.

He arched a single eyebrow down at her, silently asking if she was quite finished.

The continued silence from him raised in her an anger that made her want to slap him. "Aon! Why aren't you talking to me?"

Still he just looked down at her, with that cold, prideful smile that spoke of a man older than the mountains themselves. Saying nothing, only watching her, his gaze tracing along the lines of writing upon her face as if he had never seen them before. He seemed suddenly drawn in by them, tilting his head as if he could... read them.

But that was impossible.

"Aon!" Nothing. He kept seemingly reading the writing on her face. "Hey, asshole!" She tried to get his focus again. Spilled-ink eyes flicked back to hers. "Stop this. Let me go."

Lips ghosted over her ear as he nuzzled his head in close to her. Teeth grazed her lobe as he took it into his mouth. She couldn't help the sound that escaped her.

He chuckled low, a vibration against her where he kept her

pinned. He had proven in one movement that she still wanted him—that he still held that power over her and he could still trigger her desire like a lit match in gasoline.

With a snarl, she summoned an obsidian dagger and went to drive it into his neck. He blocked the blow quickly. Before she could react to his movement, his fist met her face. Hard. Like a battering ram of metal. She crumpled to the ground, the blow putting her into the dark sand at his feet.

He had struck her without pity. Without remorse. If she had been mortal, it would have cracked her jaw. It taught her exactly who she was dealing with and who he now was.

He was a man who would not tolerate an outburst like that.

Wrestling was one thing, but she had clearly crossed a line. A hand twisted in her hair and pressed her flat to her back, and he was kneeling over her, straddling her hips, gazing down at her with a look that could only be described as... curiosity and amusement.

The knife she had summoned was between his fingers, flicking deftly between them as though it were a practiced routine. He took a moment to ponder the obsidian blade before digging it deep into her ribs.

Time was once that it would have snapped her out of a dream like this. But now, she knew what it was like to be gutted alive. And by the very same man, no less.

This was just a dream.

And even if it wasn't, a single knife wound like that wouldn't have really killed her. Not anymore.

She cried out as the pain rushed her body, but she gritted her teeth against it after a moment and redoubled her effort of trying to glare at him so hard he burst into flame.

The more things change, the more they stay the same...

He sank down over her, pinning her down as he kept his hand around the hilt of her dagger. Her anger and insolence didn't discourage him in any way—in fact, it seemed it had the opposite effect. Lips crashed against hers, devouring her, even as he held a knife deep in her body.

When he broke away, she was breathless, the pain of the knife almost forgotten in the headiness of the embrace. He watched her, approval in his eyes.

Still, his silence plagued her. He had never acted like this before. Even when he had spelled out for her in perfect detail exactly what he wished to do to her, it was better than this. It bothered her more than the knife in her ribs that seemed more like a nuisance now than anything else. "Aon, talk to me. Please, I—"

She grunted in pain as he pulled the knife from her ribs.

He lifted it before his face, and she watched as her blood shone crimson against the black obsidian blade. A drop of it fell from the edge of the sharpened black rock and landed on her cheek, hot and wet.

Rapt, unable to look away, she watched as he began to lick the blade clean. His black eyes slipped shut as he let out a deep moan in his throat. He shuddered at the taste, seemingly overcome by the ecstasy of it. Her heart was lodged firmly in her throat, and her stomach was a tangled knot of confused emotions.

Some were extremely inappropriate.

Or would have been, about... six months ago before all of this went down.

When the knife was clean, he tossed it aside into the sand with a quiet *thuff* as it sank partway into the substrate. The wound in her side barely stung now. It was already healing. Once again, she struggled to remember that this was still only a dream, after all.

But there was one more drop of blood for him to hunt. The one that had landed on her cheek. He lowered himself further, sliding down her until he was propped up on his elbow. She whimpered as he slowly dragged his tongue along her, cleaning up what had spilled, as though it were some precious, expensive wine.

The moan that left him almost drew one from her in exchange.

She couldn't help what he did to her. There was no denying that she was trembling underneath him. Whoever he was, he could still tune her up and play her like a violin. For everything about him that was now in question, that simple fact remained the same. She wanted him. She knew she always would. And by the look on his face, the heady darkness in those spilled-ink eyes that looked down at her, hungry and half-lidded, he knew it too.

When she managed to find her voice again, it was as unsure as the rest of her. "Why aren't you saying anything?"

He tilted his head down as if to bury it into the crook of her neck. She jolted to try and smack her head into his, forcing him to withdraw. The look on his face was one of incredulousness— as if wondering how she dared deny him something he wanted.

"Please. I'm begging. Say *something*."

Another thin crook of an eyebrow. "Have you been speaking to me?"

Finally! He talked! "Who the hell else would I be talking to?"

The man over her lifted his metal gauntlet and examined it curiously, as though it were perfectly foreign to him. "I did not know whom you were addressing. You insist on using a name that *is not mine*."

History repeated itself as, without warning, he rammed the blades of his claw deep into her body.

This time, it was painful enough that the dream around her shattered as she screamed.

* * *

Lyon knelt at the feet of his one and only King. He bowed his head low and pressed his hand to his chest in prayer.

The Ancients had commanded that he serve, and he would do so without question. Now that the full truth was known to him, the whole of the picture of the world was laid bare. The centuries of railing against the true King of All felt paltry and like the struggles of a child against curfew.

Like Mortals against the Ancients.

For his King was the only one truly of this world. The only one born of the Ancients. The only one worthy of the title. Lyon may be the King of Blood, but he was nothing in comparison to the King of this place, of their world.

A fire raged in a cauldron nearby, casting flickering shadows up the walls. Ones that seemed to twist and warp into the shapes of the eldritch creatures they both called masters. The Ancients were always near their only child, now that they had been freed. The images were horrifying, and Lyon found himself casting his eyes to the ground in both reverence and fear.

Here, in the depths of his King's palace, the sun did not bother him so. His King assured him that the sun would eclipse shortly, and he may go out to feed. He was starved. He felt the cry and the call for blood as though he were newly turned. Whether it was the product of his recently performed resurrection or due to this restored old world, he did not know. He did not much care. The cause may differ, but the symptom was the same.

The King gestured his hand for Lyon to rise. "Yes?"

"Forgive me for waking you, my lord. Ini has been captured and is imprisoned as you requested." He obeyed and returned to his feet. "We are in close pursuit of Vjo. Dtu evades us, as does Edu, but we are narrowing where they may be hiding. No one has left the city."

"And what of Lydia?"

"There is no sign of her yet. Buried in the storm and yet to surface, most likely."

His King's instruction came short and concise. His voice was quiet, low and sharp. But he heard the echo of hunger, of destruction that lived within the two simple words, "Find her."

Lyon responded without hesitation in his heart. "As you command."

FOUR

Lydia awoke with a start. She was covered in a cold sweat. Grains of sand were sticking to her damp skin as she rolled over onto her side and tried to clear her head of the feeling of Aon's claws deep in her chest.

"You insist on using a name that is not mine."

Not Aon. He wasn't Aon anymore. Any hope that he was the same man was gone. Torn away from her by his own words. By the look on his cold face. She pressed her forehead into the sand and felt the tears come again. She wept for him—for her—for what she had and lost.

What now?

Hope was an insidious poison. It was the hardest illness to kill. Like a cancer, it burrowed deep and infected the cells at a nearly intrinsic level. But her other option was to give up, and so she drank that poison willingly. *Maybe he's still in there somewhere. Maybe I can talk sense into him. Snap him out of it. Break him of the hold the Ancients have on him.*

She laughed. It was weak, it was tired, and it was mocking her own stupid thoughts. *Right. Let's go fight some primordial gods. That's a great plan.*

What would *he*—whatever his name was now—do when he found her? And she knew, despite her best efforts, it would be a *when,* not an if. Maybe she could run for centuries—maybe she could hide for ten thousand years. But if Aon wanted to find her, he would. It only took time before the warlock could have whatever he wanted.

She had learned that lesson what seemed like a lifetime ago, that against him, she never really stood a chance. Not just because he was a force of nature, but because... she always wanted to give in. Deep down. But she had always had his heart in her hand in return, even as he held hers.

It was a strange, messed-up power dynamic between the two of them, that was for sure.

How did you love a man like him without giving up a part of yourself? Yet he gave himself back to her entirely in return, and she knew he would have done anything for her.

In the end, he had, after all.

For her, he had destroyed the world. For her, he had destroyed himself.

Was that still true? Would this version of him still love her like that one did? Or was everything different now? Who *was* he?

Wiping her hand across her face, she grunted as the sand clinging to her stung. Whatever. She had other problems right now.

Namely, the man she loved was possessed. He was an... elder-thing himself... and he was hunting her down. He had told her to run so he could chase her.

That was a pretty clear promise of what he intended to do with her.

She pushed up to her feet and willed herself into new clothes. Something desert-worthy. Something that wouldn't be miserable in the blazing sun she could see through the cracks in the armored monster she was still hiding underneath. The storm had ended, and now light shone through in bright streams.

"I guess I can't stay under an armadillo forever." Now, she was talking to herself as she looked up at the creature that seemed asleep over her. She had nobody else to talk to, after all.

Loneliness hit her unexpectedly.

Q hadn't been real. He had been the manifestation of a desperate mind. She took a few strands of hair from behind her left ear and braided it. She summoned a thin leather cord to secure it, and one other thing.

A single, glowing turquoise feather. She tied it into her hair and sighed. He had always wanted her to wear feathers. Now, it was too little too late, but he had his wish.

Q hadn't been real.

But he'd been real to her.

Enough wallowing. Wallowing didn't solve problems. She reached up and patted the armadillo-thing on the leg. "C'mon buddy, time to go."

It snorted, blinked its eyes open, and began to shuffle and shift. Lydia squeaked and raised her arms to cover her eyes as the sand that had built up on the creature rained off. Inches of the stuff had piled up like the worst kind of snow during the storm. The creature lifted its armored panels back onto its body and shook itself off like a wet dog—sending the grit flying everywhere.

"Gah!" Lydia laughed and hid her head under her arms as she was pelted with the little bits of rock and dust.

The armadillo finally finished cleaning itself off and took a few steps away from her. It was huge, now that she really saw the whole of it, some twenty or thirty feet long and looked as though it were actually part stegosaurus, the way the plates stood on its back when it had them all folded in. It yawned, gaping its big jaw before snapping it back shut. It scratched behind its head with a giant back claw like a dog.

"Thanks, by the way." It was a silly thing to say, but it didn't hurt to be polite. She knew it didn't really understand.

Without any further ado, it ran off—skittering through the sand and between the white clay buildings she suddenly realized surrounded her. It left a bizarre, zigzag line in its wake as it tore off through the city.

City?

Where in the hell *was* she?

Lydia took a few paces back and found herself under the shade of a fabric overhang. Pitched up by two wooden beams, the swath of crimson fabric kept her out of the glare of the overhead sun. The light made her squint, and she still had a hard time focusing on everything around her.

She had just found herself on what looked like the lost set of *Ben Hur*. The buildings were crude, tightly packed together and made of clay. The windows were holes in the structure with only rolled sticks tied together to create a covering. All of them were lowered, hiding whatever—or whoever—might be inside.

The city was silent. There was no one around, only the wind and the whisper of sand as it blew and rustled. Tiny dust-devils were kicked up in tight corners, whirling the newly placed sand up into tiny and short-lived tornadoes. As she shielded her eyes with her hand, she dared to look up. There in the sky were two moons, pale against a bright blue background. And one very brightly burning sun.

No birds. No insects. Nobody and nothing.

It looked like something ripped from her old picture books on the history of Egypt. And looking up at the horizon... the comparison was solidified.

Looming over the city was an enormous temple. It wasn't a pyramid, but a stacked-stepped building. It had soaring, black columns on every tier. It rose hundreds of feet above the rest of the city and was as foreboding as it was impressive.

She knew who lived there.

She knew *what* lived there.

Not just "not-Aon," but the Ancients that had risen and reclaimed their world. That made it the number one place she didn't want to go. Although she had the sinking suspicion any amount of running was going to wind up being hilariously pointless in the end, she had to try. She didn't know what to expect from the Ancients and their only son... but she didn't want to find out.

Giving in just wasn't her style. It never had been, and she wasn't about to start now.

Still, something about that building took her breath away. She had never seen anything like it. She had never traveled outside of the country—Canada didn't count when she was from New England. It was awe-inspiring. It was a display of power, meant to intimidate, and it worked.

It told her more about the man who lived there and called it his throne than she had learned in her dreams.

Part of her wanted to go there. To just let the inevitable happen. To find out for herself who he really was now, and if some part of the man she loved was still buried in him. But if there wasn't? If the Ancients had worse things in store for her? Then there would be no escape.

She had to leave. Get out of this city. Head for the horizon and find some dark place to wedge herself. Maybe find the others, if they were still alive. She summoned a thin cotton coat. Something with a hood that would keep the sun off her arms and her face hidden.

There was still no way she was ever going to wear a stupid mask.

Pulling the fabric up over her head, she tucked her hair in behind her. She could try to fly away. Summon a creature that could carry her somewhere else. Or even, just maybe, try to change shape herself. She felt like she could. The memory of turning into a winged snake was itching at the back of her mind, begging her to try. But something told her that wouldn't exactly be a subtle way to leave—bursting out from the rows of clay buildings as a giant monster.

Not-Aon would have creatures that could catch her, even if he couldn't do it himself. She'd have to wait until dark. Unless it never got dark again, she realized. The sun might never set. It hadn't risen for five thousand years, after all.

With a sigh, she realized what she had to do. She had to make her way to the edge of this sprawling maze of ancient clay buildings. Once there, she'd hopefully be far enough away that no one could keep up with her.

And so, she picked a direction. Pointing straight away from that towering, horrifying temple... she walked.

* * *

Edu remembered this world.

He could almost still feel the shackles around his arms, biting into his flesh, drawing fresh blood with every movement. The heavy metal bindings that kept him chained for so very long were now so fresh in his memory he had to brush his hand over his neck to ensure they were not there. As he stood in the darkness of an alleyway, cramped tight with wood and clay buildings, he could recall how the sun would blister his flesh and how the sand would sting the open wounds that he had been dealt by the King of All.

Edu had been the man's favorite plaything to whip and torture. To pit him against his pet monsters, hoping one of the warlock's beasts may finally devour him. How he remembered the arenas and the battles to the death, like a gladiator for the King of All's amusement alone.

Now, he knew why he loathed that man, so deep to his core. He hated the ghost of the King he once despised and feared.

Edu leaned himself back against the dried clay structure and felt so very tired. He felt the weight of his years, now that he saw the world from which he had come. The one he and the others had so desperately tried to forget.

And now, this place lived again. The Ancients were freed from their prison. Havoc and horror would rule once more, grasped in the palms of the creature who had come to name himself *Aon.*

A lie. A bold-faced, utter lie.

That man could call himself similar to Edu, no more than the sun might burn low and name itself a moon. He was a scourge created by the very demons that built their world.

What are we to do now?

There was only one course ahead of him; he would kill the King of All. Once and for all, he would ensure that wretched monster lay dead, or he himself would finally greet the void. Suffering through whatever tortures the beast may devise for him was far better than living in this sham of a life, pressed under the thumb of a tyrant.

The presence of two small arms clutching at his right bicep broke him of his thoughts. He turned his head to look down at the fiery redhead beside him and was keenly reminded that his place in the world was not so simple. He had others he needed to protect. Others he cared for and would see sheltered from all that this world had to offer.

Smiling behind his mask, he reached up to place a heavy palm atop her head and rock it side to side as he loved to do.

Unknowingly returning his smile, as she could not see his face, only in her eyes did he see the weight of the fear she must feel. For her world had been upended and destroyed—his had merely reverted to something dead and gone.

Though which was worse, to not understand the torture this world promised with every speck of sand or to see what lay ahead? He did not know.

A storm had come and destroyed all the world of Under

that little Evie had known, erased it, and from the depths of the whirling grit had come this place. No matter how much distance they had put between them, Edu, Dtu, Ini, and all the others had found themselves brought here in this place with the massive Temple of the Ancients in the center. There was only one city in this world... it only needed one. It hadn't even had a name, for that very reason.

It was not the only thing without a name.

The King of All was only that, a title.

He was not a man deserving of a name, but a plague.

A curse.

In the chaos that had erupted, many went missing. Ini was gone; so was Ylena. His heart wrenched for the lack of his empath. He deeply worried about her safety, the distance between them too great to even feel if she was all right or suffering. If that cretin who called himself the King of All dared lay a hand on Ylena, Edu would tear his eyes out from his sockets or die trying.

Arms tightened around his. "I know, I'm worried about them too."

Edu marveled at how easily Evie could read his body language. It brought another smile from him, and he turned to hold her, to wrap his massive arms around her small frame and hold her up against him. Ini and Ylena were merely on the long list of those who had gone missing or been taken.

For men and beasts alike stalked the streets, in search of any who did not wear black or white. The humans who had come from the lake as creatures—their beast-kin—served the King of All with blind diligence.

The monsters walked alongside the warlock's ilk as they sought out and dragged away any with masks who did not kneel to the King. And those who did not come willingly... were destroyed.

Edu had seen several already fall before the creatures, their marks torn from their faces and devoured as if they were nothing but raw meat, only worthy of being thrown to rabid dogs. There was no reverence for life here. There were no laws forbidding the true death of another.

He and the others had taken to a structure of tunnels deep beneath the city that Vjo remembered using in those days so long ago. Edu despised hiding, but the tunnels and network of chambers were easier to defend against the warlock's forces than here above ground. As much as he wished to throw himself headlong into a final battle with the man, he had to think of the others.

And it was for those others that he had come up here. For he could not sit in the darkness below and let those who may still wish to resist be rounded up and herded away like cattle. If they were to stage a revolt—if there was to be a war—he would need as many as he could save.

He had tried to leave Evie behind in the relative safety of the tunnels.

The key word there was that he had *tried*.

The little spitfire would not be abandoned. She would not listen to reason. She demanded she come "help." She had borrowed an axe from Oanr, one that was meant to be thrown with a single hand, and yet she held it with two as though it were some mighty immortal weapon of the gods.

Truth be told, she was fearsome with the thing. Like a tiny, curly-haired berserker, she had no fear of battle. No fear of what danger she may be in, as she went about leaping headlong into a fray and shrieking like a condor. Most of those she had defeated today had crumpled, caught largely by surprise. He himself would not know quite what to do with a tiny hellion like her, racing through the fight like a rabid house cat.

It made him grin.

He could not adequately express, in either the words he was now fully denied or otherwise, how proud he was of her. How his heart swelled when he watched her fight. He had found himself earlier that day laughing during battle as he watched her clamber up onto someone's shoulders and attempt to cleave their head wide open like a nut. He hadn't laughed that hard in a very long time, much to her dismay. She had accused him of teasing her, making fun of her lack of skills. He had done all he could to reassure her with a kiss that no, he had merely been reminded how much he loved her.

And it seemed he would have reason to be reminded again, for another fight was about to begin. A caravan of prisoners was headed up the broader street to which the alley they stood in attached.

Monstrous figures of every kind walked to either side of those they had shackled and chained into rows. None of those who served the King of All wore masks. And now, Edu remembered why. The masks were not to protect the marks from the world—the masks were made to protect the marks *from him.*

For only one amongst them could read the words etched upon their bodies.

The prisoners walked with their heads bowed, many bloody and beaten, having struggled before surrendering to salvage their lives. Men and women in white and black kept watch over them.

And worse still, mixed amongst the enemy beast-kin and the monsters who wore the faces of men and women... were the dead. For the warlock had always fought with the corpses of those he could raise from the sand and dust. And now was no different.

Under was a world that had been built upon the dead. There was no shortage of corpses for him to pull from the depths.

Evie pushed away from his arm and began to ready herself. She was inhaling and exhaling in deep breaths as if she were warming up for a morning workout, not a bloodbath. Edu tried not to laugh. He had to wait for the signal that would be given to himself and the others who waited in the other narrow passageways or atop the buildings nearby. He had not come alone with only Evie for help—he was not a fool.

The caravan of prisoners pushed into the main street where it widened slightly. A perfect place for an ambush. Edu looked up as a figure cast a shadow across the packed sand and dirt road from where it was perched atop a building. A creature that stood some twelve feet tall, fur hackled up and striped in tones of oranges and reds with blacks and whites.

Kamira in her true form was something to behold, beautiful as she was terrifying. Elegance that carried the promise of a quick death under several tons of muscle, sinew, and fang. She roared loudly at those below. Bits of clay rained down from where the clay roof did not stand a chance against her giant claws. A challenge, a warning, and a signal for them to attack.

Edu hadn't stepped one foot forward before Evie was charging ahead at full speed, axe overhead, hollering her own version of a war cry.

For the second time in two days, Edu found himself laughing his way through battle.

FIVE

It still got dark in Under.

Lydia had an answer to that question now. She had a dozen other unanswered questions, but she'd take what she could get. But the sun didn't set—not exactly. The sun never moved. Never tracked through the sky. It was like it was frozen, trapped at about three o'clock. Just far enough over to cast shadows. *Naturally.*

When it suddenly began to grow dark, she stopped walking and looked up to see what the hell was happening.

It was an eclipse. A dark disk was sliding over the sun. It only took a matter of moments before the disk slid into place, far faster than it should have been. And then, it didn't move. It just stayed... parked there. It was as though a great, all-powerful creature had simply said, "And let it be dark." For all intents and purposes, she figured that was exactly what had happened.

The blazing sun was stunning. She had never seen an eclipse on earth—not in real life—and it was beautiful to watch. The halo and arcs of light that curled out around the black disk was so fascinating she almost forgot where she was. Along the horizon in all directions, it looked like sunrise or sunset.

To say it was surreal would be to put it mildly. She could see the arcs of sun flares jumping from the edges of the disk, and she was tempted to stand there and watch. But she shouldn't be standing here, in the middle of a deserted street, staring up at the eclipse like an idiot. It wasn't safe.

Not like she'd seen any imminent signs of danger in the past two hours she'd been walking. No one was around—no whisper of people. And that made her nervous. It meant either they were all gone or they were all hiding. Either way, it wasn't good.

Shaking herself out of watching the eclipse, she pushed the hood of her cotton coat off and was glad the sun wasn't so damn hot anymore.

It was funny how adjusted to the dark she'd become. She had only been in Under for six months at this point. Maybe seven, tops. But she had become so used to the never-ending night over that time.

She kept walking, keeping close to the edge of the buildings, her eyes darting down the alleys she passed in case something was about to leap out at her. Precisely for that reason, she saw them before they saw her. She ducked in between two of the wood and clay buildings and pressed herself against the wall. The streets were empty, until the exact moment they were filled. But not with a normal kind of crowd. These people were wearing chains.

It was the kind of thing you only ever saw in movies. Dozens of people, shackled at the wrists and chained together, being led through the streets. Prisoners surrounded by the imposing force.

At the first sight of a walking skeleton, she knew who the imposing force belonged to. *Huh. Zombies. That's new.* Add it to the list of weird shit she'd seen in the past six months. She watched as the crowd was marched along drearily, surrounded by men and women in black, the undead, and the soulmarked beasts that were the human souls that came out of the pond more changed in body than others.

Not-Aon commanded his House, the corpses he could raise, and now apparently the beasts of Under. Well, the ones that weren't hers. "Great. That's great. That's just freaking fantastic. No biggie." Letting out a long whoosh of air as quietly as she could, she finished muttering to herself and tried to think through what to do.

Should she get involved?

She could probably—*maybe*—take out the men and women wearing black, the monsters, and the freaky walking corpses. But then what? Where would they go? If Not-Aon had an army, what the hell was she supposed to do about it by herself?

Maybe she should lie low. Bide her time. Stay out of this. That was the safer bet.

All debate ended when her eyes landed on someone in the chains. One of the prisoners, his face bruised and bloody. He had been beaten, and badly. But he was still walking, even if he now had a stiff limp in one leg.

Maverick.

Beside him was Aria, her clothing torn and stained in blood, clearly having been through a nasty brawl. Whatever fight had landed them where they were now, it hadn't been a fun one. And Not-Aon's people weren't taking their prisoners gently.

And wait. Was that *Gary?* It was! That poor, soft-hearted Englishman she met so briefly in a time that felt like a decade ago. He had a split lip, and one of his eyes was swollen shut. He looked bleaker than the rest of them, if that was possible.

She grunted.

Well. So much for biding her time and lying low.

* * *

The swarm of glowing, turquoise locusts he saw rising in a cloud over the city was Lyon's first clue as to where he may find the Queen of Dreams. He had taken to the skies himself as a thousand white bats, covering more ground in such a way than he could as a man.

There had been no sign of Lydia since the world was restored some days ago. Three eclipses had come and gone with no indication of where she may be. His King had informed him that the girl was facing down the brunt of her full powers and had likely needed to rest. He had managed to invade her dreams once but had not managed to do so again through what she was suffering. Her resting state made her difficult to find.

Prey that held perfectly still made for difficult quarry to hunt.

Yet, his orders were clear. He had been instructed to find Lydia and find her *personally*. He had been told not to return to the temple until she had been retrieved. And so, he dove low, reformed himself on a building, and swiped his hand at a locust that came too close to his face for his liking. Looking down into the street, he smiled faintly.

What a creature she had become.

He remembered the mortal girl who had valiantly tried to run from him on Earth. The one who walked into the Pool of the Ancients a mortal girl and miraculously had returned the same. The warm-hearted, blazingly strong young woman. He felt as if he had known her for centuries when only months had passed. He should have recognized her as a queen the moment he first saw her. He was a fool not to have seen the Ancients' plan for her when it was so very clear now in hindsight.

For ones who were as old as he was, where time stretched on endlessly, it was astonishing to him when time could still find the means to seemingly change its tempo. For the woman he watched in the streets below was a force to be reckoned with, and time seemed to slow to allow him to watch her work.

The insects were a perfect distraction to level the scales. She was outnumbered—until he considered the creatures she had summoned to fight with her.

Creatures born of nightmares, twisted and futuristic, cartoonish yet bizarre—their strange proportions doing nothing to hamper their destructive capabilities as they devoured and ripped to pieces the walking dead who guarded the prisoners.

Caught off guard, those who were meant to escort the prisoners fared no better. Some were felled. Most, understandably, fled from the Queen, heads ducked as they tried to protect themselves from the insects that viciously and mercilessly chased them.

Once the foes were fallen or gone, the locusts cleared, and the monsters dissipated. Lydia quickly worked her magic to snap the chains of the prisoners, and ran to greet a few of them, hugging them eagerly.

Lyon could recognize Maverick and Aria from where he stood. Lyon felt no small amount of relief that they were alive. Oh, how he wished he could join them, but he had come with a job to do.

Yet... he would wait. Let them converse. Let friends find shelter in each other, before he came down to ruin it all. He could spare them a few moments.

But his master's forces were not to be deterred.

In fact, his presence was not the only one that had been drawn by the ruckus caused by the fight. Although the squall beneath him had ended, it was merely a pause in the violence. From his vantage point, he could see several more battalions of forces drawn in by the noise, weaving through the maze of ancient buildings toward the unsuspecting prisoners and Lydia.

The new queen's strength was about to be tested.

* * *

Lydia hugged Maverick so tight that he grunted.

"Thank you." He hugged her back, propriety for once be damned, as she squeezed him. "Thank you, Lydia."

"It was about time for me to help you for a change, doc," she teased him. "It's so good to see you."

"You as well. After I heard what Rxa had done, and then when the world fell apart, I did not know what became of you." Maverick's visible brow furrowed. "I found myself rather worried."

"It means you're feeling an emotion called 'friendship', Mav. It's normal." She grinned. Hope. Insidious thing. Hard to kill.

Aria was chuckling from beside him, mustering as much amusement at Lydia's jab as she could, even with how battered and pained she looked. "I am so glad you are well. These past few days have been... trying."

"Days?" Lydia blinked. "How long has it been?"

"Three," Maverick answered simply. "If that abomination," he pointed up at the eclipse, "counts as the passing of a day."

Sighing, she ran her hand over her face. She must have been out for a lot longer than it felt. Oh, well, no point crying over spilt milk. Especially when she had bigger issues to deal with, and—

She squeaked as somebody hugged her rather abruptly. She hadn't seen them walk up with her hand over her eyes. It was Gary, and he looked as though he was about to cry. She laughed and hugged him back. "Hey, man!"

"I was so c-certain this was the end. It is so wonderful to se-e—" he stammered and then started the tears. The poor man was at his wits' end, and he wiped at the parts of his face that he could while wearing his mask and stepped back. He was clearly embarrassed that he had just jumped onto her.

She knew how good hope could feel, even if it was a dangerous trap. How wonderful it was to think you might have a chance when everything grew dark. And that's what she was to Gary—he had thought he was doomed, until she burst from nowhere and set them all free. She smiled and stepped into him, hugging him again, less urgently this time. "Glad to help."

Gary smiled down at her and returned the gesture before managing to collect himself and step back. He let out a long breath and tried to calm his tears. She hoped someday she could really get to know the man and be a real friend to him.

"What happened?" Lydia sighed. "What've I missed?"

"Aon, well, what has become of him, is in command of the greater beasts, as you saw. He has raised his armies, and he is gathering any who do not kneel. Those of us who wear masks are being rounded up regardless." Maverick was trying to brush himself off, although it wasn't really doing much good. Blood-stains were hard to wipe off wool.

"He's taking people with masks? Why?" That made no sense.

"I do not know." Maverick looked up at the temple that still loomed high over the city, although it was several more miles away than it had been when she first saw it. "I fear you would have to ask the *man* himself." It was clear how much he thought of the *man* in question.

"I'd rather not, thanks." Lydia couldn't suppress a shudder.

"I am surprised he has not come for you." The doctor's statement was blunt, and it was unapologetic. She looked away and let out a small sigh. It was enough for Maverick to put the pieces together. "He already has spoken to you, hasn't he?"

She couldn't suppress a wince. "More or less."

Maverick went to open his mouth to pry for more details, but a roar cut them off. Whirling, she saw armed undead creatures, as well as men and women wearing black, pile into the courtyard. A monster had been the source of the noise—a great, hulking mass of flesh that looked almost toad-like in its rolls of fat and giant eyes.

"Do you have somewhere safe to go?" Moving to step in front of her friends, she asked Maverick the question without turning to face them.

"Yes. It's—" Another roar cut him off. The group of men and monsters were coming at them *fast*.

"Go! I'll find you, just go!"

"But—"

"I can hold them." She thought she could anyway. Well, she was going to try. "Just *go!*"

Maverick and the others turned and fled. Smart.

Letting out a breath, she cracked her neck. The squadron looked at the running forces, then looked at her, and ignored the prisoners.

They knew her on sight.

They knew she was far more interesting a trophy than a bunch of bleeding prisoners. They began to form a half-ring around her, as she was blocking their path to following Maverick and the others.

"All right, kids. You wanna dance? Let's dance." She had no idea what she was doing. But she was actually kind of *excited* to fuck around and find out.

Time was once she would have turned and run. Dropped to her knees and begged and cried for help or tried to hide behind someone who could fight for her.

Not this time.

She took off the cotton coat she had donned and tossed it aside. This was going to be a real fight, and it would only get in the way. She held out her hand and called from the nothingness a spear. It was tipped in obsidian, like her daggers. The staff was decorated with carvings and markings, and turquoise, glowing feathers hung from it near where it became a blade. It felt familiar. It felt right. She grinned, feeling a strange joy come over her at the idea of a good fight.

She was still herself. But maybe, just maybe, a little bit of her remembered what it was like to have been Qta.

A creature like a rotted, destitute hyena came bounding around the crowd, leaping over several rows of men to try to catch her off guard. She stabbed her spear up and through its head from the jaw, bursting out the other side in a spray of gore. It should have knocked her over with the weight of the attack. Or as she was now holding the horse-sized creature half off the ground, impaled on her weapon. It seemed she was stronger than she used to be.

Okay, that's cool.

With a twist, she dumped the creature onto its side and planted her foot on its face to yank the blade free from its body. She swung it just in time to smash a man in the side of the face with the end of her wooden spear.

This is fun!

The feeling of spilling blood.

Of fighting, of killing. This felt like freedom. This felt like power.

She barely noticed the rest of the fight as it went on. She was moving by instinct, dodging swipes of claws, swords, or axes. She could easily maneuver out of the way of crackles of magic that the warlock's House fought with.

She might have even been laughing, she didn't know. So far, she didn't even have a scratch on her. None of the blood on her body was hers.

This wasn't like her at all.

Nor was her ability to handle a spear. She fought with it like it had been an extension of her own arm. No, more like an extension of her whole body. Like she had been using it since the dawn of time.

The fight was easy—almost *too* easy—until she heard another roar. The large, toad-like pile of fat was now coming toward her. She knew it was more dangerous than it looked. Its arm had been replaced with a metal bludgeon, spikes sticking out of it in odd angles.

It looked like something Nick would have fought in one of his stupid video games.

That thing gave her reason to pause and wonder if she was going to win this. She took in a breath and let it out, wiping some of the sweat from her brow with a clean spot on her arm.

The ones she had only wounded and not defeated were standing up, staggering back and forming a front once more. She had only taken down about half of them, and the other half were still ready and raring to go.

Fine, then. She might not win, but she was going to try. And if they thought she was going to go down without trying, they were very wrong.

Wait, why're they backing up?

Every single one of them, even the giant lard-monster, was backing away from her with looks of nervousness and fear on their faces.

It wasn't because of her.

Suddenly, she felt like she was missing something very important. Something that was behind her. It wasn't until the men, women, and monsters either vanished or began to retreat that she found the nerve to see what had chased them off. Turning slowly, her mouth gaped open at who she saw.

A thin, kind smile met her. She knew the man's face, even if it bore many more white marks upon the alabaster surface than usual. A man dressed all in white, thin and tall, a doleful expression ever etched into his eyes. She felt her heart lift in hope.

She let her spear fall to the ground as she rushed to him. He held out his arms and caught her in an embrace, hugging her tightly as she wrapped her arms around his neck. He stood as she did, lifting her off her feet and twirling her once before setting her back down, but didn't release her from the tight hug. She wasn't ready to let him go yet either.

She was crying, she was laughing. She was so happy to see him. She couldn't form words. All she could get out was a choked out, "Lyon!"

"Hello, Lydia. It is so wonderful to see you."

Hope.

She should've known better.

<h1 style="text-align:center">SIX</h1>

There weren't words to describe how much relief Lydia felt at hugging Lyon, at seeing her friend after what had happened to him. She was sure he would know what to do. Or what to say. How to fix this.

How to fix the world.

He always did.

He would know where to go and how they should handle this new world. How to handle Not-Aon or whatever the man she loved had become.

"I'm so sorry, Lyon."

He released his grasp around her just enough for her to look up at him. He looked down at her, confused and quizzical.

"I'm so sorry about what happened to you. About Rxa—about what he did, and…" She'd have nightmares about that damn pool of blood for as long as she lived, she knew.

He reached up and gently stroked her hair. "You saved me from oblivion. You spared my life when you could have freed yourself. I admit, perhaps it was a bit foolish, in light of all that has occurred in the wake of your decision. Yet I cannot help but thank you from the depths of my soul."

Chuckling at his comment, she looked up at him as a thought occurred to her. "How do you know they gave me a choice?" No one else knew, except her, Aon, and the Ancients.

"I heard their voices in my mind the moment I awoke. Our creators told me of the gift they offered you, that they would spare only one of us." He shook his head like a mildly disappointed parent. "Whatever made you decide as you did? I cannot truly be worth so much in your mind."

"That's not true. You're my friend, Lyon. You're the only person in this godforsaken world who's been... just nice to me. Nice for the sake of it or who didn't want something in return. I couldn't let you die for me. I couldn't let another person I cared about die before my eyes. I just couldn't."

He leaned down and placed a kiss on the top of her head. He folded her into his arms again and held her. "Thank you, my dear, dear friend."

"Besides," she smirked, "Kamira never would've let me hear the end of it."

That got a laugh out of him, and she felt him rest his cheek on her head. She had never known him to be this touchy before, but she figured they had a bond now. "Yet I mourn for how many more may die in my stead."

Gently pushing away, she looked up to meet his ice-blue gaze. He had resumed the expression of a mournful cemetery angel. The thought had already occurred to her. How many people had already died, let alone how many more would join them? All because of what Aon did to save her from an eternity at the bottom of a lake.

"I never said I was smart." She couldn't hold his gaze, feeling like she had let him down.

"You are not a fool, my friend." He placed a finger under her chin and tilted her head back up to look at him. He was smiling again, if faintly. "I am not casting judgment upon you, for I would have done the same if I were faced with your dilemma. You are compassionate, and your heart defines you. Never let this place or the passage of time take that away from you. Certainly, you should never feel guilty for it."

"Thanks. I'm just so happy you're okay." Furrowing her brow, she realized what she was looking at. She had seen his extra marks, but it hadn't really sunk in yet. "What's all this?" She reached up to point at the extra white lines that ran along his pale skin.

"I am now the head of the House of Blood. With Rxa dead, there was a need to be filled. A king needed to rise, and so the Ancients took their opportunity, it seems. To grant another the power of a royal, the body must be lifeless. As you were, and now, as was I."

"Huh."

Lyon shrugged. "Not that it matters anymore. The Houses are not what they were. We only remain as such for their amusement. Kings and Queens like toys in a box to be played with."

She nodded. The Houses were dissolved, for all intents and purposes. If Not-Aon was now the King of All, who knew what they now were or what roles they played in this world? The arrival of the Ancients had effectively thrown the game board across the room, and now they were all starting from scratch.

She fought back the encroaching dread by reminding herself that Lyon was here—he was alive. And because of that, she was no longer alone. There was someone with her now in all this madness. The Priest and his ever-present voice of reason was more than a little welcome. "How is Kamira? She must be so relieved you're alive." She took the opportunity to steer the subject away from their now uncertain futures.

He seemed reluctant to answer at first. "I do not think she knows. I have not been able to locate her. Dtu and all the others are in hiding, and she likely—and correctly—believes me dead." He was clearly saddened over the suffering his wife must feel.

"She'll be okay. Nothing can keep that woman down."

Lyon smirked. "I am not concerned for her. She will be quite fine. This new wild world will pose no threat to her. Indeed, she may find it more enjoyable than most."

She laughed and had no problem believing that. She could easily picture Kamira having a blast in this primal and brutal landscape.

He reached out and placed his hands on her shoulders. "I am so glad to find you are safe. I am glad to find that you are finally now yourself, as well."

"What?"

"The marks on your arms. The way you fought. It is clear you are now whole and unafraid. It brings me great joy. While I know you must mourn your snake, as he was an amusing creature, you are now what you were meant to become. You look magnificent."

She felt her face go warm, and she shrugged sheepishly. "Thanks. I think I'm still me, mostly. I just have so much extra shit running around in my head right now, though. It's weird. I don't feel..." She trailed off, not knowing what to say.

"Human?"

She nodded. He really did always know what to say. "Yeah. I don't feel human."

"As you shouldn't. I know this world has not been kind to you. Not in any sense of the word has your coming here, or your time within it, been gentle. But do not rail against what you have become for that you feel resentment over such a thing."

"I don't. I'm just sorting it out. I only wish I knew what to do next. Every time I feel like I catch my footing, the world changes the rules on me."

He tilted his head to the side slightly. "What do you mean?"

"Well..." She was confused. Wasn't it obvious? "Aren't we all on the run now? Hiding from Not-Aon? What does he want? What do the Ancients want? What is our life now? I don't know what I'm supposed to do, except try to find you or Edu or any of the others. Hell, I might even settle for Dtu at this point." It was a poor attempt at hiding the fear that was rising in her again. Fear of what was to come.

The Priest pulled her into another hug as if sensing her growing nervousness. She wrapped her arms around him in return and ignored the feeling of his odd tepid skin. He was so cold, even in the hot air. He had no warmth of his own, after all.

"That is why I am glad I have found you. And so quickly, as well. You were not subtle, I must say. The giant cloud of glowing insects was not an effective method of staying hidden, you realize."

Laughing quietly, she shrugged. "I didn't really think it through, instinct just kind of took over. I'm getting better at this whole 'being a queen' thing, but I'm still working on the details."

He shifted and leaned his head down toward her shoulder. He was really being unusually touchy. At first, it felt like two friends seeing each other after they learned they both had survived a train wreck. But now, it was becoming strange. The alarm bells began to ring. He was so polite and so shy usually, not nearly as hands-on as all the others. "What're you doing?"

His voice was a faint murmur. "Our Master has sent me to find you. It is by his command that I have come. Though I am glad for it, and I left with a happy heart to see you again. I truly am so grateful you saved my life. I praise the Ancients that you are well. I have come to bring you home."

Home? What the ever-loving hell was he talking about? Master? She went to pull away and ask him as much. "What're you—" Lydia never got the rest of the question out of her mouth before it was too late. Lyon's hand twisted in her hair and yanked her head sharply to the side. She let out a small, choked cry in her throat as something sharp pierced her throat. Like a pair of needles.

Teeth.

The feeling of his teeth buried in the tender flesh of her neck stung hard enough to bring tears to her eyes. His arm banded around her lower back, squeezing her tight to him, keeping her from struggling. He kept her head wrenched to one side as he pressed her body to his. It felt like being held by a marble statue.

"Stop—" she gasped through the pain, feeling his lips close around the wound. Feeling him *pull* from her, drawing her blood into his mouth. The sensation was inescapable.

Every time he took a mouthful from her body, she let out a small whimper as a rush of every kind of feeling overwhelmed her.

"Lyon!" She tried to push him away. He simply held her tighter. It was like being stuck in a metal vise. He was so much stronger than she was. Immovable and unstoppable.

He was going to drain her dry and bring her unconscious body to *him.*

There was a bizarre noise coming from him, like a strange, deep purring noise as he drank from her. It was a rumble that seemed to vibrate through her as he fell into a slow pattern, the fangs buried in her neck keeping the wound from closing.

The sound made her freeze, and she couldn't explain why.

The pain faded, even as he continued. What it was replaced by was far more dangerous than the stinging had been.

It was pleasure.

Sheer, utter, and total pleasure. Like being on morphine, that time she had broken her ankle. No. It was more than that. It was numbing, yes. It was a warmth that spread over her. But it was... erotic. It felt *intimate.*

A veil was being pulled over her mind, as though someone was wrapping her up in the most perfect warm blanket by a fire and she had a strong drink in her hand. It felt like trust, like being safe, like being tucked away during a winter storm. There was a low throb that filled her in time with his pulls from her throat—in time with her heartbeat.

It felt like bliss.

Each time he pulled, she let out a gasp as her body bloomed in warmth. Wouldn't it be so simple? To sink into this and to let it take her? Why not let him wash away all her fear and worry and wake up safe, away from all the uncertainty of this new world? Wasn't that all she ever wanted?

It would be so easy, just to let it all go.

It was Lyon. She was safe with him. He'd never hurt her. Right?

It felt so good to be his prey.

To let him take her.

She wanted this to never stop.

She wanted to melt against him and give up. To stop fighting. The struggling was so pointless, wasn't it? Her life was like quicksand. The more she struggled, the more hopeless it became. *Let go. Let this happen. It's already too late. Just let go. Let him take you home.*

If she just let her eyes slide shut, it would all be over.

No!

She didn't know where she found the strength, but she summoned a dagger into her hand and dug the obsidian blade deep into Lyon's neck. He howled in pain and whipped his head back and staggered away, half throwing her from him.

The clay and wood wall of the building behind her met her back as she leaned heavily against it, her hand going to her neck. The wound stung now that she was out of his control, and it was damp with blood. But she was in better condition than Lyon.

She had dug her dagger to the hilt in the side of the vampire's neck and twisted it before he could react. When he yanked it back out, blood splashed onto the dusty ground at his feet, speckling his white clothes with crimson. Morbidly, she observed that a large portion of that was probably hers.

"What the hell is wrong with you?" Her shout wasn't half as loud as she wanted it to be, still feeling weak from the blood loss and still shaking off the weird reverie he had put over her. Her spear was back in her hands, having summoned it from where she had dropped it.

His face was drawn in pain as he placed his hand over the wound in his neck. It was already healing and closing. He coughed, and his lips were suddenly flecked with blood. It took him a moment to stitch back together enough that he could speak. She should probably stab him now, but... he was her friend.

Betrayal or not, he deserved a chance to explain himself.

When he did, his voice was low but strained from the wounds she had given him. It was raspy and a little wet, blood still in his throat. "He sent me to find you. The king wishes you to join him. The others will be along shortly. Come, please. You know this is fruitless." He held out his hand to her, just as he did that night on the streets of Boston when he had come for her and Nick. "You know this is inevitable."

He was right. She knew it was very, very pointless to fight what was going to happen to her. The King of All *would* find her.

In Boston, she had been a human girl with no idea what she was up against. She had done okay, all things considered, with a gun, her wits, and a hobby knife. Now, she had real power. She had a chance. If she was going to go down, she was going to go down with a fight.

She paced a step away and held up her spear. "I take it this means you serve him?"

"I serve the Ancients. I am their High Priest. I bow before my rightful King, as should you. Will it not bring you joy to see him? To hold him? Do you not still love him?" There was a flash in Lyon's eyes when he talked, an odd and unfamiliar glint.

Oh, *shit*. She knew that look; she'd seen it enough times on Aon.

Lyon had lost his mind.

He was a little bit insane, or he wasn't entirely himself. He was the same man but with clearly different priorities. He had become another puppet of the Ancients. They seemed hell-bent on taking *everyone* away from her.

Focus. One problem at a time. He had asked her a question, and the longer she stalled him, the more she healed before they were going to have to fight. "I don't know who he is anymore. He's not the same. So no, I can't."

"Are you so sure?"

"He's shown up in my dreams once. He's not the same."

"I mean are you so certain you cannot love him?"

Growling, she decided she didn't want to argue about it. If she did, she might start questioning the value in his statement, and that was not a road she wanted to go down. "Lyon, you aren't okay. They're controlling you. Can't you tell?" She stepped away from the wall slowly. She was tired, and the blood loss was creeping up on her. The adrenaline was giving her legs to stand on, but she knew it wouldn't last forever. "Snap out of it!"

He was almost fully healed now, and he straightened back up to his full height. The wound on his neck was gone. "Lydia." He said it like a scolding parent again. "You once more find yourself fighting against the weight of the world. You struggle against the will of the Ancients. You know you cannot escape. You have nowhere in this world where you can hide. Why do you fight?"

"Because I can't just give in. Because rolling over and taking it isn't in my nature." She began to pace away from the wall, circling Lyon, putting some open air behind her back. There was going to be a fight, and she didn't want to start it by being stuck in a corner. "Ask Kamira why she and Dtu are running. Ask anyone."

"They are merely scared. They are frightened of what our Master may do to them, but you have nothing to fear. He loves you. He is devoted to you. He will not harm you. Do you not want to love him? Do you not wish to find if you still can? Return to him. Come with me, please. Do not draw this out needlessly." There was an overeager glint in his eyes. The edge of madness, the edge of a zealot.

He took a step toward her slowly as if trying to calm a wounded, cornered animal. "Do not deny yourself peace over a misguided sense of what you believe is the right thing to do."

Oh, how badly she wanted to agree. How badly she wanted to just let go. But like every time she had chosen to fight before, she had to do the same this time. There was no surrender, not yet. She could still stand on her own power. "No." She took another step back. "I'm leaving now."

"I am afraid I cannot let you."

"Don't make me hurt you, Lyon." Fighting her friend was the absolute last thing she wanted to do for a whole lot of reasons. Least of which being that she knew she wouldn't win. "I really don't want to fight you, but I will."

Lyon held out his arms at his sides, and she went wide-eyed as she watched gold armor appear on his arms. Gauntlets with talons like the claws of a dragon in ornate, golden and shining armor appeared on him. The armor stopped at his upper arms. He fought with his bare hands, and the claws he now wore put the ones on Aon's prosthetic to shame in how vicious they looked.

"Huh," Lydia said, surprised.

"You did not think I could hold my own?" Lyon smiled sadly at her. "Do not underestimate me, my friend."

"I guess I figured you'd use a sword is all."

"If I am to cause harm to another, I wish to do it personally."

All right, that suited him. She nodded and readied herself, trying to pretend she wasn't terrified. "Please don't make me do this."

"I beg of you the same."

They stared at each other in silence. Neither wanted to fight. Neither wanted to hurt the other. But she couldn't give him what he was asking for. And he couldn't let her go.

In a blur, Lyon disappeared. The man moved quickly. He hadn't teleported; he had just gone almost too fast to be seen. She swung her spear and clocked Lyon across the jaw with it as he reappeared standing next to her. He staggered back with a grunt and put his hand to his face. Lyon looked at her, surprised she had connected the blow.

"Do not underestimate me, my friend," she echoed back at him.

"I see you have accepted the power of Qta as your own. Finally, you are a true queen of Under." There was real, genuine pride and happiness in his eyes. "How glorious. I cannot wait to see our King's reaction when he sees firsthand what you have become."

Lyon rushed at her again, golden claws raking through the air. She ducked out of the way and dug the tip of her spear into his side. She sank it into his ribs and twisted it as she yanked it out. Lyon snarled in pain as blood poured down his side. When she went to attack him again, he vanished into mist. A crack into the back of her head sent her sprawling to the dirt. She rolled out of the way in time for his golden claw to dig into the sand, right where her torso had been.

The fight raged on for several minutes. Lyon was fast, and he hit *hard*. More than once, he raked his claws into her skin, tearing welts in her. They burned and stung but didn't slow her down. Not at first, anyway.

She was used to the touch of claws, after all.

It was only a few moments before they were healed, only stains of crimson reminding her of where she had been hit. But they were starting to add up, and the more he hit her, the slower she healed.

Lyon very clearly had the upper hand. He had taken a lot of her blood. Her adrenaline and her fear would only last for so long. She would tire before he would, she was sure. He was a nearly two-millennia-old vampire, and now a king. Lydia was still the new kid in town, a queen or not.

Dents and cracks were left in the buildings around them. A stack of straw baskets was destroyed when she hurled Lyon through them. She, in turn, reduced a wooden beam to splinters in much the same fashion.

Lyon backhanded her viciously across the face, sending her sprawling to the dust. She tasted blood in her mouth. Lydia's head was swimming, and it took her a split second to blink her eyes back into focus. It was a split second too long.

Lyon rolled her onto her back and clasped his golden-armored hand around her throat. "I did not wish to snap your neck. Though now I see it would have been the kinder way." He reached his other hand down to her head, and she knew her world was about to go to black any moment. "When you wake, all will be well." There was a twinge of regret in his eyes.

"Yeah, right."

"I am sorry, my friend, for what it's worth."

"I believe you. For what it was worth." Shutting her eyes, she braced herself for what she expected to be brief pain before the darkness consumed her.

SEVEN

Golden claws grasped her head, and Lydia prepared herself to learn what it was like to have her neck snapped. She had no doubt Lyon would do it. He had lost his mind to the Ancients —to Not-Aon.

But it never came.

Instead, she felt the blast of fire. The heat washed over her like she had thrown open the door to her oven. Lyon's weight on top of her and his hand around her throat vanished. She opened her eyes, stunned, and saw him staggering backward, snarling, his fangs bared at whoever had been responsible for attacking him.

Who the hell?

A giant sword swung for Lyon a second later, and she had her answer. A hulking, mountain of a man in full armor.

Edu!

She never thought she would ever once be happy to see the nightmarish warrior, and yet, here she was, feeling exactly that. Rolling back up to her feet, she felt a little wobbly, but she managed to stay vertical. The blood loss was still affecting her, and the backhand to the head hadn't helped. Neither did all the cuts he had dealt her. Many of them were already healed, but some were struggling to get there. It seemed like the more hits she took, the longer it took to mend.

Lyon was struggling to catch his footing, and Edu wasn't letting up. The warrior knew how to keep the other man on the defensive, unable to plant his feet to strike back. After another swing of his massive blade, Edu found pay dirt. Lyon hissed in pain and disappeared into a swarm of bats, reappearing some twenty feet away. He was holding his side, where the white of his clothing was beginning to turn dark crimson from the deep gash.

Edu stood, his sword raised, ready to attack.

Lydia moved to stand beside him and summoned her spear back to her hand. Two against one. Sure, she was injured and exhausted and would probably lose in a heartbeat on her own, but the vampire didn't need to know that.

Seeing that he was now horribly outmatched, Lyon sighed and straightened his shoulders, even as he winced in pain from the wound. "Edu, this does not concern you."

Edu shook his head, clearly arguing otherwise.

Lyon knew trying to convince Edu wouldn't work, so he tried a different tactic. "Lydia. Please, come with me, I entreat you. Our King means you no harm. All the opposite, I promise. Running and hiding will only delay and irritate him."

"I'm really good at irritating him. He should be used to it by now. It's basically our form of foreplay." Lydia couldn't help but smirk as Edu snorted in laughter. "No, Lyon. I'm not going with you. I'm not going anywhere near him. Not willingly."

"And you know it shall come to that. It will only be a matter of time before you fail. You cannot hide in a world that is his. Not when he seeks you so adamantly."

"I know."

"Then why bother fighting?"

"Sometimes, it's the only thing you have left to do."

Edu glanced at her. But neither of them kept their eyes off Lyon for long. The vampire seemed to concede the inevitability of how the conversation was going to end. He squared his shoulders and let his hand drop from his side. The wound Edu had dealt him was already healed. All that was left was the crimson stain on his white suit.

"Then he will be the one who comes for you. This was your one chance to make this relatively painless, Lydia. Regardless, I will grieve for your troubles, but I am glad to have seen you." There was such sadness in his face. The eyes of a man wishing her to make a different choice. He was a puppet being danced about by the Ancients—but unlike Aon, she could recognize her friend.

"I'm glad you're alive, Lyon. Even if you are being an *abject* dick right now."

He smiled thinly and bowed his head to her in thanks. "Farewell." And with that, he exploded into a swarm of white bats and took off into the sky.

She let out a breath she had been holding and felt some of the tension slack out of her shoulders. "This sucks."

Edu chuckled and nodded. She watched as his sword disappeared from his hand. As he started walking, his armor vanished as well. He changed into his somewhat subtler Viking clothing, even if he did seem hilariously out of place in the ancient sandy city. At least now he didn't look like a walking angry bus that fucked a scarab beetle like he did in the full plate mail.

After about ten feet, he stopped and looked back at her, gesturing for her to follow him. Lydia took a second to debate it. Could she trust him? This was Edu, after all. He had tried to kill her twice—wait, three times. Succeeded once. What kind of stupid bizarro-world was she living in where *Edu* was the ally and *Lyon* was the enemy?

What were her other options right now? Give herself up or try to escape alone. The first option was out of the question, and the second hadn't gone so well already. She scratched the back of her head, the feeling of her nails on her scalp providing some small amount of comfort while she thought. Going with Edu was the only logical choice she had.

Once she started following him, he turned and led them through the alleys and streets of the city. It still looked abandoned—no one was on the streets. "Where is everybody?"

Without turning back to look at her, he pointed at one of the buildings, then opened his hand so his palm was facing down and moved it a few inches lower as if pressing something.

"Lying low?" she guessed.

He nodded.

Edu was pretty good at communicating, even without being able to speak. *Fifteen hundred years of practice,* she reminded herself. *He's been mute longer than most countries on Earth have even existed.*

Everyone was hiding? Well, if Not-Aon's people were rounding up everyone wearing masks, it would make sense. Of course, they'd hide. She'd be doing the same thing if she thought it'd amount to anything. There was no doubt in her mind that *he* could send hounds to sniff her out.

She had to get out of the city. For her own safety, and everyone else's.

"Thanks for saving me."

Edu shrugged. Not dismissively. Maybe saying "of course" or "no big deal." She sped up her steps to walk next to him and put her hand on his arm. The big man turned his head to look down at her but didn't stop. The streets weren't safe, after all.

"No, really, thanks," she reiterated.

He reached up his hand, and she fought the urge to flinch away. He then patted her on the back with such force it sent her staggering forward a few steps. She laughed, finding herself grinning at his goofy gesture. He had done it very clearly on purpose.

She fell in step beside him and didn't bother pestering him anymore. He kept a driving pace. His legs were long, and they took the city in stride. She almost had to jog to keep up. The city itself was a winding, tangled mess of ramshackle buildings. It looked as though there was no rhyme or reason as to where they were placed or how they were laid out. This was from an era long, long before city planners had been a thing. There were very few main roads, just streets that became wider from time to time.

They were doing their best to keep away from the open areas also, which made the backsy-forthsy nature of their wandering even worse. More than once they had to duck into a dark nook between buildings to avoid a marching group of the undead or those wearing black and white ink. Or monsters. Or all the above, in some cases.

She was sure Edu could take them. And even as tired as she was, she figured she could have done the same. But to do so would reveal their location and draw the attention of someone neither of them wanted to see—*him*.

"He showed up in my dreams again," she commented after another group of people passed by and it was safe to talk as they resumed their dodging and weaving path through the sprawling, ancient acropolis. "Whoever he is. Aon. But he said that isn't his name."

Edu nodded.

"You remember him from back then, don't you?" She was guessing. She didn't want to resort to playing twenty questions with the man. It'd be insulting to him, she figured. Also, because she had always sucked at that game.

Another nod was what she received in return, as he lifted a hand to rub at his neck unconsciously. There was a scar there, she saw. It ran around his neck in a circle. Like it had been put there by something having been wrapped around his throat for a very long time. The scar was old—ancient. And now, she knew who had put it there.

For as much of a nightmare come to life as this was for her, she suddenly realized that for Edu and the rest, they were reliving a very real and very old pain. "I'm so sorry. I'm sorry this happened."

He nodded again, but fainter than before, accepting her apology but signaling it truly didn't do anything to change how he felt. It wouldn't do anything in the end to soften the reality of what had happened. It was a platitude.

The statement of sorrow for another person's loss at a funeral. It didn't do any good, but it didn't hurt to have.

She fell silent again, her mind taking the opportunity to wander back over all that had happened. Some part of her felt relief at having found Edu. Or, rather, him having found her. There was comfort in not being alone. And even though it was clear that Lyon was very much not himself, and that his motivations were now driven by the Ancients, she was happy he was alive.

Hope truly was an insidious poison. *Maybe I can talk some sense into Lyon, break him out of this. Maybe Aon's still in there somewhere. Maybe I can get through to them both.* So many maybes. But like all her maybes up until now, she knew they would fall flat. But her hope would simply not die, no matter how loudly she screamed in her head for it to stay down.

Finally, Edu stopped in front of a building. He pushed the wood door open and walked inside. She knew she had to follow, even if the idea of now being cornered in a tight space with the big man was making her just a little bit nervous. Old habits died hard. She stepped inside in time to see the man opening a hatch in the ground. It looked like they were going to be forced to hide quite literally underground.

Edu pointed into the hole, indicating he wanted her to jump down. She walked up to the edge of it and investigated the pitch-black darkness. She couldn't see how far it went, what was down there, nothing. "Um. Not to be blunt, but... how do I know I can trust you?"

Edu sighed heavily, a beleaguered and tired sound. Before she could open her mouth again, he picked her up by the back of her shirt and lifted her off her feet like she was a kitten and he had her by the scruff of the neck. "Hey!"

He held her over the hole and dropped her into the pit without any further pomp and circumstance.

Lydia yelped as she fell. But the ground met her after ten or twelve feet. She landed with a hard *unf* and groaned at the impact. At first, she worried she might have broken her ankle, but the second after, she remembered she wasn't so easily injured anymore. Hearing a scuff of boots and a creak of wood above her, she rolled out of the way just in time for Edu to jump down after her, slamming the lid down after him as he jumped.

"Asshole," she said into the darkness.

A whoosh of fire and she saw him holding a torch. He was on his feet standing over her, looking down with a silent shake of his shoulders. He was laughing at her. He reached his other hand down to help her up.

She took it and he hefted her vertical as though she weighed an ounce. "You're still an asshole."

He nodded, agreeing with her assessment. With a jerk of his thumb ahead down the tunnel, he began walking. He was taking the light with him, and although she could probably "magic" herself up her own solution to the darkness, she had already committed to following him. She fell in step behind him, the tunnel too narrow to walk next to him. The man had to turn sideways to fit through the narrow bits as it was.

The tunnel looked carved out of rock, roughly and probably hastily. But it was definitely manmade, judging by the chisel marks and the few rings she saw pounded into the surface, meant to take a torch. But they sat empty and abandoned, much like the rest of the world above them.

Questions nagged at her. She wanted to ask him who else was with him, who was safe, if he knew what was happening. But he was mute, and without Ylena. It'd do no good to ask. She desperately wished she could communicate with him, and she realized with a pang that probably, so did he.

She didn't bother asking Edu why Aon wouldn't release the curse that kept his tongue from healing and his hand from regrowing. Spite was the answer. Aon had said something to that effect once as well, in a life that felt so far away now. Aon had said he had made out on the better end of the deal, as he only had to relearn how to write with his other hand.

She had come to love a man who was not known for his generosity or kindness. She knew that. She wasn't an idiot. But walking in the darkness, following a man who couldn't answer her questions past the basics that could be communicated via charades, it sank in once more.

A few times they came to a fork or an intersection, but he didn't even hesitate. He knew where he was going. "This isn't the first time you've had to use these tunnels, is it?"

He shook his head, confirming her theory.

"Is Evie okay?" Stick to yes or no questions for now. Edu nodded, and Lydia let out a sigh of relief. "You two are a thing now, huh?" Another nod from him. She shoved at his elbow playfully. "For realsies? Or just because you're a serious whore? Although I guess since you aren't getting paid to do it, that's not technically true."

Edu huffed a laugh and shook his head, amused at her insult. He nodded again, and she knew it was in response to the first half of the question and not the second half. He patted his hand over his heart. She barely caught the gesture, as they were walking single file and the man was basically a plug in the narrow passage.

"You love her?"

A nod.

She couldn't help the smile that was now on her face. That was adorable. Evie was so big-hearted, she was shocked no one had fallen for her sooner. Or maybe they had. She realized how little she knew about someone she considered a friend. "Yeah. That girl's a keeper. I just hope you don't screw it up."

Edu huffed another laugh.

"How does she feel? The same?"

Edu nodded again and rubbed the back of his head with his massive hand, ruffling his long, curly hair. It was an almost boyish gesture. That was just so damn cute, she couldn't help but grin. Big man, falling for the little spunky redhead. Big, five-and-more-thousand-years-old, powerful, inhuman, ancient man. But still.

"I bet when she told you, you didn't lose your freaking mind. That must have been nice."

Edu glanced back at her and tilted his head to the side curiously, clearly asking what she meant.

"Before Aon killed Nick, he took his mask off and told me that he loved me. I loved him then, but I couldn't tell him. I didn't know how. I had just died and become... well, you know." It felt weird, talking to Edu about how she felt. But she needed to try to trust him, just a little bit. And the man seemed like a softie, deep down beneath it all. If he loved Evie, there was something in there she could be friends with, she knew. "It didn't feel right. I didn't know if I could trust him. I knew he had killed Qta, but I didn't know why. He wouldn't tell me. It hadn't mattered before, when I was human, and suddenly it *really* did."

Lydia chewed on her lower lip as she thought it through. "He's... I know I shouldn't feel the way I do about him, Edu. I know he's a monster. I know he's a violent, vicious jackass. I know what he's done. The more I learn about his past, the more

I second-guess how I feel. But when I'm with him, when he looks at me, I can't help it. I love him. I just *do*."

Edu switched the torch from one hand to the other so that he could turn himself part way to watch her as she talked. His head was still tilted to the side just slightly as if he was trying to process what she was saying. It must sound impossible to him, she realized. Nobody could love Aon in his mind.

"I didn't tell him how I felt until after the trial. He snatched me right after it ended. He was furious—I thought he was going to seriously hurt me. But he couldn't. After what he told us, about that poor thing he made in an attempt to be loved, I had to tell him how I felt. It didn't feel right to let him keep going without knowing someone felt that way for him. It'd be selfish otherwise. And when I did, he... cracked. He's waited five thousand years—or longer, I guess—to hear somebody say those words."

Edu grunted and let out a sigh. Whatever he had to say in response, he couldn't.

So she continued. "He... um... had an episode. Between the choices of someone loving him or me being a figment of his madness, the madness won. That's how convinced he was that he'd always be alone."

Edu's shoulders were tense, and he just walked. She knew Aon would be furious at her if he knew she was telling Edu about a moment of weakness on his part, but she didn't care. She had to try to mend her relationship with the big man.

Her thoughts circled Aon again, and she looked back behind them down the dark tunnel with a sigh. She missed him, even as she was afraid he'd step out of the shadows at any moment. "I can't even imagine what that must be like. That kind of loneliness. That kind of self-loathing."

He looked back at her then, a curious tilt to his head.

"Oh, buddy. Don't you get it? Aon *hates* himself. He just

hates you all a whole lot more. He only thinks he's superior by comparison." She snickered and then sighed as her heart ached.

Edu chuckled and nodded. They fell into silence for a long while, and Edu heaved a long, heavy, weary sigh.

"But it... doesn't matter anymore." She let out a breath. "I've talked to this new version of him. Or, rather... old. He isn't the same. The man I loved? I don't know if he's still in there somewhere. Or if he's really—" *Gone,* she finished silently, unable to say it out loud, unable to finish, tears stinging her eyes.

She missed Aon so desperately.

She wanted him here with her so badly it hurt. To step out of nowhere, to laugh at her silly concern over him and tease her over her fear. To say this had all been a massive game on his part.

Abruptly, Edu stopped and turned to face her. Before she could even react, he wrapped an arm around her and hugged her. *Edu is hugging me.* She froze, unsure of what to do, just locked solid as he crushed her against his frame hard enough to pop a portion in her spine that needed a realignment.

When he let her go, he took that same hand and plopped his palm heavily onto the top of her head, rocking her head back and forth. It was a gesture of—she hoped, anyway—affection. He was seemingly trying to comfort her.

Edu was trying to say he was sorry for what she was going through.

What the hell is wrong with this world?

She couldn't help but laugh now and try and swat his hand away as he continued to rock her head from side to side. That apparently had been his goal, to cheer her up. Stupidly, it worked. He clapped his hand on her shoulder and squeezed it.

Try as she might to fight against it, it made her feel better. "Thanks, man."

He rolled his shoulders back, cracking them, and ended in a gesture that they should keep going. It was clear that it was making him a little uncomfortable to talk about her feelings toward Aon. She chuckled and nodded. "Lead the way, Rambo." That was going to be her new favorite nickname for him, she decided.

The reference was lost on him, but she didn't care. It seemed he didn't either, as he patted her shoulder one more time before turning and heading farther into the caves. Silence stretched on for minutes. She didn't pester him with more comments; she just followed behind him and thought.

If there was somebody in this world who knew what it was like to be haunted by someone who should be the person you love, it was Edu. He and Ziza had been together before Aon had ruined everything. The big man in red leather and black fur knew precisely how she felt.

After walking for another ten minutes with her mired in circular internal conversations about what to do about Aon, they stopped at a small wooden door. He pounded his fist on the worn surface. Really, he was just knocking. But a man with fists that large sounded far more impressive than what she would have managed. He knocked in a pattern, a signal to whoever was on the other side.

The sound of a creaking, rusty metal latch filled the tunnel, and then the door swung inward. A man stood on the other side. He wore a blue mask that covered the lower half of his face. He looked up at Edu and stepped aside. She couldn't help but notice how his eyes widened when he saw her.

Maybe someday they'd get used to her. Hell, maybe someday *she'd* get used to her. She tried not to laugh at the silliness of it.

The man in the blue mask wasn't alone. There were three others there, two men and a woman in green, red, and purple, respectively. Lydia did her best to smile at them as she stepped inside the chamber. The first man in blue swung the door shut, and the group of them worked together to drop a huge metal bar across the back of the door. No wonder it had been so loud. No wonder it took four people to move it.

It was meant to defend against an army.

Yet another reminder of who they were up against and of what that man would do to capture and control them. She knew that giant piece of metal wouldn't stop the "King of All," but it might slow everything else down long enough to let a few people escape. It was an act of desperation in desperate times.

The room looked carved out of the rock, rough and utilitarian. The floor, walls, and ceiling were all made of the same sandstone material. Torches in hooks burned on the walls. There were probably forty people in the chamber, and she saw several other archways leading into other rooms with more figures in them, sitting or standing about, talking in hushed tones. Many were glancing at them, the Queen of Dreams and the King of Flames. Wondering what their appearance might mean.

"Lydia."

She turned to face the voice. Maverick. His clothing was still ripped and a little bloodstained, but the blood on his face was cleaned off. He looked utterly exhausted, and she couldn't blame him.

"Mav! I'm so glad you got away!" Rushing over, she hugged him again. He chuckled quietly and patted a hand on her back.

"Yes. We all did. Well, those you intercepted. Aria is resting in the other room. Garrett as well."

"Garrett?"

Maverick made a face as if he hated saying what came next. "Gary." It was clear the nickname offended his sensibilities.

Lydia snickered. She couldn't help it; she really was growing fond of the doctor.

"We fled. As we did so, we found Edu and a few of his own. When we told them what you had done, Edu left to assist you. The others led us here." Maverick's hand moved to touch her neck. She realized there was probably dried blood there. "I see that you did not have an easy time of it."

"Lyon."

Maverick pulled in a sharp breath through his nose. "The Priest?" When Lydia nodded, Maverick glanced to Edu, and he did the same. Maverick's brow furrowed. "He has always served the Ancients. I suppose it is not unexpected. The House of Blood has consistently stood in league with the shadows. While I am pleased he lives, I am less so now that I know to whom he swears fealty."

"Who else is here? Who else is safe?"

"Safe?" Maverick's yellow eyes darkened. "No one. Presently hiding with us? Most of the higher-ranked souls, save a tragic few."

She wouldn't bristle at his arguing semantics. He was allowed to be bitter. "Who's been taken?"

"That you may know? Ylena and Ini, most notably."

Lydia cringed. "Ini." She couldn't imagine what was happening to the floating, cheerful, and somewhat irritating sprite. Whatever Aon was doing to them was guaranteed not to be pleasant.

"Shit. Oh, Edu." She looked back at the big man, who merely hung his head. His hand tightened, clearly thinking the same thing she was. Until now, she had assumed Ylena was left behind because it wasn't safe. Not because she was imprisoned. She had nothing to say that wouldn't feel insulting or pedantic. No platitudes to give.

"More of us would be in his dungeons if you had not intercepted us," Maverick reminded her. "For that, I thank you."

"Dungeons. Of course, he has dungeons." Lydia cringed. "Why is he taking people? And why only those with masks?"

"When we were captured, Navaa was there and bare-faced. He demanded we remove our masks and pledge our loyalty to the 'King of All.' It seems that those in the service of the warlock now do not wear them. We refused, of course. As to why, or why it is important? I do not know."

She ran both hands through her hair and scratched her scalp, thinking. She had no clue what was going on. Although she should really be used to that by now. "What's the plan?"

Maverick let out a small breath. "I am not sure. Vjo is sleeping. Her escape from the warlock's regimens did not... go well for her. She lost her arm, and while it is healing, it takes all the rest of her energy to do so."

Well, that was one thing Aon hadn't done to her during her "training" in captivity—remove a piece and let it grow back without killing her. She shuddered at the thought.

It seemed Maverick shared her opinion, judging by the thin look on his face. "As she is our tactician, we wait upon her. For now, I would recommend you too get some rest. I expect there will be little chance for it in the future."

Solid advice. Especially since she had been kicked around by both the warlock's armies and then Lyon. She felt like a spent battery. Looking over at Edu, he nodded, confirming what Maverick had said. With another pat on her shoulder, he walked away, through a stone archway and into another room. His version of good night, she figured.

"I am glad to see you and Master Edu are mending your relationship."

"Funny what an apocalypse will do to grudges." She looked back to Maverick and shrugged. "I never really disliked him. I was furious at him and terrified, and I still disagree with what he did. But I never hated him for it. I'm glad that we might—if we survive this—get to be friends."

"He is a good man, and has always sought to be a good king. For all his flaws, he understands precisely who he is and carries no shame in it. There is an enviable quality to that." Maverick rubbed his hand across his visible brow, and his features drew up in pain.

"Are you all right?"

"A headache. Forgive me. I am not much of a fighter, as they say."

"Follow your own advice and get some rest." She put her hand on his elbow. "Doctor's orders." She cracked a grin up at the man, who had to chuckle once at her bad attempt at humor.

"Yes, yes. I suppose so. Good night, Lydia."

"You too, doc."

Now on her own, she looked around the room. People were hunched down in corners or standing near the walls. Eating, sleeping, talking. But one thing was pervasive—fear. Everyone looked tired and afraid.

It reminded her of the cave she woke up in after being dragged to Under. Only this time, everyone here wore masks instead of bearing a mark upon their body they hadn't put there. History was repeating itself, it seemed. Just... in a backward and messed-up fashion.

This time, she didn't have Edu to worry about. There was a plus.

She walked from the main chamber into another one. There were bed rolls and cots scattered about, clearly scavenged from the city above, mismatched and crude in their construction. Many were taken, but there was still plenty of room.

She took one by a corner, flopped down onto the uncomfortable swath of fabric, and did her best to fluff what could be excused as a pillow and shoved it under her head. She could summon herself something nicer, she knew. But she was already exhausted and spent, and something told her she should save her strength.

Clearly, she underestimated how tired she was. As soon as she let her eyes shut, sleep came for her with a vengeance.

EIGHT

Lydia should be expecting this shit by now.

I mean, really, why am I surprised? She knew she was dreaming.

There was no way she wasn't.

Suddenly, she had just found herself standing inside a building that left her turning around in amazed silence. There was no other phrase for it but... awe-inspiring. It had been built to impress. If it had been built to demonstrate the power of the Ancients and make her feel small and helpless, it worked. She had never seen anything like it.

Maybe if she had gone to Rome and seen the Colosseum, or to Egypt and seen Karnak or Luxor temple, she could have something to compare it to. But she only had the images she had seen of those places to reference. The stone columns, made of what looked like black sandstone, soared up over her head some fifty or sixty feet tall. Carved to look like lotus leaves at the top, they bloomed out and supported a ceiling that had many sections open to look up at the star-spattered sky beyond. Every surface was painted and inlaid with gold.

It was dark, with the sun in its eclipse visible through the square openings in the ceiling. Beneath those skylights were shallow pools of water, several inches deep, decorated in mosaics of painted alabaster and depicting figures she couldn't make out from where she stood. Lily pads and other aquatic plants dotted the surfaces.

Upon every surface were painted and carved symbols and images of the Ancients. Twisted, horrible depictions of monsters tearing apart humans in a bloody feast. Devouring everything in their sight and celebrating the gore. This was a place meant to worship them. This was their temple. Their *home.* Something told her they likely dwelled here, and this was the center of their power.

The Ancients weren't really gods, after all. They weren't omniscient. That thought gave her a small, brief flicker of comfort that didn't last terribly long. Turning away from the art, she pulled in a startled breath. She should have known.

It was him.

Standing some ten feet away from her, watching her with an unreadable expression, was the man she knew as Aon.

The man who had been him once.

A face of stone, but in his eyes glittered something she couldn't name. She froze, her breath catching and her chest tightening. She felt as though she couldn't move. Something about him arrested her, locked her up, and made her feel tiny in a way Aon never had. Aon had been many things, but *this* man?

He was the King of All.

The moment shattered unexpectedly as he turned from her and walked away. He passed between two columns, through a massive archway, and out of sight. Lydia stood there, confused. He had just left. Without a word, without a gesture.

Why was she a little disappointed?

Shaking herself out of that line of thought, she peered around one of the huge columns to see him standing on a balcony. There was no railing in front of him, where he stood between two of the massive columns. It was just an opening into the drop below. She knew they were high up in the temple at the center of the city. He stood with his back to her, looking out at the world in front of him. He cut an impressive figure, the dark tendrils of his hair flowing down his pale, inked, and muscular back, blowing slightly in the breeze, like some nightmarish Pharaoh.

The game he was playing snapped into view as she realized what he was up to. He was making her come to him. Making her admit she was curious about who he now was, just as she was afraid of what she'd find.

Swearing silently in her head, she knew he was right. Besides, standing here in this massive chamber was fun and all but would be a terribly boring dream. Hope tugged at her, just as much as the curiosity.

Maybe he was still just a little bit of the man she knew. Maybe she could get through to him. Maybe she could snap him out of it.

Maybe this wouldn't be so bad, after all.

There were all those maybes again. *Holy hell, I'm stupid, aren't I?*

Questioning her intelligence on many levels, she followed him out onto the balcony. When she was five feet behind him, she could see the view he seemed so taken by. The view from the temple that sat at the center of the city, down to the sprawling metropolis below was stunning.

Lydia gasped. Now that she could see it from above, she realized it wasn't just a mindless maze of buildings. The whole of the city was laid out to create a large, circular symbol, much like the marks they all wore. Monuments dotted the buildings, large statues of creatures or obelisks at the center of lines created by aqueducts or wider roads. Palm trees and grassy areas were grouped wherever she could see the aqueducts lower into waterfalls that fell into great pools and ponds.

It was beyond beautiful. The way the faint light of the eclipse and the colored tones of the moons cast shadows against the pale clay buildings took her breath away. Surrounding all the city that she could see was a desert. Miles and miles of dunes and windswept sand. There, on the horizon, barely visible in the darkness, were mountains.

They stood there in silence for a moment that seemed to stretch on forever. He didn't speak. She didn't know what to say to him. She wanted to call out his name and beg him to turn around and hold her and tell her everything was going to be okay. *But Aon isn't his name anymore. I don't even know what to call him.*

It was as though he could sense her turmoil. Maybe he could. This was a dream, after all.

His voice, no longer a knife in velvet, somehow a sword made of steel instead, broke the silence. "I finally awaken from my fever dream. A cursed nightmare of pointless cruelty, of blood and madness. I opened my eyes from that darkness and found that the only thing I had in that terrible vision worth keeping—the only shining jewel in that muck and mire—I had gripped in my hand so tightly that it was with me when I arose. A miracle made of turquoise."

Still, he kept his back to her. He held out his hand in front of him, the metal gauntlet, looking at it in front of his face as if he didn't understand it. Or didn't recognize it. *He might not,* she realized. She didn't have time to debate the thought.

He dropped his hand and continued speaking. "Now, I find that the only treasure—the only boon granted to me in those five thousand years of wandering in broken thoughts, in *endless torment,* indeed the answer to the only thing in this world that I have ever desired—looks upon me in fear and utter revulsion."

He said it without judgment or anger. Just... sadness. The loneliness of a man whose hopes were crushed.

There was no way around it. It broke her heart. "You're half right. I'm not repulsed by you."

"I disappoint you."

That was a kick to the gut. She took a reflexive step back, as the impact of the statement was almost visceral. He wasn't wrong. As much as she wanted to argue to defend herself, it was true. She wanted *her* Aon here. Not whoever this guy was or whatever he'd become. Whoever the Ancients made him when they were busy plugging all the holes in his head.

"I'm sorry," was all she quietly managed to say. "I wish... I don't *know* you."

His tone turned cold. "Wishes are a worthless currency in Under." He shook his head as if reminding himself of exactly the same thing. His tone softened once more. "But your sentiment is appreciated."

He turned to look at her, dark eyes catching her gaze. He held out a hand to her, his flesh-and-blood one. He made no demands. No hypnotism. No glowering. Just a silent request for her to join him.

Damn it all. Damn her and her soft spot for him. For how her heart beat just a little faster when he looked at her. Even if he was a stranger wearing a familiar face, he had the same power over her as before. She was drawn to him like a moth to a flame.

He was patient as he watched her wrestle with herself. But it was, like everything else, just delaying the inevitable. When she slowly approached him, he smiled at her. It was faint, barely there, but it was something.

She knew that look.

It was *hope*.

And that caught her more than any dark gazes or sensuality.

Hope.

Aon's expressions had always come so quickly—a man used to hiding his face and who had no need to practice restraint.

This man schooled his emotions, and she was reminded of how hard Lyon was to read sometimes.

But she knew how insidious hope could be.

When she put her hand into his, he drew her closer. It was such a gentle action, so careful in his movements, she worried what he was going to do next. But despite how she held her breath, the violence never came. He simply lifted her fingers to his lips and kissed them, warm breath washing over her skin.

Her cheeks went warm, and she cursed herself silently.

Dark, spilled-ink eyes flickered in something close to enjoyment.

Silence hung between them, even as he held her captured in his gaze. She couldn't take it anymore. "What's your name?"

Sorrow, old as time and as cold as stone, deadened the glint in his eyes. "I do not have one."

That she didn't know what to do with. "You... what? Why not?"

"I am from a time far before you humans assigned names to anything. Before you had words and language. And why should I need such a thing? I am the only one of my kind. This city has no name, for there is only one of it. Your Earth has but one sun and one moon, and neither you saw fit to name. I have never been in need of one before now, before you."

"But you're..." She looked out at the city, breaking her gaze from his dark, unfathomable eyes.

"The King of All?" Fingers under her chin turned her to look back up at him. "Yes. But I am the child of the Ancients, their slave, made of dust and blood and given life by their will alone. They did not see fit to name me, for why would they? They had no other. The name you know is one I chose for myself to pretend I was ever like them—ever once a human. It was a lie I wore like that mask of metal you knew."

Aon wasn't a lie. He wasn't. Arguing wasn't going to work

with him. Taking shelter in pragmatism, she looked up at him warily. "Then what the hell am I supposed to call you?"

"King. Lord." He smirked. It was not nearly the fiendish expression of the man she knew, but it was almost there. His face inched closer to her as his voice dropped. "Master."

"No." Now, she knew her face must be bright red. "Nope. Not happening. Not now, not ever."

What she expected was anger at her insubordination and defiance. What she got instead was an amused smile and a shrug. He leaned in to whisper to her, brushing his lips across her ear. "Lover, then?"

When she went to pull back, he chuckled and let her. Her foot hit the edge of a column base. She tried not to jump out of startled fear and failed. That only amused him more. She must seem like such a silly little thing to him.

Looking away, she suddenly felt like a fool. While she was always very much out of her league with Aon, now she was little more than a child. She froze as he let out a quiet hum and stepped back into her, trapping her between him and the column. He moved slowly so as not to startle her. He didn't want to scare her. Not right now, anyway.

"You are ashamed," he observed. "Why?"

"I..." There wasn't any harm in telling him the truth, she figured. "I feel so stupid and small."

"You are neither of those things, my love." He drew up near her and lifted his hand to brush his knuckles gently down her cheek. "Not now, not ever," he echoed her words.

Her face felt warm, and she looked away. She couldn't help it.

"You are so shy," he said, clearly deeply amused. "Were you always this way? I only have but the shattered memories. Pieces, here and there."

"Jerk." She tried to shelter in her annoyance with him. It was safer than the attraction. "And...yeah."

He chuckled. "I would prefer you did not choose that name for me, if you do not mind."

"Then I still don't know what to call you. And trust me, you don't want me making up names for you. You won't like any of them."

His smirk broadened into a smile at her playful threat. "Very well. Call me Aon, if you must. But know that it is a falsehood I accept for your comfort and in acquiescence to how confused you are in this new state of being."

She was a little bit more distraught than confused, but okay. No need to be rude. "Thanks."

His hand tilted her face up to him, and he leaned down to kiss her cheek. Again, and again, featherlight and in a line, the action lodged her heart in her throat. He was tracing the ink on her face as he moved. Down one line of marks and then up another.

Captivating. That was what he was. There really was no other word for it. She felt trapped in his palm as if he could wind her around his fingers without any say from her. And whatever he wanted, she'd be helpless not to give him.

When he finished, he settled a single kiss against her forehead and looked down at her. His eyes traced the lines his lips had just touched as he tilted his head to look at them. The way his gaze moved over them, it looked like a man reading.

"You know what they say, don't you?" she finally worked up the nerve to ask.

"Of course."

He said it like it was the most obvious thing in the world. Maybe to him, it was. *He can read the marks. The things that nobody could understand. He can read everything about you—your soul itself.* She suddenly felt naked in front of him, far more than if she hadn't been wearing clothes.

He smiled thinly at the look on her face but stayed silent.

"That's why he—you, whatever—studied them." She blinked at the realization. "Why you wanted to control them."

"I yearned to remember what I once knew. Within that dream of darkness, I recalled that which I should be. I scrabbled at the walls of the pit I had made for myself. But, as the written word evades us in our dreams, so did this gift in my nightmare of madness."

She remembered Aon poring over pages of his research, attempting to decode the language of the Ancients. All because he was haunted by what he used to know. She couldn't wrap her head around that. It was too big and too tragic, like everything else about this conversation. So she went with her pragmatism once more. "What do they say?"

"I cannot translate them. It would be as if you asked me to translate a literal physical rose into French. It does not work that way."

"Okay, then I'll rephrase." Of course, he had to be difficult. Some things apparently didn't change. "What do they mean?"

He smiled, proud of her. "A much better question." He stepped in closer to her, and it was hard not to melt against him. Hard not to give in to his touch as he traced the writing on her face with his fingertips and followed the line of it down onto her throat.

Harder still not to let her hands fall to his hips and pull them against her, wanting to feel the strength of his body nestle against hers.

If he saw her turmoil, he ignored it. "What do these markings mean upon you? They speak to me of who you really are. Resilient, unbreakable, empathetic, and powerful. That you would rather follow your heart than your head. They tell me that I stand no chance in bending you to my will, but that I might entice you instead. They show me your very soul. Every part of you is laid bare to me by reading them. But most of all, they tell me that even if I could not remember you... the moment I laid eyes upon them, I would love you more than life itself. Each time I read these words, I love you more."

Her face was on fire, and she knew she must be beet red at this point. He smiled calmly down at her, the face of a patient man. The coldness in his eyes was warmed, softened at the edges. Just because of her. Now, she could see the faint glimmer in his eyes for what it was. Adoration.

He still loved her.

That stung her fiercely. He loved her, and she didn't know how she felt about him anymore. All she felt was a sense of being lost, confused, and distraught. Once more, her world was upended. Once more, he was at the center of the storm. She forced herself out of that realization and wished she could retreat from him. But up against the column, she was utterly trapped, so she steered the conversation away from where he clearly wished it to go. "Why're you taking the masked as prisoners?"

He seemed irritated that she ignored his profession of love, but he went along with it regardless. "They seek to hide from me their very natures, as they did in days gone by."

Her eyes widened. That was why the masks existed, so long ago. Not to protect the marks, not to hide them from each other. But to hide from *him*. Seeing her understanding, he smiled and leaned in to kiss her forehead. "Never once have you embraced a mask. Never once have you sought to shroud yourself from those who might pry. You have forever been open to me, even when you were a mortal and my mind was so horribly muddled. You have nothing to fear from me."

"What about everyone else?"

"Those who fall in line will prosper. All war is over. All politics and games have ceased. There is only one King now. This world beats with one heart—mine."

"And those who don't fall in line?"

Aon met her gaze, and the expression in his dark eyes chilled her to the bone. "I have no need for false genuflection. I am no tyrant, though others may think otherwise. Forced servitude is a brittle leash and shatters at its first opportunity. Where there are lies, there are traitors."

The threat was clear. Kneel... or die. Her heart skipped a beat in fear. She knew so many—cared for so many—who wouldn't think of obeying him. "No, please."

"You ask for leniency for them? For those who would betray me?" His eyes glittered in the first show of mischief she had seen of him, the first small hint that buried in there somewhere was the man she loved. "What do you bargain in return?"

"I—I—" What the hell could she even offer him?

He cut off her useless stammer and made his price known. "Come home to me. Pledge to be my queen. Stand at my side."

She felt cold, and she knew all the color had drained from her face.

He let out another hum and watched her as she frantically tried to come up with something to say, before looking out over the city once more, his expression drawn tight. "This is why I have been so quiet. The more I speak, the more I remind you of what has transpired."

The more he reminded her that he was not the Aon she knew. Not entirely. Not even mostly, it seemed. Aon bargained with her, yes. But not like that. Little games and wagers. Putting books away in exchange for information. A game of poker, not the Treaty of Versailles. Not a promise of marriage and swearing allegiance in return for the lives of others.

"Debate my deal. Take your time. I am patient. I am... so very old, my love. I have waited for you for longer than you can perhaps even fathom. This curse that your Aon suffered—this loneliness—know that I bore it long before he did."

"Exactly how old are you?" she had to ask. Aon said he hadn't remembered. This man, *this* Aon, might. He said he dated from a time before language, before things had names. But that was an awfully large range.

"I walked your world in shadows when you humans were but tribal beasts struggling to control fire. I am the darkness that has always haunted the fears of your former race. It all traces back to me."

Lydia's eyes went wide. That was... tens of thousands of years. Maybe a hundred thousand or more. He was older than humanity itself. Older than recorded history. *What the hell am I up against? I can't fight him. I have no hope. This is who he really is.*

Aon smirked at the look of realization upon her as the weight of his statement sank in. "Needless to say, I am capable of waiting."

"Don't hurt them." She couldn't even wrap her head around how old he just admitted he really was. It was impossible for her to comprehend. She couldn't even really try to understand what it must have been like to live for so long.

"That I cannot promise you." He paused and took a moment to consider his words. "But, for you, I will not kill them. Not until you have made up your mind. For you, I will suffer a surplus of dissentious rabble." He leaned in to kiss her and then paused, hovering his lips a hair's breadth away from hers. "For you, I would endure far more than you can imagine."

And with that, he zeroed the distance, and it was like her heart shattered. He was so utterly foreign and yet so familiar to her. She couldn't help but slide her hands to his chest and let him take what he wanted. She felt pulled under by a tide—knocked over by a wave and dragged beneath a power that was as unfathomable to her as she would be in the ocean.

He was a force of nature.

A demigod.

The King of All.

She was just... Lydia. Lydia with super-pets, maybe, but still just Lydia.

Sinking in the tide of him, feeling him threaten to wash away all thoughts of fighting or resisting him, she grasped the first thought that floated by her like the battered plank of wood from a wrecked ship in a storm. He had revealed his goal. She knew what his game was. He wanted her to be his queen. To stand willingly at his side... that was why he hunted her. But she couldn't say yes. Who was he? Who was he, really? He wasn't the man she had known. He merely wore his face.

Which man was the lie? Her warlock or the King of All?

And who was worse?

What would the King of All make of this world?

Sensing her tense, he broke the kiss slowly and cradled her head in his metal hand. "For five thousand years, I lingered in dreams of lunacy. All I have are shattered, fragmented memories of those centuries. But I remember you, as clear as the daylight sun. And I will earn your love, my starlight, just as I had once before. For you are my shining gem in the darkness."

Beautiful, flattering poetry. Something Aon had never done. "You aren't him."

He winced as if she had slapped him, and he pulled his head up and straightened his shoulders. His pain faded to resignation. This was a conversation he must have known they were going to have. "I am he. I have not driven who you knew away to some dark corner of my mind. He does not rail away in chains, a passenger to who you see before you. I am the man you loved."

"You're different."

"You knew an illness. I am the man you knew *made whole*."

Now, it was Lydia's turn to cringe. She remembered what Aon had said to her—her Aon—as the sun was rising. That the Ancients had filled in the missing parts of his mind. "You're possessed. They're controlling you. You're 'made whole' only because the Ancients are plugging you up like corks in a sinking ship."

He smiled. "Would you prefer the madness?"

"No, but—"

"Or did you merely love me because I had lost my mind?"

"What?"

"I wonder if you only cared for me, for that I was weak and vulnerable. That you saw me as something to be pitied." There was an angry growl there, accusing her of only loving him for his weakness.

"That's not true. You weren't weak or vulnerable."

"I was to you."

"That's... that's different." *Great argument, idiot. You'll ace debate club with that one.*

"Then what benefit does he have over me? Am I not superior to what you knew? I am far more reasonable. If you could love me then, why can you not love me now?"

She sputtered. "I don't know how I feel. But love doesn't work like that. I don't know who you are—I don't know what you're going to *do* to people—"

"Oh? I am mended. I am *whole.* You saw quite well what I was willing to do to the world in my madness. Wage wars. Murder thousands. I do not suffer from the kind of paranoia and jealousy that sent your dear friend to his grave."

"No. Don't you dare bring up Nick."

There was no stopping him. "I would have protected him. Not killed him for my own sadistic glee. He relished in your tears, in your grief—"

"He." She caught him in his misplaced word. Referring to her Aon as someone separate from himself. She turned it on him in her anger. "I thought you were the same man. Which is it?"

"It is easier for me to think of that man as something outside myself, yes." He winced. "Otherwise, I would have to reconcile the actions I took in my delirium. Such pointless bloodshed, such needless war. All that pain I caused in the fruitless attempt to fashion from dust that which I desired. Qta suffered and died for no reason. How could I not have understood that what I desired cannot be made but must be *earned*?"

She looked away. He knew where to hit her. She tried to dodge as best she could. "You couldn't have protected Nick. Not from Dtu, not from Rxa."

"Those children?" Aon scoffed. "If I had been whole, they would have bent a knee to whomever I demanded. They were my playthings."

"Playthings? Is that all we are to you?"

He smirked idly at her attempt to use his words against him once more. He leaned into her, forcing her to press back against the column as he caged her in by resting his forearms on either side of her. "That is why they were brought here, so long ago. That is why we still rob from your world. The Ancients saw my loneliness, my desire for company. They brought me those idiots to amuse me and to pass the time. But I found them all lacking. It did nothing to settle my soul. Not... until you."

"We're just your plastic army men, then? Your ego never fails to amaze. You two still have that in common."

"I do love your tongue..." He chuckled. "The Ancients molded me in their desire to create something for once in their eternal lives. But they are beings of destruction, of bloodlust and monstrosities. Once they had made me, they did what they could to provide for their child. This world was made for me." He looked at her haughtily. "Quite literally."

She jabbed a finger into his chest, and he drew back an inch, seemingly startled by the gesture. "That doesn't give you an excuse to be like *this*."

"How, precisely, am I to be humble when the very moons you see were made for that I wanted them?"

She snorted in laughter. "You can try."

"I do not think you loved me for my modesty." He pressed up against her, pinning her to the stone with the length of his thigh. "I think you loved me for anything but."

The action made her face go warm. In fact, she felt warmth rush her whole body at his gesture. It'd be so easy to give in. So easy to just let him have her. That was what he wanted, after all. And deep down inside... she wasn't so sure she didn't want the same thing.

"I can't give up trying." She felt like she was reminding herself almost more than she was telling him.

"For now. I know. I will wait." He nuzzled his head in close to her neck and placed a slow kiss there, making her hiss in a breath. "As much as I wish to pin you to the ground in this dream and take you, I think it is better to let you linger in your own desire. I will let you run. It amuses me to give chase. To hunt you brings me joy. Hide in the burrowed dens with the sewer rats, if you wish. I will find you all in time."

"You don't know where I am?"

"No. The Ancients wish to watch this sport unfold fairly. They wish to watch our little drama play out upon their stage." He sighed. "They obscure you from me. But fear not. I will earn you back to me. I will have what is mine." His voice lowered to a deep rumble that vibrated through her.

I will have what is mine. Aon had never laid claim to her. Never pretended she belonged to him. Not once, not even when she was his prisoner. But this man had done just that. "I don't belong to you."

"Ah, but you do. You will come to see it in time." He lifted a hand from the column to catch one of hers. He slid her palm up to rest over his heart. "And I, in equal turn, belong to you."

"That's a lie."

"How so? Whatever you wish, you shall have it. Whatever you desire, it shall be yours. I shall take or spare the lives of anyone you want. I will remake this world into a jungle oasis, if it would make you smile but once. I will wear that oafish and childish mask, wear a suit of wool and sculpt for you a home of ostentatious pride and glowing blinking lights if that is for what you yearn."

She called his bluff. "Then do it."

"I have made my fee known. Only if you agree to become my queen. Stand at my side. If you think I am such a vicious mongrel, then temper me. Show me how to better wield my power, if you think my ego is so insufferable."

"But I don't know how I feel, and—"

"It matters not," he insisted, cutting off her excuse. "You loved me as a broken, shattered thing. I understand that what has become of me has come as a terrible shock to you. To ask that you dive into my arms would be too much to beg of anyone. But... you will come to love me again. I am sure of it."

Which one of them was he trying to convince? "That's not how this works." Lydia tried to pull her hand from his chest, but he kept it pinned there, his grip tightening. She saw then that she was balancing on the edge of a knife. At any moment, she might push him too far into anger. She stilled her attempt to snap free from him.

Black eyes were as dark as pitch. "Let me fight for you. Give me a chance to have you."

"How exactly do you think you're going to earn me back? By chasing me? Imprisoning the people I care about?"

"It worked once before, did it not?"

With a growl, she balled up a fist and slammed it into his chest. Now, he was making fun of her. She could tell by the glint in his eyes. He laughed at her indignity and wrapped his arms around her, pulling her tight to him in an embrace. "Oh, now, now... I am merely teasing you. Forgive me. Calm yourself."

"Fuck you."

He arched an eyebrow. "Hm. While I am not accustomed

to someone making such a direct and forward proposition, far be it from me to refuse. Turn around and let us begin."

Her face flushed warm again at his directness. "I'm swearing at you."

"I know."

He was playing with her. Toying with her the same way he had done so many times before. His face was still far colder, far more stoic than she was accustomed to. But that was a flash of the same man. A hint that he might be telling the truth and that there was still some of the man she knew mixed into the whole.

This was too much. Why couldn't it be simple? Why couldn't he just be a monster, a laughing despot, and nothing like the man she knew? Why did there have to be hope? The world was destroyed. Everyone was hiding from him, running and scared for their lives. And yet, here she was, faced with the very real fact that he may not be the monster she wished him to be.

He might still be the monster she wished he used to be.

Nothing was ever that simple, was it?

He wasn't Aon. He wasn't the man she loved.

But he wasn't somebody else either.

It brought tears to her eyes. She went to wipe them away, but he beat her to it. He lifted his flesh-and-blood hand to her face and gently stroked his fingers along her cheeks to brush them off. He let out a deep, weary sigh. "I am sorry. I am sorry I am not as I was. Would that I could be, I would do so in a heartbeat."

"Stop," she begged. She couldn't take this anymore, this taunting reminder.

He pulled her into a hug once more, cradling her head against his bare chest. His skin was warm against her cheek, and she let her eyes slip shut. But he didn't smell like old books. He smelled like hot sun and warm wind. It only made her cry harder.

"Sleep. Rest. You will need it, for I will come for you, my love. I will find you."

It was meant to sound comforting, same with his embrace. But it didn't bring her anything of the sort. As the world faded back into blissful darkness, she felt one thing, and one thing only—dread.

NINE

She woke up with tears on her face. The janky pillow underneath her head was stained damp with them. She was shivering. Not from cold, but from adrenaline. *Damn the Ancients.* Damn them for doing this to her. To Aon. To everyone.

If Aon were nothing like the man she loved, the whole situation would be simple.

It would be horrible and heart-wrenching, but simple.

And if he were still the man she loved, she could adjust to this new way of being—maybe.

But he was neither of those things—instead trapped somewhere in between. It left her also stuck in between, rolling in a turmoil that was going to eat her alive like a vat of acid before too long.

Could she love this version of him?

Should she?

Was the King of All truly evil? Or just different?

Was this version of Under better... or worse?

She didn't know yet. After all, everybody had told her for six months that Aon was the worst of the worst. That she *shouldn't* love the warlock. Even Aon himself believed that nobody *could* love him. Other people's opinions didn't factor into this, then.

No, she had to sort it out for herself.

Who was the King of All, really?

What kind of Under had he made?

And *could* she love this... mended version of Aon?

"He sacrificed it all for you."

She jolted, having not realized anybody else was there. Rolling onto her back, they were sitting right beside her, leaning up against the wall. Her white hair hung long around her face, tangled and limp, no longer set in perfect curls or done up behind her in a bun. Her eyes were staring down at her lap. Unfocused and... not white, but emerald green. They might have been bright once, but now they were left dull and vacant.

"Ziza?" Lydia blinked in surprise. The woman made a small hum in response. As if she heard her but didn't know how else to respond. "Are you... okay?" Stupid question, by the looks of things.

"No."

It hit her then. Ziza was the Oracle to the Ancients. The voice of the primordial creatures that ruled their world. But they needed her to speak for them when they were captives at the bottom of a lake of their blood. Now... they were free.

They didn't need her anymore.

Her eyes weren't white. She was the woman she must have been before they had taken her as their mouthpiece.

Well, whatever was left behind after fifteen hundred years of being ravaged like that anyway. And judging by the glassy expression and emptiness she saw? Not a whole lot.

"Ziza, I'm so sorry." She sat up to sit cross-legged next to the *former* Oracle. "Oh God. I didn't even realize..."

"There is no god here, Lydia. There never was. There never shall be." Still, Ziza didn't look up. Just picked at the sleeve of her dress that was tattered and torn and stained with blood. She, too, had been in a fight to escape. "Do not mourn for me. I served my purpose."

"That doesn't make it right." Sitting up, Lydia shifted to sit beside her. "They had no right to do this to you."

"They have every right. They made me. Without them, I would have died long ago of the consumption or famine that both plagued me. I lived at their pleasure." Her tone was empty and flat. But it wasn't icy like it had been before. Now, it was just barren, a wasteland, as if she had become the same as the sands outside. "I would have lived a month, maybe two, had I not been taken to Under. My life was worthless to the 'god' you reference. They came to salvage me instead. They saw value where no one else did."

Lydia reached out and took the woman's hand and squeezed it gently, trying to do what she could to comfort a woman, even though she knew anything she did was pointless. It was just another sad platitude. "I'm still sorry."

Her gesture brought a faint smile to Ziza's lips. "You are so kind and caring. I hope that part of you never dies. I felt fondness for you even when I could feel little else. All because they feel the same."

"They?"

"The Ancients."

The Ancients were *fond* of her? "They have a funny fucking way of showing it."

Ziza chuckled. "I came to say I was sorry I could not tell you what Rxa planned. I knew Nicholas would die for nothing. They forbade me from speaking of it." Ziza cringed as if the memories were stinging her like bees. Lydia knew that expression well. Aon wore it many times when he was fighting off instances of his madness. It was the fight of a beleaguered mind fighting off the pull of insanity.

"It's all right. It's not your fault. I don't hold you responsible for any of this." She squeezed the other woman's hand a little tighter. It felt like she was talking to a woman on her deathbed.

Maybe she was.

"Thank you, Lydia." Ziza shut her eyes slowly and leaned her head back against the wall. She watched for the second time in as many days as someone's face simply shifted into another's. As an actor slipped into a role.

A fiendish grin split Ziza's face, one that looked utterly wrong on her austere, beautiful features. It was toothy and wicked. It was a grin that promised blood.

Lydia watched, yet again, as the Ancients took over someone she was talking to.

"Do not weep for Our child."

Eyes reopened and sought hers. They were no longer emeralds—they weren't even white—they were *blood red*. Red and glowing as the pool she hated so damn much, from lid to lid. Ziza smiled still, that sick expression of excitement and hunger.

Lydia tried to pull back, but Ziza grabbed her hands tight and yanked her close. For such a small frame, she was suddenly very strong. When Lydia went to scream or shout for help, Ziza lifted one finger in front of her lips and shushed her. "We have come to speak to you, child. Only to you. Listen."

"Don't hurt her."

Ziza's brow creased in confusion. "Hurt her?" She laughed quietly as if she finally understood. "Oh, how you fret so much for others, when you should be far more concerned for yourself. We care not for what happens to Our Oracle, poor thing. A doll, broken and discarded. Let her live or die on her own. We no longer mind."

"That's the problem. You don't care."

They laughed again. That was what Ziza was right now. Not a her, but a *they*. They smiled at her with such sudden and sincere sympathy that it caught her off guard. "Oh, poor thing... forgive Us our callousness. We have lived longer than your world has hung in the sky. We are sorry for her pain and passing as you may mourn a fruit fly upon your table for that it kept you company for a fraction of the tick of a clock. It is our age that makes us so. Not our hearts."

Lydia couldn't help but shudder at the way they hissed the words. She was learning tonight just how very small she really was. First from Aon, and now from them.

Maybe there wasn't a real difference between the two anymore.

They were playing with her hand now, toying with her fingers as if she was fascinating to them. Lydia had the distinct fear that they were going to snap her fingers for the fun of it. Just to watch her scream, or maybe just to see what happened when the joints failed.

Because it was no more impactful to them than if she stepped on an ant in the parking lot by accident on the way to the car.

"No, no... do not fear. We will not harm you, little fragile thing. Not like that, not now."

"You can hear my thoughts?" That was unsettling at best.

"When We are this close, yes. You bear Our marks. Our blood flows through you. Our power beats in your very veins. Those who go into the pool emerge with Our life flowing through them." They smiled as if they were lying on a grassy field on a warm summer day. The idea of it brought them bliss. "Such is as We make you."

Lydia fought down the urge to yank her hands free and run for her life. There was nowhere she could hide. And it seemed they just came here to... talk. Maybe this was her chance to get some answers. "Why do you make everyone hate him so much?"

She wanted to know the answer to that for a long time. Now, she could ask the source.

Ziza grimaced. "For that he turned them against Us, five thousand of your years ago. For it was his childish spite that buried Us in the lake. Without him, the others would never have succeeded. We punish Our Son for his misdeeds. There is nothing that he loathes more than to be alone. We ensured he stayed that way. That was, of course, until you came along. But We needed to ensure you were strong enough. That you could endure what this world might bring. That you were worthy of him! Oh, your sweet suffering. It was so delightful to watch."

"You need to get better hobbies."

They grinned, leaning in closer to her. "You are far more fun. You have yet to break. Yet to yield."

"Okay, so... why did you have Edu kill me?"

"Your body needed to be devoid of life, such that it could take the power of a Queen. The only way We could raise you as a dreamer was to end your mortal life in its entirety." Ziza—they—reached up a hand to stroke her hair. She let them do it. The only thing she'd accomplish by yanking her head out of the way would be to insult them. When she flinched at their touch, though, they smiled. "We corrupt the life of those who enter Us. But to impart such a gift... We needed a blank slate."

It had happened twice now, she realized. "Lyon." The vampire had said he suspected that was how this had worked. Now, she had confirmation.

"Yes."

"You planned that too."

"Prisoners even as We were, We found Our ways to pull the strings of Our children. Rxa, the precious and most loyal child, such a loss. But it was required, to set Us free."

"So... that brings us to now. Why do all this?"

"Could you live happily in a cage for eternity? Trapped and stagnant, when you once knew the whole of *existence itself* in which to roam?" They snarled, hatred flashing across Ziza's features. "We wished to be free."

"This whole thing was about Rxa freeing you?"

"Mm, no." They shifted to sit closer to her and flashed a wicked smirk. "But it is to be enjoyed regardless."

"What was it about, then?"

They took in a lungful of air and let it out in a long, breathy sigh. "We only want you to love him. To bring our Only Son peace. To mend what within him could not be fixed with paltry toys and playthings."

They were calling the whole world and millions of souls paltry toys and playthings. They were echoing the words Aon had used. Great. *They really are connected. Shit.* She tried to focus on the matter at hand and not how terrifying that was. "You only want him to be happy?"

"Of course. We love him. More than you can imagine. Yet again and again, like the orbit of planets, he is miserable. He wails and cries, he moans and weeps, wishing for someone to hold. Wishing for someone to love him at his side. Our love is not enough, for We are not like him." They grimaced in pain, like a tired parent recalling what it was like to listen to a howling toddler in the night. Full of love and bitter exhaustion, all at once.

She sat there, stunned. At first, she had no idea what to say. "Then... give him back to me. I love what he was before."

"It is not so simple. Part of Us is within him. We took pieces from Ourselves and made him from what We could sever from the whole. We can no more free him from Our influence than you could free your body from your very soul."

"But before..."

"We were prisoners. Hostages in a cage, severed from Our link to him. Without Us... you saw what remained, a broken creature deeply ill of mind." The grief on their face was sincere. "He was suffering."

Lydia flinched. "I loved him anyway."

"Would you wish him to suffer? For all eternity, simply so

you could embrace him?" They tilted their head to the side in curiosity. "You saw his pain, his agony. You saw how he writhed in his madness."

They were right. She had. More than once, she had watched him push his claws into his own body as if to dig out his pain. More than once, she had been in close proximity to that agony. Looking down into her lap, she found she couldn't meet the Ancient's gaze. "I..."

"We understand. You fear what he has become. You wonder if this world is crueler now—if this world is now *wrong* and must be made right." A hand on her cheek was shockingly tender.

The Ancients gently tipped her head up to look at them as they continued to speak. "You fell in love with pieces of a shattered stained glass window, lying about on the floor. Pieces of a whole. Now, you turn away from the image for fear of what you may see in it."

"Because *you're* in it." She finally bit out the words. "Sorry, but you and I haven't exactly been on great terms."

They chuckled. If they were offended, it didn't show. In fact, there was sort of a calm, smooth sympathy on Ziza's borrowed features. As if they honestly felt *bad* for Lydia. "You suffered only as much as We required you to. Did We delight in it? Of course. But never an ounce in abundance to make you what We needed."

Lydia held perfectly still as they reached out a hand and placed a palm over her heart, just as Edu had done to stop it when she had died. Ziza frowned.

"What do you want from me?" Lydia whispered, feeling angry tears forming in her eyes. "What's the game, now? You want me to love him. He wants me to marry him. But I know you well enough to know you've got some kind of *scheme*."

Those horrifying, red eyes were fixed on her. "Love him. That is all We require of you."

"And if it turns out I can't?" This was the other shoe. The *or else* that was lingering at the end of their statement. The one that would really tell her what was going to happen to her.

Ziza's expression turned cold. "He loves you too much for Us to let you go. It would destroy him. You must understand."

"No. No more veiled threats. No more half-statements and *prophecies*." Lydia snatched Ziza's hand away from over her heart. "If I decide I can't love him, what will you do to me?"

Ziza smiled, seemingly tired. No, *exhausted*. That same expression of a parent after long hours of taking care of a needy child at night. "We will ensure that does not come to pass."

The meaning was clear.

Lyon. They'd go inside her head and scramble her brain and *make* her love him. They'd take away her *soul*.

"You—you can't. He wouldn't let you. It'd be a lie." Fear ran down her spine like cold water.

"Do you think so?" They hummed thoughtfully. "We believe Our Son would rather keep the only soul he has ever truly loved close by his side, even in a lie, than lose her again. He has sacrificed it all for you—and you will not even *try* to love him in return."

"I..." She hated that they were right. She hated that they made sense. "I've lost everything. My home, my friend, now him—you *killed* me. I'm not even human anymore, and..."

"We are not asking you to kneel to Us in this moment. We are not asking you to love him come the dawn." Ziza shifted closer to her. "We are merely asking you to try."

"Or you'll make me." Lydia shook her head. "That's the problem. You're not giving me a *choice*."

Delicate fingers—feeling very wrong for the power that burned beneath them—tilted her head to look back to them a second time. They were scrutinizing her. Memorizing every reaction she had to their words. "What would you do, to protect your Only Son?"

She was up against the worst helicopter parents in existence.

They laughed, and she reminded herself that they could hear her thoughts. "Perhaps. Perhaps We protect him too much. But he is fragile. You have worked your way into his very core... you can destroy him in ways no one else may dare imagine. You saw this come to pass the night he stood trial."

She couldn't argue with them, as much as she wished she could. They had her on the end of a line. It felt so hopeless, trying to win a game of poker against creatures that might as well be gods. "I can't outplay you."

"Nor do We expect you to do so. We simply ask you to let the pattern repeat. To let him woo you as he did once before."

She had noticed Aon was following in his old footsteps by haunting her dreams. Threatening and promising to come for her in the same breath. It had all felt eerily similar. Now, she was trapped in caves with frightened masses who had been taken from their homes and dumped into a new world. The context had changed, sure... but she had been right.

And it was all because *they* wanted it to be that way.

"We control this world. We control all."

Lydia deflated. Felt her shoulders slump. This was pointless. She was helpless. Utterly powerless against them. Whatever they knew, *he* knew. If the Ancients were here, then Aon was on their heels. Fear plucked at her like a string on a guitar. She had to get out, she had to warn everyone—

They answered her thoughts once more. "No, darling one. We will not tell him where you are. We will not help him in any way. We wish to see this opera play itself out. We wish, most of all, for you to love him without Our aid."

She realized it wasn't a game of chess with her against the Ancients—it was a game of chess with them as the *very game itself.* She was playing Aon and talking to the computer system controlling the rules. She was just a couple of bits inside some awful game like the ones Nick adored so much.

Goddamn, she missed Nick so much right now.

"Do not weep for him. He lives on, within Us. He was a valuable soul."

"Don't mock me."

"Mock you? No." Ziza shifted closer to her. "None of this has ever been to mock you. We love you, Lydia." They gathered her hands in theirs and bent down to kiss the backs of her knuckles tenderly. "You have done so very well. You have exceeded all We have placed before you. We have... *faith*... you shall continue to do the same."

"You have a fucked-up way of showing love."

A grin of madness and hunger spread slowly across Ziza's face. "We are what We are." Elder things, monsters and powerful creatures that were older than Earth. Things that fed off blood, and terror, and madness. This was probably as close to expressing "love" normally as they could, she realized.

Tears stung her eyes at the reality of what she was up against.

Learn to love him.

Or get her mind scrambled and be *forced* to love him.

There was no option three that she could find.

"Poor child. Poor little thing. So frightened, so alone. Lost and wandering, helpless and afraid. You suffer so needlessly. Go to him. Love him."

"Please, I—" She just wanted them to stop tormenting her.

"If you wish Our games to end, do as We ask, darling child. You will no longer feel such suffering. You will no longer be alone. No betrayal from others shall be thrown in your path. You will reign above all, unchallenged and safe."

"I... I can't."

"We know." Another grin as they leaned in and kissed her cheek. "And We could not be more delighted."

They wanted her to fight. To struggle. To suffer. As she pulled back from them, she felt Ziza go limp. Her light frame slumped against hers, and Lydia had to catch her to keep the poor woman from collapsing.

They were gone.

She laid her down on the bed roll and summoned a blanket to throw over her.

Love him.

Or get turned into a lobotomy patient like Lyon.

There had to be a way. There had to be a third option. There *had* to be.

Accepting that there wasn't would be as good as surrender.

Hope was an insidious poison.

But right now, she'd drink that bottle happily. Doubling over, she leaned her head against Ziza's shoulder and cried.

* * *

Lyon hissed in pain as the blades of a claw, burning in black fire, pushed slowly deeper into his rib cage. They cut through sinew and tissue as though they were nothing, the fire charring all that it touched. The agony sent his vision flashing to white and nearly emptied his mind of thought.

He had failed in his task, and this was Lyon's rightfully due amercement for having returned empty-handed. It was a sign of personal respect, for his King was doling out the deed himself and not giving the duty to Navaa or one of the others.

Lydia had become a true queen of Under. She wielded her strength well, although it was clear she was still learning and refining her gifts. But she was no match for him with the hundreds of years heaped upon him.

How he wished his deceit had worked. How he wished he could have drunk her dry and let her wake here in the hands of her beloved.

Instead, Edu had intervened. Of course he had. Lyon considered himself to have truly terrible luck.

And now, he suffered keenly for his failure.

This was deserved, and he accepted it without a struggle. The pain would only be temporary. It would pass.

With a vicious yank, his lord removed his clawed prosthetic from inside his body, sending much of Lyon spilling out onto the stone floor. Several of his internal organs landed with a wet splash around his feet, torn free of their housings by his King.

Lyon sank to the ground and fell to his side, shuddering in pain, feeling the world begin to dim. His Master had been lenient and not made the punishment linger. He would not suffer for long before darkness took him and he was left to heal.

The man standing over him began to speak as crimson dripped from his claw onto the ground by Lyon's face. "I watched the fight unfold. I stood atop a building nearby to watch my Queen do battle. She was... breathtaking. Edu is at fault for your empty-handed return. You did as well as you could. But failure is still failure." His voice was darkened with a twinge of excitement, his next words spoken with a heady mix of anticipation and desire.

"In truth, I am glad, for I will have to do this myself."

TEN

Tears always ran out, no matter how awful the pain.

They left like a passing storm, and Lydia felt about the same as if a tornado had come through her home. Everything was thrown about and barely recognizable.

But it was hard to complain with Ziza still unconscious beside her. That poor woman had been brutalized by the presence of the Ancients. She couldn't even imagine what it must be like, to have creatures of that magnitude cramming inside your head like an elephant trying to drive a compact car, only then to have them suddenly leave you in the dust.

Eventually, Lydia had to gather herself up as best she could, comb her hands through her hair, summon herself some new clothes, and try to face what was before her. She had other people to worry about.

Evie. Maverick and Aria, Gary, and all the rest. She wasn't alone in this new hell. There was some solace in that, some comfort. Misery really did love company. It was that need to be around others who might understand how she felt—even if they didn't know the new depths of her dilemma—that finally drove her to walk out of the smaller chamber she was in and into the main cavern.

She saw Edu first. It was hard to miss him, standing against a wall with his massive trunk-like arms crossed over his chest. Surrounding him were several figures she recognized and some she didn't. Vjo, Kamira, and Maverick she recognized. There was a man sitting on a rock with his back to her. Standing at Edu's side was a familiar and happy sight—Evie.

Upon seeing Lydia, the girl's face split in a bright grin and she tore across the room, throwing herself into Lydia's arms.

Oh, how she needed a hug right about now. Lydia clung to Evie tightly, squeezing her hard enough to make the girl giggle. "Bunny, you're gonna crush my ribs."

"Sorry, sorry." She let up a little.

"You're a lot stronger than you used t'be." Evie was still smiling brightly up at her, mop of red curls loose around her head. "Now that you're really a queen like you should be. I'm gonna miss your little friend, though."

"I miss him too." What she wouldn't give to have Q with her here to help her along.

"You okay?" Evie looked up at her, seeing the misery that must have been clearly written across her face.

"No... no, I'm not."

Evie hugged her again, this time trying to squeeze her as hard as she could. Lydia smiled and just enjoyed the moment for what it was. So many of her friends were gone, but she still had a few.

For now.

Cold dread washed over her with that sudden realization. The Ancients were taking everything away from her. Knocking out her support structures one by one. Her world, her friends, then Aon. How long before they—or their only son—came to take the rest?

She was a danger to all of them. If Aon was coming for

her… she'd lead him straight to everyone else. She gently pushed Evie away and did her best to smile down at her, even with the feeling of ice rushing through her. She had to leave before that happened. She couldn't let others get hurt because of her. So many had already.

"Lydie?" Evie blinked up at her curiously, seeing right through her fake expression. She'd never called her that before, and it was clear she was concerned.

Edu waved her over, saving Lydia from having to answer.

"C'mon. I'll need your help translating the big idiot." Lydia took Evie's hand and led her back to the group.

Evie giggled, seemingly forgetting her worry in that one moment. "It's not so bad."

As they walked up to Edu, the man sitting on the rock turned his head. Over his face was a full wooden mask, etched in green and carved into the shape of a wolf. He had chin-length brown hair that looked like it was only long because he didn't give a crap about it. His back was crisscrossed with scars and green ink on a tanned surface. He wore a pair of ratty trousers.

She'd never seen him before. But something in her recognized him, all the same. "Oh, hey, Dtu. I didn't recognize you with pants on."

The man grunted in response.

Kamira grinned and laughed, and it was her turn to walk up for a hug. "I will not bother to ask if you are well. You are not. None of us are. I am glad, though, that you are alive and not a prisoner. Either of the Ancients or of what they have made of Aon."

"Thanks." Both for the sentiment and for not pretending like the world was going to be okay.

The wild woman placed a kiss on her forehead that lingered a little too long, and for once, Lydia didn't fuss about it. "We are trying to make a plan for escape. Come." She turned to take her place back standing by the wall.

With a sigh, Lydia joined the circle and sat on a rock, as far away from Dtu as possible. It landed her near Edu, and he distinctly felt like the better option.

It was funny how things changed.

In fact, he leaned over to put a heavy hand on her shoulder and squeeze it. Looking up at his masked face, she smiled at him weakly. She very much appreciated the gesture. Especially from him.

"How do we know she is not a spy for the warlock?" Dtu huffed.

"You're still stuck on hating me? Great." Lydia glared over at the wolf.

"I will suffer your existence only if I must."

"Go find something to hump, Cujo." Lydia was in no mood to play this game.

Dtu stood with a low growl in his throat.

Edu lifted his hand to instruct the other man to calm down.

Grumbling, and with body language that clearly demonstrated the desire to do anything but, Dtu sat back down. "My concern still stands."

"I'm not a spy."

"You're his—" the wolf began.

"Do not start, Dtu," Vjo cut him off. "We have enough to concern ourselves over than rehashing your continued distrust of the girl."

"Such as the end of the *fucking* world," Kamira muttered and looked off worriedly. It wasn't like her to swear like a modern person.

Lydia turned as Edu was snapping his fingers to get her attention. She looked up at the big man. He pointed at his neck, then her, then at Kamira.

Lydia blinked. "I... Sorry. I don't follow."

Edu sighed heavily. He gestured his hand as if to reference the height of a thing, and it was nearly as tall as he was. Then to the side of his neck, then again to her, and then to Kamira. This time, slightly more frustrated.

Suddenly, it dawned on her. "Oh!" It took her a second, but she finally got there. He was referencing Lyon.

The poor woman didn't know her husband was still alive. Mind-controlled by the Ancients, yes, but... alive.

The Regent of Moons was in exactly the same predicament as Lydia.

"Kamira, um. So. Lyon's alive." Lydia winced, bracing for the woman's explosion.

"*What!* How?" Hands twisted in her coat, and Kamira dragged Lydia back up to standing. Green cat's eyes nailed her to the spot. "Tell me."

"It's kind of a long story."

"None of us know what happened to you," Vjo said from where she sat. The woman in purple looked tired, leaning up against the stone wall. They all looked ragged. But she couldn't pay them much mind with Kamira staring so intently. "I, for one, would also like to know what transpired."

"You say he lives, though?" Kamira shook her once, snapping her focus back to the angry tigress.

"Yeah. But... um. He's not himself. Not exactly."

The wild woman cringed, swore in a language Lydia didn't understand, and sighed. She let go of Lydia's coat and let her hands instead settle on her shoulders. "Dtu has told me of the days he can now remember. When the sun burned high and the Ancients could take those they wished. Lyon is their Priest. He always has been. I admit I do not know if I am dismayed that he is no longer of his own mind or overjoyed that he still lives."

"I know how you feel." Lydia paused. "Trust me."

Kamira furrowed her brow briefly, and then her expression smoothed into one of understanding and pity. "Yes. I suppose you do." She pulled her into another hug, much softer than the first. This one was an embrace of real sympathy. Lydia hugged her back. "We are sisters in this, it seems."

After a moment, Kamira parted from her, let out a sigh, and walked back to where she was standing. "Tell us all the tale. I would like to know why our world has burned."

Lydia sat back down on the rock, and even though she was surrounded by other people—several of whom she would count as friends—she felt so very distinctly alone. "Rxa demanded I surrender to the Ancients and that I swear fealty to them. He saw Q's separation from me as an abomination."

"It was." Dtu sniffed. "And you are."

Edu walked across the circle, reared back his hand, and smacked Dtu upside the head, nearly sending him sprawling to the dirt.

Dtu growled like a spurned dog up at the bigger man. Edu pulled back a fist, ready to knock the King of Moons unconscious. But the dog sighed through the snarl. "I am done."

Edu shook his head and jammed a finger into the other man's chest, a silent and very clear warning that the second time would not be nearly so polite a rebuke. Edu turned back to lean against the wall and gestured for Lydia to continue.

"We have to teach you sign language," Lydia commented up to Edu.

"He has not the patience to learn it. I have tried," Vjo commented dryly. "He says he wishes not to flail about in such an undignified manner. He believes he can communicate just fine on his own with his fists if the need arises."

Edu crossed his arms across his chest once more. Lydia couldn't help but laugh and shook her head. Slowly but surely, she was starting to like the big man. There was something endearing about the tank, even if it had taken her some time to get a chance to see it.

"Anyway," Lydia shot a glare at Dtu before continuing, "Rxa wanted to force me to kneel to the Ancients. I refused. He couldn't kill me, since he'd just doom the world back to the void. So he planned to chain me to the bottom of the lake with the Ancients themselves instead. To drown for eternity."

Evie's hands went over her face, and Kamira visibly blanched. Even Maverick looked unsettled at the thought. Lydia continued. "Lyon tried to save me. He tried to stop Rxa. But Rxa killed him and dumped his body into the lake. I went in a few moments later." Lydia shut her eyes for a moment but decided it was better to stare down at her boots. Shutting her eyes brought back the image of falling backward into that lake, of Rxa pushing her. Of the red water flowing over and around her, consuming her as she sank deeper.

"They talked to me, then, when I was nearing the bottom. They gave me a choice. I could I either spare myself... or spare Lyon." She sighed. "They'd either free me or bring him back to life. I chose Lyon."

"Why?" Kamira asked, curious and in disbelief.

"I'm sick of people dying for me. I'm sick of people sacrificing themselves or hurting themselves just because I *exist*." Anger rose in her, and she clenched her hands into fists. It took everything to keep from accidentally spawning monsters around her. "He... he's a good man. He was one of the few people here who cared about me. I couldn't let him die. I'd rather spend eternity at the bottom of a lake, losing my mind, than let him die for me like that."

Kamira bowed her head, her eyes shut. She looked both touched and deeply in pain. The woman remained silent, clearly lost in thought.

"He's the King of Blood now," Lydia added with a smirk.

That broke Kamira out of her dour mood. She cackled in laughter at the absurd thought. "Him? A king! Oh, now I deeply wish to see what travesty the Ancients have wrought."

"Aon killed Rxa in order to free you." Vjo pieced together

what obviously must have followed. "But to shatter one chain is to shatter them all."

Lydia nodded. "I woke up a little while later. He was there with me. But I watched as... as they took over." She cringed at the memory of watching the man she knew disappear into someone else. "What he is now isn't..."

"We know. We remember." Vjo looked off. "I remember the chains. I remember the torture, the pain, the blood. I remember burning beneath a pitiless sun. No, my sister. He is not the man you knew. He is far, far worse."

"Do you remember when you chained up the Ancients? Do you think we could do it again?" Lydia asked, searching for hope wherever she could find it.

Dtu huffed a laugh. "*We?* We barely helped, girl. That putrid bastard turned his back on them. That is the only reason we were ever freed. Without his help, we do not stand a chance."

"Why'd he do it?" Lydia thought she might know the answer, but she wanted to be sure.

"The only reason that man has ever done anything, it seems," Vjo answered. "For love. They could not fill the void in his soul as he so desperately wished. He begged for them to make for him a queen to love him. Something even they could not do. In his wrath, in his spite, he sought our help to imprison them. But Dtu is correct. Without his assistance, we would be useless."

History was repeating itself. Again and again, over and over, they were stuck in this loop. Aon destroying the world because he could not be loved. Lydia gritted her teeth and looked down at her boots again as she thought. "Maybe I can convince him to do it again."

Dtu snorted in laughter. "You do not know what you are talking about. Even if you were successful, we only pulled it off the first time because they did not think he was capable of such betrayal. They would see it coming now. They would predict the blow."

"What other option do we have?" She looked back up at the wolf. "How else do we set the world back to the way it was?"

"We cannot." Vjo sat up from where she was leaning against the wall. The woman moved slowly, clearly exhausted and sore. "I see no path forward like that. None that do not end in ruin."

Lydia shook her head. She couldn't accept the fact that this was the way things had to be. But Vjo was clearly a master strategist. Arguing with her was going to be utterly pointless. But she couldn't give up hope.

She had to try to talk Aon into imprisoning the Ancients again. There was no other way to set things right. If not? "What other options are there?"

"We run. We escape. We lived like this once before. Back then, we left the King of All to his Acropolis and his loyal servants. Those of us who did not serve him, did our best to flourish elsewhere. Farther from his reach, from the shadow of the Ancients." The spider's words were matter-of-fact. "He will capture us, torture us, and we will escape. The cycle will continue, as it always has. The game will continue. As it seems it always will."

"You're all trying to escape? Out of the city and into the hills?" She had seen mountains on the horizon in her dream with Aon.

"Yes. That is the hope." Vjo sighed. "Those of us he has not taken prisoner already."

Ylena. Ini. Who knew who else. Lydia flinched. "And fighting him is useless?"

"Even if we were an army, we would stand no chance against him. He commands the greater beasts who walk this world, armies of the undead, and two full Houses serve him without question. Many of those who never wore masks have fallen in line beneath him. Better to live in safety and servitude than to suffer in hiding," Kamira provided. "Cowards."

"No. They are not cowards. They merely wish to survive," Vjo rebuked the tigress gently. "We cannot fault them for staying out of a fight that they could avoid. But her point is correct. Whatever battle we would stand against the warlock would be for dignity's sake alone." Vjo looked out upon the group of people in the caves. "But we have others we must think of. Those we serve as royals. We must think of those who live in our Houses. If we can reach the horizon, we can live a life as well as we are able."

"In hiding from a tyrant king," Lydia muttered.

"Yes. But it is life, all the same. And with those they have come to think of as family. They will craft, they will write, build a new world and go on. Earth and Under will align again, and we will hunt our marked prey as we always do. We will persist. We have for thousands of years, and we will continue for thousands more. I seek to move what remains of the Houses of Fate and Words as far away as I can. There, they may find ways to live their lives devoid of as much of the King of All's influence as is possible. He is not a god, and neither are the Ancients. Their powers are immense but finite."

Running still felt wrong. It seemed she wasn't the only one who felt that way. Dtu snuffed. "I would rather die a free man in battle against that cretin than run and hide."

Edu nodded, clearly agreeing. Two votes for war, one vote against.

Lydia sighed darkly. She didn't know what she wanted to do. A fight was probably useless, but hiding felt... empty. "I'm glad I don't have anyone else wearing turquoise to worry about." She did her best to try to find any upside to her situation.

"You are concerned enough with the rest of us," Maverick

dutifully pointed out. That was true. The thought of anybody suffering at Aon's hands twisted a knife in her side.

"Regardless of our choice to either fight or leave, we cannot wage a war from down here," Vjo concluded. "We may decide our choice once we are clear of the weight of the city bearing down upon us."

"What's the plan? How do we get everyone out of here in one piece?" Lydia asked Vjo.

"Do you agree that our priority is ensuring that all those here escape this city?" the spider queen asked. "Are you willing to help us?"

"Of course. They might not wear my color, but Maverick's right. They're all my people. I'm a queen, and I'm going to try to act like one." Lydia took in a long breath and let it out in a sigh. "And that's why I'm not going with you to the mountains. I'll get you as far as the edge of the city, but then I can't go with you. If I run, it'll be in a different direction."

No one said anything. She looked back up to find everybody staring at her. "You know I can't go with you, and you all know why. And no, it isn't because I'm a fucking spy." She cut Dtu off at the pass before he could start. "He's... coming for me."

"How do you know?" Kamira asked.

"He's haunting my dreams." She shot a look to Evie. "Again." She decided not to tell them about her conversation with "Ziza." With the Ancients, and the game they placed in front of her. It was too messy, too new. She didn't even know what she thought about it, let alone trying to describe to them what had happened. "And the longer I'm here with you all, the more danger you're in."

Edu shook his head and *whunked* his fist into the stone wall behind him. He pointed at Lydia and then circled his finger to point at them all.

"I think he's saying you're one of us. And that we don't

leave people behind," Evie provided helpfully. Edu nodded, confirming her theory.

"You're not leaving me behind, Edu. You're not abandoning me." Lydia shook her head. "This isn't a failure on your part. I'm making a conscious choice. Wherever I go, he'll be on my heels. Now and forever. I can run as hard as I can, but where could I possibly go where he couldn't find me? Even if I left this city, I couldn't stay with you all. He'd just use you against me. Like Nick and then Lyon. You're all next. It's just a matter of time."

Edu let out a deep sigh and leaned back against the wall, lowering his head. His long, curly hair fell alongside his masked face like a curtain of auburn. He was trying to come up with a retort. But everyone—even Vjo—was silent.

"I'll help you get everyone out of the city. And if things go wrong?" Lydia paused. Well? If it had to happen, it might as well count for something. "I'll be the bait."

ELEVEN

The plan was simple. It made sense. It would work.

Lydia wasn't thrilled about it.

But it'd work.

They waited out the night until the sun slipped from its eclipse into full glow overhead. It seemed counterintuitive—trying to escape during the day—but Aon wouldn't be able to call on the House of Blood to help him. The vampires would be trapped in the shadows. He still had plenty of power to hunt them down, but he would be missing one portion of his strength.

The plan was to split into three groups. The House of Flames and the House of Fate would leave in one group and the House of Words and Moons in the other. Mixing the fighters in with the rest would give everyone a better chance. Splitting most of the refugees into two groups would better the chances that one half would escape.

But the regents and the royals would split away as that third group. Aon would not be able to resist the chance to take them all down at once. They were a distraction to allow the others to escape.

Only then, when they had drawn Aon's attention, would the others leave her and go. It was then, and only if it came down to it, that Edu agreed to leave Lydia behind.

She had very much appreciated the sentiment. It was really weirdly touching, even if she was pretty sure it was only to keep from giving Aon what he wanted.

She also had no doubt that it would absolutely "come down to it."

The pack of them—several hundred or so—would come out of the tunnels underneath the city, as far to the outskirts as they could get. Vjo, Edu, and Dtu knew the mountain range that was a few dozen miles off into the desert, and it was in that direction they'd head. If anybody else was looking for shelter, it was that or the open sands. They would have headed there.

There was safety in numbers, even if it meant they were all clumped in one place.

Vjo predicted that the warlock would give chase before they made it too far out of the city, and that was where Lydia would come in. She was the safety net. Aon would focus on her.

She could hold off Aon's armies for a little while. She would lose eventually; she wasn't an idiot. But if it got everyone out of the city and to relative safety—whatever it was worth, and even if it was temporary—it was worth it.

She was also the only person Aon wasn't going to kill on sight.

Probably.

There was one thing that was bothering her, though. "Vjo?" She looked over at the other queen who was walking beside her as they made their way through the tunnels. The spider knew her way by heart and had no trouble leading the gaggle of people through the tight corridors as far out to the edge of the sprawling acropolis as possible.

"Yes?"

"I need to tell you something. I don't want you telling anyone else. Not Evie, not Edu, nobody."

"Of course."

Somebody had to know. Somebody had to understand what Aon and the Ancients were after. "Aon came to me in my dreams. He told me what he wanted. He wants me as his queen."

"This is no surprise."

"No, you don't understand." She took a breath in and let it out slowly. Somewhere in the pile of people behind her was Ziza, on a stretcher. "He isn't the only one who came to talk to me."

"Oh." Vjo paused. She let out a quiet *hmm* and tapped a finger against the chin of her mask. "Ziza. They can still use her."

"Yeah." She shouldn't be surprised that Vjo could put that together. The woman was brilliant. Beyond brilliant. It was a little freaky, if she were honest. "Remind me never to play you in chess."

"I adore playing chess."

"Yeah, but I'd lose every time."

"If I did not mind not having a challenge, I would never move the pieces." Vjo chuckled. "I would be honored to play you. Perhaps even teach you what I can. Someday, perhaps."

"Someday."

"Tell me of what the Ancients said to you."

"Everything they've done to me was by design. Everything that happened. Leaving me a mortal, Edu killing me, Q, Nick's death, Rxa, Lyon... now this. All of it was to test me. To see if I'm truly worthy of loving Aon."

Vjo let out a tired sigh.

"They told me to love him. And said if I didn't... they'd make me. They'd go in my head, and remake me like they did Lyon." She cringed.

"And how did you respond?"

"I didn't, really. I still don't know what to think. Only that I don't... I don't ever want to be like that. Like Lyon. I don't want them to *make* me love him. I'm myself. I didn't kneel to them for Rxa, and I won't do it now." Not like she had a choice. "Not willingly."

"Good." Vjo squeezed her hand. "Hold onto that part of you for as long as you can. They will likely tear it from you. But you can fall in battle knowing you did not bend your head to the executioner's block."

When Aon had held her in his prison and tortured her after she came back as a dreamer, she knew that he hadn't really been trying. If he had wanted to break her mind, he could have. He could have kept her there for years—hundreds of years—and broken her down. He hadn't wanted a slave; he said so much himself. He had wanted to be free of fear, not shattered.

But now?

Now, she wasn't so sure.

Aon had been terrified when the sun had risen. He had told her to run from him, and that what he would become would be worse than anything else. The man she had met in her dreams was terrifying. He was not the same.

But he wasn't a complete stranger either.

Would this King of All try to break her?

Or would he want to keep her whole?

Lydia sighed drearily. "I can't beat him, Vjo. I know I can't. If he shows up, and I have to stand my ground so you can all escape, it's only a matter of time before he wins. Either because he's stronger than me, or because..." She trailed off, unable to put it into words.

"Because you still love parts of him. And if, upon meeting him again, you find that you love the whole of him? You may not have the desire to resist him. I understand," Vjo provided for her.

Lydia nodded weakly. "But if he's a monster, if he's—if he threatens you all, I don't know if I *can* love him."

"Why?" Vjo's tone was deeply curious. Not vindictive or doubting. "Why are we worth the pain of what the Ancients will do to you, if you deny him?"

She laughed and looked ahead down the tunnel with a smirk. "Because you're all my friends. And because that's just not what you're supposed to do. If he's a tyrant—if he's wrong —I can't be with a man like that. I can't let him win."

Vjo went silent for a long time, then let out a small breath. "You sound like Edu, just there."

Lydia snorted.

"It was meant as a compliment. I wish you had known him when we were younger and he owned a tongue. He is noble, and he was kind, then. He laughed a great deal, and I think you two would have been dear friends. I laud your strength and determination. To face down the King of All—to face down our creators—and know you will fail? I could not claim such strength. I would seek shelter in their promises. I will not speak of what you told me. I may only wish you the very best."

"If he finds us, if he comes for me, you may never see me again. Not... not really me." Lydia cringed. "I don't know how to feel about that."

"You may only do your best. Do not weep for what could have been. Do not think you could have done any better." Vjo let out a small sigh. "I will do what I can to honor your sacrifice. I, too, do not look to the horizon with anticipation. I do not wish to live once more within caves and blazing sunlight."

"Hey, well, it could be worse."

"How so?"

Lydia grinned at the woman cheekily. "I'll trade you."

Vjo chuckled and shook her head. "No. I do not think I would take such a deal. Your point is quite well made, my friend."

Lydia looked down the tunnel, and like the light at the end of the proverb, she saw a thin wood ladder leading up to a hatch. It was time.

Well, shit.

The plan was simple. It made sense. It would work.

Right until the exact moment *it didn't.*

They made it out of the tunnels and into a city square—large enough to hold the few hundred of them. They were starting to divvy up into their different groups. It had only been seconds since the last few had come out of the tunnels before everything went wrong.

It had taken next to no time for their plan to come crashing down.

They had been expected.

They were surrounded.

Havoc descended around them from all sides. It was utter mayhem. She ducked as something flew over her head, too close for comfort, and she had no idea what—or who—it was. Shouts and screams and cracks of lightning echoed around her. Fire roared, and she found herself quite instantly in the middle of a fight.

When she finally caught sight of where she was and what was happening, she saw men and women wearing black blocked off every alley and road out of the square. They weren't alone. Around them were creatures whose lives had ended a long time ago. Rotted flesh fell from their bones as they stepped into the fray, unconcerned about what would happen to them.

Monsters, bizarre and unique in their litany of horrors, joined behind them. The King of All's forces had been waiting for them. They knew where they would be. This fight was doomed before it even began.

Because of that, the scuffle was brief. Brutal, but short. She felt something smash her upside the head, and she felt like she had been hit by a car. She fell to her knees, and when she looked up, there were only a few dozen or so around her. Maverick, Aria, and Vjo were among them. The warlocks had managed to corner off a few of the weaker House of Words, and she had been caught up with them.

"Son of a *bitch*," she swore loudly and spit the blood that had formed in her mouth into the dirt between her hands. It was already healing, but goddamn if it didn't still hurt. She saw nobody wearing any other color besides purple. Hopefully, they all managed to escape. Hopefully, Edu and the rest were already heading for the hills.

There, moving to the head of the group that surrounded them, was one man she recognized. Although this time, he didn't wear a metal mask. His face was exposed. Navaa—Aon's regent and second-in-command. He stood as the leader of the pack of men and women. Many of them had dozens of marks on their faces, but none wore masks.

They all surrendered them. They all took them off in servitude.

"Lydia?" Navaa said upon seeing her, surprised. His face quickly transitioned from his momentary shock and bloomed into a broad and wicked grin. He turned his head to say something to the woman next to him. She disappeared in a swirl of black smoke, and she knew where Navaa had sent the woman.

He had sent her to fetch *him.*

Great.

"This is a wonderful surprise!" The Elder of Shadows held out his arms as if to greet an old friend. "Here I thought we were only bound to catch a spider, a dog, and a brainless boar. Now, we have the prized snake as well."

Vjo stepped forward as if to attack, but when several bows pointed straight in her direction, arrowheads tipped in black fire, she stopped.

Lydia pushed up to her feet and wiped her mouth on her sleeve. It came away red, but the cut it came from was already closed.

As shitty as everything was, immortality had its benefits.

"This makes no sense," Maverick asserted from her side. "It is not possible that they would know where we were. There were too many options. We chose this location at random."

"We were betrayed, Maverick," Vjo replied, her voice low in a quiet and angry hiss. "Someone in our cadre has recently sent a messenger and told them where we would emerge."

"Very astute, as I would expect you to be, Queen of Words." Navaa laughed and began to walk forward. He seemed utterly unafraid of them. And Lydia could understand why. A bunch of scholars, doctors, and her? They weren't fighters. They were horribly outmatched without Edu, Dtu, and the rest. "Yes. Someone has betrayed you."

"Fine, but why?" Lydia summoned her spear and held it at the ready, stepping forward and away from the frightened group she was trying to protect. She was also trying to space herself out from Vjo. If the spider managed to take her other form, she would need some room to fight. Not to mention, Lydia was making her own plans on what to summon to give Aon's army a run for their money. "Why would anyone here join you assholes?"

"Ask her yourself." Navaa pointed to someone standing behind Lydia.

Afraid to glance behind her but too curious not to look, she turned. Navaa was pointing at... oh, no.

Aria.

Maverick had his arm around her but was now looking down at his wife with his single visible yellow eye wide in concern and fear. "No. No, my Aria..." he mumbled to the smaller woman at his side. "Say this is a lie."

Aria had her hands clasped to her chest, and she shook her

head. Tears were streaming down her visible cheek. "Forgive me, my love. I could not stand the thought of—they said if I helped them, they would spare you. I could not bear to see you harmed. I would rather serve the warlock than lose you!"

Maverick's face twisted in pain. He took a step away from his wife and covered his face with both hands, seemingly unable to handle what had just transpired.

"You are an elder. They were going to string you up by your toes, they said! They swore no regents would live. All would be killed as a warning to others. I could not let this come to pass." Aria pulled at his hands, begging at him to look at her. "My love—"

Maverick pulled farther away from her. His shoulders curled in on himself, the betrayal seemingly too much for him to withstand.

"Lady Aria," Navaa began with the same toothy, aggressive grin he seemed to always wear. "And we will hold true to our promise. Maverick will live. You, however? We thank you for your service." He laughed. "But we have no use for traitors."

Lydia reacted a moment too late. A figure in black rose out of the sand. Materialized out of nothing. He grabbed Aria's head in both of his hands from behind.

It happened too fast to stop it.

Just like it had with Nick.

Just like it had with Lyon.

Aria screamed as she burned, her body incinerating in black flame. A woman in a purple mask stabbed the man in black, sending him to the ground, but it was too late. The fire did not extinguish.

"*No!*" Maverick screamed and went running to his wife—went to embrace the inferno that was her body. Several others held him back, dragging him to the ground as he screamed, kicked, and thrashed, reaching out for the woman who was already a crumpled heap upon the packed dust. "*Aria!*"

The black fire worked quickly, and her struggles ceased.

Aria didn't suffer for long.

Chaos erupted once more after the flames went silent. They had taken one of their own, betrayal or not.

And they were not alone in their anger. Lydia let out a howl of rage and tore at Navaa with a fury she hadn't known she possessed.

Strange turquoise glowing creatures exploded from the ground, crawling out of every pocket of the earth, until they were a swarm of leathery-winged, ghastly, bat-like creatures that descended upon the warlock's armies like a plague.

"I will kill you all *myself!*" Lydia shouted as she dug the end of her spear through the head of a man in black who stood in her way.

Navaa was not expecting her wrath, nor the creatures she summoned. For a moment, she had sent Aon's legions into disarray, scattering over each other and swinging their arms to defend themselves against the enormous insects under her command.

Her ghostly, glowing, insectoid bats were tearing his men to pieces, and the elder did not know what to do.

Lydia drove her spear through another man's chest and pinned him to the ground. "Vjo!" she shouted to the woman who was now a massive spider. She was doing her best to defend those who could not fight. "Get everyone out of here. Take them and go. I can take these little shits myself."

"Lyd—" Vjo began.

She cut her off. "*Go!*"

Navaa was backing away from Lydia, wide-eyed and unsure as to what to do with her as she stalked toward him. There was fear on his face. Nobody here had ever been afraid of her.

And it felt *amazing.*

Lydia was furious. How *dare* they. Maverick was her friend. Aria was her friend, driven to betrayal out of terror. She was at the end of her rope. No more of this bullshit. She slammed the end of her spear into the ground.

She'd had enough.

Eyes began to appear in the shadows cast by the blazing sun. Glowing slits that blinked into turquoise, eerie faces. Too sharp and angular, like they had been cut there by knives. Flickering like jack-o-lanterns, toothy grins, wide and sharp, split open and began to cackle in sharp-pitched, hissing voices.

She had one command for them. "End them all."

Navaa stopped abruptly in his retreat. He looked down at his chest, and from it protruded several long, ghostly fingers. A long-taloned hand had reached through him like a ghost might pass through a wall. Fingers appearing on the other side like he was insubstantial. But when it snapped its hand back, it carried with it the man's entire spine. It had reached through Navaa's body and ripped it loose like it was nothing.

Navaa coughed blood and collapsed to the ground, a useless and limp pile of limbs without the column of bone to hold him up straight.

The sight of their leader falling in such a graphic manner sent the greater beasts and those in black running away, scattering and disappearing in swirls of black smoke.

"You want to see an army of freaks?" She began to walk toward a pack of men and women in black who were cornered against a wall. "Here it is!"

Lydia swung the end of her spear, knocking the head off a walking skeleton who got too close to her, sending it rolling away from her across the sand.

Her wraiths were destroying everything in their path, cackling and giggling like the nightmares they were, as they dismembered whoever was not smart enough to run.

Those horror movies she watched all her life were finally coming in handy.

When Lydia looked up from the carnage, she saw Vjo and

the others were gone. There was a smattering of bodies on the ground of those wearing purple, but not many. Barely a few in comparison to those wearing black or the piles of broken corpses and monsters. Good.

Two more undead fell to her spear. Then three more. One of them managed to land a blow to her shoulder, but it lost its head a moment later. The battle was mayhem, a mix of wraiths and shadows versus skeletons and corpses.

Lydia was laughing, the fury and the joy of the fight mixing into a strange kind of manic glee. This felt so wonderfully cathartic. She had this frustration pent up for a long time, it seemed.

She was furious. They were going to pay.

And she was winning.

Too bad it didn't last.

It was funny how history was repeating itself. It seemed the past six months of Lydia's life were playing back out in front of her like someone had hit rewind.

Lightning struck the center of the city square.

Lydia turned her head and shielded her face from the impact. When the flash of light and the deafening crack resided, there was no noise.

All her creatures were gone. So were all the bodies and the undead. The sounds of battle, of panic and death, were ended in that one moment.

Only silence remained.

Nothing moved, except for the wind.

The whole of the city square was empty. Save for her and a figure standing in the center of the square. He was shirtless. Around his waist was a wrap of black fabric that hung to the ground. It was adorned with sections of black metal that banded around his waist and hung down at his side. It looked ancient, ceremonial, and matched the thick bracers on his forearms. A metal gauntlet decorated one hand.

He had long black hair that hung along his slightly lowered face, with just a few gray hairs in the mix. His exposed chest and arms were covered in jet-black lines of ink. Marks that she would never forget. Marks that she had kissed more than once.

He wore no mask, and as he slowly lifted his head to look at her, spilled-ink eyes found hers. Power filled the air like a cloud. It made her ears ring. This was the first time they had met in the waking world since the world was remade.

In dreams, things between them had always been different.

Now?

All bets were off.

Lydia readied herself, despite the fear in her stomach and the lump in her throat. She lifted her spear and aimed the obsidian tip at the man.

"Aon."

TWELVE

"We have to stop meeting like this." Lydia didn't know where she got the strength to quip. There was safety in the humor, she supposed.

The man who was standing before her was as much a stranger as he was achingly familiar. He was dressed the same way she had seen in her dreams, garbed like a dark god or an ancient pharaoh. And now, that really was what he was. He was beautiful. He was unearthly.

He made her stomach twist in knots of desire and fear in equal measure.

The dreams hadn't done him justice. The feeling of him washing over the city square made her skin break out in goose-bumps. She shivered despite the warm air and blazing sun over-head. She could sense his power around her like a thunderstorm rolling in from the horizon.

And like a storm, she felt as helpless to stop him—just as caught in the force of nature that was the man before her. He was as terrifying as he was awe-inspiring.

He didn't speak. He just watched her silently from where

he stood, his face unreadable save for a strange, eager look in his jet eyes.

There was no question that she was terrified of him. The seconds dragged on with them in silence. It made it somehow far, far worse than if he had spoken. Her hands began shaking, but she realized with a sad creeping kind of dread that it wasn't from fear. It was from exhaustion.

Shit.

The adrenaline from the fight was wearing off. Lydia had been so engrossed in the battle—so desperate to kill Navaa, to get everyone out safely, and to get revenge for Aria's death—she had forgotten that Aon was on his way.

Now, she didn't know how deep her well of power went, but she was pretty damn tapped.

Lydia shifted her grip on the spear, trying to stop her trembling.

It seemed that was what he was waiting for. He smiled faintly as he began to walk toward her. He moved methodically, in no rush to cross the thirty feet between them. The dark metal of his belts and adornments swung along the black fabric he wore around his waist and barely brushed the ground as he walked. He was barefoot.

He moved like a panther—slow, graceful, purposeful. His eyes never left hers as he called her bluff. He gave her every chance in the world to turn and run. If she even had the strength to still do anything of the sort. She was already out of breath, and the pounding of her heartbeat hadn't slowed, though the reason behind it had changed from rage to fear.

She shifted back a step reflexively—she couldn't help it. "I know your name isn't Aon. I know you're just putting up with that. But... Aon, say something, please."

He ignored her and did nothing but merely walk toward her. As he got within range of her spear, she lifted it and put the point underneath his chin at his neck. All she received for a reaction was that he simply stopped walking.

"Say something!" Lydia cried, half pleading with him now to stop his unnerving and terrifying silence. She had expected him to come blasting in and making demands. He had always loved the sound of his own voice. "You said you weren't talking because it reminded me you aren't the same man I love. The silence isn't helping either."

He raised his hand and with the back of it tried to push the spear away from his neck. It wasn't a forceful motion. It wasn't even quick. It was him, testing her. He seemed to want to see if she would hold on to her conviction and keep her distance.

For a moment, she resisted and kept her spear where it was. But what was the use? Why should she bother fighting him? She could feel the power coming off him like a fire. It reached deep into her, and she felt like it was pulling her closer.

This was safe. This was home. This was right. She belonged here, with him, like this.

Slowly, she allowed him to push the spear away from his throat and step in closer to her. She let it fall to her side, nearly forgotten as he closed the distance between them.

Reaching up his flesh-and-blood hand, he brushed his fingers against her cheek. His touch was warm, and it set something off in her like the crackle of electricity.

He was a warm blanket on a cold night. She could feel her eyes slip half-shut, wanting nothing more but to lean into his touch and let go.

It would be so easy, to sink into that embrace. To let him wrap his arms around her and to let all her worries and fears merely wash away.

Something screamed in the back of her mind. Some small part of her sent up the flag. He had done this once before. This felt wrong. Lydia snapped out of it and jumped back a step from him, her eyes wide. The moment shattered, and she felt the cold reality sink back in.

"Stop it with the stupid hypnotism trick!" she snapped.

He had been trying to worm his way into her mind. He smirked at her darkly, seemingly amused that she managed to break the spell. "Can you blame a man for hoping you might make this easy?"

"Yes, I can." If he thought she was going to give in that easily, he had another think coming. Lydia picked up her spear and thrust it at him with an angry growl.

Aon's servants and the undead had been slower than she was. Weaker and afraid of what she could do. The warlock was none of these things. He dodged, grabbed the end of the spear, and yanked her around. Dragging her back against his chest, he used the body of the spear to pin her against him, the wooden staff up against her throat, choking her. He chuckled, a rumble in his chest as he cut off her air.

"You are beautiful, my queen," he purred into her ear. "More so when you are angry. How transcendent you will be, defeated and surrendered, pledging to me your love and your loyalty as I ravish you."

Snarling, she winced in pain as he pressed the spear harder against her, cruel and unapologetic. If she wanted to do this the hard way, it seemed he would be happy to oblige. She summoned daggers into her hands and stabbed them behind her and into his ribs.

Aon let out a hiss of pain and let go of the spear, letting it fall to the ground.

Whirling to face him, she put some distance between them. The warlock gripped the gold handles of her daggers and yanked them out, letting them fall to the ground beside her spear.

Lydia's eyes went wide. He didn't even bleed, the wounds closed so quickly.

As Aon stepped toward her, she staggered a step back. His face bloomed in another smile as he watched her realize precisely how hopeless this was going to be.

"Aon, please, wait—" she said and held up her hand as he stepped toward her again and she another one back. "Please, just wait."

"You desired a fight. I am merely granting your wish."

She was too spent to summon monsters to fight for her. And even if she weren't—even if she could create a horde—he would simply destroy them all in a snap of a finger as he had done when he appeared. Everyone had been brushed away, wiped clean from the slate like they hadn't even existed. They weren't worth his time.

"You killed them all. Your own people." Not even her warlock would have sunk that low.

"Hum?" He looked around as if confused for a moment and then laughed when he realized what she was talking about. "You think I *killed* them? Of course not. I merely relocated them. I wished for privacy. What manner of monster do you think I am?" he asked quizzically as if amazed she would think such a thing of him.

Small favors. But he had let one person die. "The kind who would kill Aria."

"Traitors should not be suffered to live." He sighed. "I have few laws in my world, but that one is paramount."

"She was afraid. She was bargaining for the only thing in her life that mattered to her—the man she loved. Does that sound familiar?"

"What will you bargain, should you fail to love me and the Ancients come to remake you, I wonder?"

She went cold once more. "The Ancients told you?"

"I am their son."

Grimacing, she took another step away from him. "I won't

let them in my head—I won't let them turn me into what they did to Lyon. To—" She broke off.

"To me?" The King of All tutted and shook his head. "I am in need of the Priest's unwavering loyalty. We may... negotiate for his freedom in the future, once your fealty is unquestionably mine. As for myself? I am not *turned*. I am *whole*." He placed his palm to his chest. "This is how I am meant to be—do you not understand?"

"I get it, I just—I don't—" She winced. "I don't... you didn't kill them?"

"Not even those in purple. Not even those who thought to flee." He tilted his head to the side slightly. "You think me worse than the warlock you knew. You think this world some manner of travesty. But you have not given me a chance to prove it otherwise. All I ask for is that opportunity."

"You say that. But then your *parents* come in and tell me that if I don't, I'll have no choice!" That was the problem. Not that she didn't think she could love him. But the fact she was being forced to, one way or the other.

"A path that may never need be trodden, my starlight. A nightmare you may never need to live." It was clear he thought it was so simple. So sensible. He was so *certain* she'd love him.

"You don't get it."

He chuckled again. "And you are stalling to catch your breath. A clever tactic, but an old one." He lunged for her, and she dodged and swung her leg, kicking him hard in the side. He let out a small *unf* of pain. She could still hurt him.

That was something.

Not much, but something. He raked his claws through the air, intending to tear her right arm open, and she barely managed to get out of the way.

Two steps back and she summoned her spear back to her hands and stood off against him. "Stop this."

"Why? Are you not having fun?" He swept his human hand

through his hair, brushing it from his face, before holding out his hands at his sides as if to invite her to take the next shot. "I admit I am finding this delightful."

"This isn't a game."

"Isn't it? You are stalling to give them enough time to escape, are you not? What other purpose does this serve? You know you cannot win. Furthermore, I think you do not wish to win." His eyes raked down her body. "I believe we both wish for the same thing, at the end of this little sparring match."

This was a pointless fight, and she knew it. The faint smile on his face said *he* knew *she* knew it.

But she wasn't going to give up—wasn't going to let him just win without trying to stop him. Maybe she could get a few more solid hits in before it was over. But to say that she didn't want to win? "You're wrong."

"Oh, you are simply this poor of a fighter? My mistake. I forget you are only a child." The bastard was goading her. And it worked.

Lydia snarled and this time lunged at him, trying to jam her spear into Aon's heart. He only laughed.

The next few minutes were a blur. Every movement she made was out of pure instinct. She couldn't stop to think about it—he was too fast. If she even took a breath, it felt like he would be there to snatch it away from her.

He was landing more blows than she was, but he wasn't going for the kill. Why not? More than once he had the opportunity to tear her open, to end the fight, and yet he would throw her into a building or through a wooden post, sending her sprawling to the sand and dirt.

He isn't trying to kill me. He's trying to wear me down. He's making a point. She was already tired when he'd arrived, and now she felt as though she barely had the strength to stand. Each time she pushed herself up from the ground, it took her just a little bit longer to do so.

This is about giving up. This is about being beaten.

Everything in her hurt. Everything ached. He was *not* pulling his punches. More than once she knew that if she were still mortal, she'd be dead from a punctured kidney or broken bones. It was only her more resilient state and her ability to heal that kept her lungs from filling with blood.

When she took too long to get back up to her feet, he took the opportunity to lecture her. "This world is simpler, better. I am the strength of this world. Through me lives the will of the Ancients. Here there are no more politics, no more strife, no more betrayal. Is that not preferable? Superior?"

"No." She spat blood into the dirt and knew her lip was split. "I want things to go back to the way they were."

"But why?" He tilted his head slightly as he looked at her, his brow furrowed in thought. As if what she said was utter nonsense. "That world tormented you. Tortured you. Killed you and imprisoned you. Betrayal and loss dogged your every step. Yet you wish to return to that cruelty?"

"Because..." She stood slowly and grunted in pain as she felt something in her side snap back into place. *Because I had him.* "It was fair. You're a despot."

"Am I? You do not know me. You said so yourself. You have not seen how I rule—how do you know if I am unfair?"

Lydia only glared.

He smirked at catching her in his words. "The world you knew was doomed to fail." He took a slow step toward her. "It suffered from neglect. Caught in the strife of children, bickering over broken toys. There was no way to salvage that place you knew. It was far beyond repair."

"You're wrong."

"No. You know I speak truth. If Rxa did not betray you, someone else would. The dog, perhaps. I sense his hatred of you, even from here. You were too dangerous to them—too new. They hated you for that you were unlike them. They had from the very beginning." He took another step closer. "They hated you because you dared to love me."

"I loved him. Not you."

"We are the same man. Look at me."

"Made into a sock-puppet to some asshole puddle gods, you mean. Aon wouldn't have..." She coughed.

"Would not have what? Fought you without the need to dampen his blows? Which would you prefer I do, my starlight? Treat you as a something precious to be protected, or as my equal?"

Shutting her eyes for a moment, she shook her head. He was letting her catch her breath, whether or not that was the point. "You're not yourself. You're a slave."

"We all serve the Ancients. It is simply a matter of perspective. Did you not serve a king in your world?"

"No. We had governments. We had democracy."

He laughed, deeply amused at the comments of a child. "An adorable concept. Was it not deeply flawed? Was it not still ruled by those with enough money and power to steer it? You served an established law. As do we. I merely *am* that law."

Lydia gritted her teeth and felt her jaw tick in frustration. "This isn't right, rounding up and imprisoning anybody who doesn't like what happened. That's not better."

Aon gestured behind him toward the main street out into the desert sands and the mountain range beyond. "I let them go, did I not?"

"What?" She blinked.

"I could have taken them all. I could, even now, send my legions out to fetch them. I could command the sands themselves to swallow them whole and end their lives. But I do not. Why?"

"I... I don't know."

He was on her in the blink of an eye. Suddenly, he was behind her, his arm around her neck, pressing her back against his chest. She gagged and tried to yank his arm away, but he was far too strong. His other hand banded around her waist, holding her still.

"I would let them live their lives in peace. Believe me or not, it is the truth. I have no desire for sycophants or traitors in my midst. Let them be free, let them seek out what happiness they might where they do not trouble me. But you know they will return here before long. They will form an army and march against me. I know Edu too well to think he will sit idly by and learn to live in this new world." His breath was hot against her ear. "Besides... I have what I came here for. Do you surrender this fight?"

She managed to form words, although she was growing lightheaded with him pressing against her throat. "Not going to happen. Not now, not ever."

"Once more, we shall see."

She summoned another dagger, and this time went for his face. But he deflected before she even got within a few inches. It meant he had to let go of her, and that was some progress. She stomped on his foot, and when he grunted and recoiled, she rolled out from under his grasp.

A fight that had started off as hopeless was now pathetic. Lydia couldn't move fast enough to even get close to him. Now, he was just kicking the ever-loving hell out of her.

He certainly wasn't treating her like she was fragile, she'd give him that.

His fist met her face and sent her toppling to the dirt. She thought perhaps he might leave her there, but his clawed gauntlet twisted in her hair and pulled her forcefully back up to her feet.

The ground flew by underneath her as he hurled her into the side of a clay and dirt building. She didn't know if the cracking she felt came from the wall or her.

She tasted blood in her mouth. Her lip was split and wasn't

healing as fast as it should have. The more she was injured, the less she was able to mend. The more of her strength she spent, the easier it was to damage her.

A single idea came to her mind. A single chance to play dirty. She had no other hope now, after all. Fighting fair wasn't doing a damn thing, and his efforts to tire her out were working.

Lydia pushed herself up from the ground by sheer force of will alone. Her lip was still bleeding, as was a cut on her side. All she wanted in the world was to stay down. All she wanted in the world was to give up.

No. Not until every ounce of her was gone. Not until she had nothing left.

She ran a trembling hand through her hair to push it back from her face. Aon stood some ten feet away from her, looking utterly unscathed. He was smirking at her, one eyebrow arched as if to ask her if she was still willing to fight.

She was battered, bloody, and beaten.

And he was untouched.

Once more he held his hands out at his sides, inviting her to start another round.

This wasn't the way to win. But it was too late, now. Her legs were wobbly. This would be her last ploy—her final attempt. If this didn't work, it was over, and she knew it. She took two slow steps forward, and his smirk turned into a grin, seeing how worn out she was.

It wasn't a hard task to pretend to faint. It wasn't a long stretch of her debatable and untested acting skills to let her eyes roll into her head and let her knees give out. She fell to the ground hard, and pain lanced through her as her head impacted the ground. But she didn't stop herself with her hands. She had to be "out."

The rustle of fabric near her was the only hint he had approached her at first. A hand on her shoulder turned her over onto her back. Lydia kept her eyes closed, lips parted, body limp. What would he do, if he thought she was out cold? Rip out her heart? No. If he wanted to do that, he would have done it already. He had been playing with her and letting her tire herself out in a pointless fistfight.

The backs of his knuckles ran tenderly down her cheek. She felt the tips of his black hair brush against her face as he knelt over her. The pass of his thumb ran against her lower lip, as she felt his warm breath flush against her cheek. He was going to kiss her, stealing an embrace while he thought she was unconscious.

It was now or never.

This had to end.

THIRTEEN

Lydia had one shot at ending this fight. One.

Grabbing him, she mustered everything she had left. She threw him onto his back and straddled him, one hand pressing all her weight down onto his shoulder. In the other, she summoned another obsidian-bladed dagger and held the knife against one of the black lines of esoteric writing on his face.

The look of surprise on his face didn't last for long before it faded into one of... pride and admiration. He was impressed. Pleased with her. He was smiling up at her, seemingly unafraid of the knife against his soulmarks.

"Enough!" She wasn't sure at all if she could cut him faster than he could defend himself.

"Go ahead." He laid his arms down at his sides.

The proverbial record skipped in her head. Whatever she had expected, it wasn't that. "What?"

"If you wish to destroy me, do it."

Like a deer in the headlights again, she completely froze. He lay there beneath her, watching her with a faint smile. He wasn't daring her to do it out of some sort of cocky spite. He was just lying there, calm as could be. If anything, there was *adoration* in his expression.

"I..." She didn't know what to say.

"Go on. I belong to you, my queen. I am yours to destroy." He watched her through half-lidded eyes, resting his head back against the sand, making no movement to defend himself.

"You're bluffing."

"If the only soul I have ever loved in all my eons judges me unworthy to live, I accept my fate. Put me in my grave, Lydia. My starlight."

She flinched as if he had slapped her. It stung her and felt like a physical blow. Really, she should just slice the marks in half now. Destroy as many of the lines of black ink on his face as she could before he killed her.

That would be the intelligent thing to do.

But since when had she done the smart thing, recently?

And there was the tragedy. She couldn't kill him. Her heart seized at the idea, and her hand began to tremble. Just the thought of doing it threatened to make her cry right then and there.

He had her in more ways than one.

She expected him to grab at her wrist. Or to throw her off him. What she didn't expect was him to grab her hips with both hands and pull her down against his own where she straddled him. Her eyes shot wide as she felt his body pressing against her.

He had clearly enjoyed the fight in more ways than one.

The low moan that left him nearly covered the small squeak she made at the unexpected action.

Her moment of shock loosened her grip on her knife, and it was all the opportunity he needed. He rolled them over, pinning her far more effectively to the ground. He knocked the dagger from her hand as if it were nothing. Before she could track what had happened, her hands were pinned over her head.

But not by his grasp. Something felt like it had wound

around her wrists like vines— tangling around her palms and in between her fingers, cinching tight. She looked up and saw black tendrils of power had come from the sand itself and were holding her prisoner.

"Damn it, let—" She kicked at him, struggling and thrashing as hard as she could. But he was kneeling between her legs with his hands on either side of her head, and there was little she could do to budge him. "—me up!"

The smile on his face told her he was going to do nothing of the sort. It was a smile of pride. Of victory. And of desire. Slowly, he closed his human hand around her throat and squeezed, tightening her airway but not cutting it off.

"I remember this, as if from a dream." His words were a low rumble, dusky and thick. "I remember how you would moan. How your body would tense in pleasure as I danced you on the edge of danger. Show me, now that I am no longer caught in that terrible nightmare."

He pressed his hips against hers, grinding the proof of his desire against her. The sensation was too much, and he got what he wanted. A moan spilled from her lips as she reflexively lifted her hips to meet the pressure.

It might not be her Aon in his head—not all of him—but his body was the same. And his body could still do things to her that she couldn't stop. And things she didn't *want* to stop.

The moan that left him matched her own, as he dropped his head closer to her ear. "Surrender this fight to me, my queen."

"N—"

His hand tightened, just a little, as he drove his hips back into her again, mimicking the dance they both so desperately wanted.

Fine. Maybe he wasn't the only one who had found their fight a little bit of a turn-on.

Lips, hot as lava, trailed over her ear. "Just this fight. Just this moment. Nothing more. Surrender to me... say it."

Another roll of his hips and he had her fighting the urge to wrap her legs around his waist.

His lips were hot against her skin, accented by the nip of his teeth. She jolted underneath him, unable to help it. An unexpected fire crashed through her at his touch.

She wanted this.

Oh God, she *needed* this. Needed to feel him, even if he was a ghost—she needed the hope he brought.

But more than that, in some terrible way? He'd won the fight. And now... she wanted him to take what he'd earned.

Two words left her in little more than a whisper. "I... I surrender."

Releasing his grasp on her throat, he groaned in bliss and ecstasy at her words. Bowing his head low, he kissed her skin where he had just been squeezing her, almost reverently.

Lifting his head to study her face, he propped his weight up on one elbow, before running his tongue along the cut on her lower lip. He was licking up the blood that he had spilled, and the sound that left him was utterly *primal*.

The warlock closed his lips around the wound, and she couldn't stop the choked moan that left her throat. "Aon—"

He shushed her and put his finger to her mouth. After a moment, he leaned down to replace his finger with his lips. It was possessive—it was forceful—it was reminding her who was in charge. When their lips met, he pressed his body against hers, rutting against her. Her eyes went wide at the feeling, and she arched up against him, moaning against his lips again against her will.

He let out an appreciative noise as he kissed her harder, slipping his tongue into her mouth and claiming it for his own. Now, she felt as though she were going to pass out again for a very different reason.

He was going to fuck her. Right here, in the middle of the empty town square.

And she would be driven mad if he didn't. The image of it —of being taken by him, ravished by him, like he threatened— was keeping her robbed of breath nearly as much as his grasp around her throat had done.

He was right.

She hadn't wanted to win the fight. He was as alluring to her now as he ever was, even if he was not the same man. Even if she wept for who she had lost. The darkness was still there, drawing her in.

He parted his lips from hers and ground himself against her again, watching her writhe underneath him.

"You are flawless," he breathed down at her. "I hope we spar like this frequently. I have not found anything quite so... arresting... in many thousands of years. Perhaps next time I will even let you win."

"Shut up." She ground out her words through clenched teeth as he pressed himself against her again in a slow pattern, keeping her on the brink of begging for more.

"Mm, and I am sure you would assert that you are not enjoying this moment between us."

She glowered up at him.

"Oh, that *look*. But who is that frustration meant for? Me or you?" Still, he didn't relent. He was tormenting them both for the joy of it, and she could see him shudder as well. She watched as his breath quickened for the first time since he had shown up.

He leaned down and hovered his lips over hers for a second, teasing her with the promise of another kiss. Her breath caught in her throat, and she froze beneath him at the gesture. He smirked, having earned exactly the reaction he was looking for. "Have I proven that you still want me? That I am not so loathsome as you may claim? Can you at least admit that to me?"

She was trembling—looking up at him afraid and unsure of

what to do or what to say. His words and his touch were overwhelming her. Her own words failed her.

"I remember little from before," he said to her gently as he lowered himself onto his elbows to get closer to her, settling against her like a lover, still grinding his hips into her in that repeated, slow pattern. "From those five thousand years I spent in that twisted nightmare of madness. Pieces, fragments, shards of glass that bite and sting at my mind. But I remember one thing as clear as the sun. I remember one shining light—you, my love. But what I recall as a girl, a mortal child in danger of the shadows that would consume her, I open my eyes from that slumber to see before me a queen, full of fury and power."

Aon had never been a poet. He'd never spouted words like that to her. He had too much ego to sink to that level, and he likely assumed she should merely know how he felt. But this version of him... this man was different. So similar and yet... not.

"Tell me that you want me," he whispered into her ear.

She felt her stomach cinch tight at his words. Felt herself shiver underneath him.

He turned his head to look down at her and found her wide-eyed and uncertain. He smirked and tutted, shaking his head at her. "Still such false dignity... such delicious *pride*."

He kissed her, passionate and violent. It stole her breath away, robbed her of thought. He slipped his tongue into her mouth, ravaging her. It was possessive, needy and selfish, and full of control—as if he would consume her whole. He was marking her as his territory—as his to possess. When he stopped, she was gasping for air and quivering underneath him. He smirked at the result of his work. "Good."

"Wh—what?"

"I hoped you would not give in so easily." He stood from her, and she felt the tendrils of power that kept her hands bound to the dirt release her. She scooted away from him but stayed sitting on the ground, unsure if she could find the strength to stand. "You likely think to run away, far from the others, do you not? You think you are a danger to them and that where you are I will find them all to use them against you."

"I... uh." *Yeah.*

"I will release you this time. I will not take you this day. But I will need you to promise me something in return."

"Depends on what it is." She rubbed her wrists.

"Go to the others where they will undoubtedly gather in the hills. Tell those who wish to leave in peace they may do so with my blessing. But those who wish to fight me? Tell them to gather their forces and do so quickly."

That was just a little bit of the Aon she recognized.

"I don't, I—" she stammered uselessly. "Why?"

He held out his arms at his sides as if inviting her to start another fight with him. "I find myself... eager for a climax to this little game." The look on his face made his innuendo quite clear. But, my dear, sweet starlight... know that when I win next time? You will be mine. And I will not be so lenient."

With that, Aon was gone in a swirl of black smoke.

And she was alone.

FOURTEEN

It felt wrong, abandoning a fight. Edu never retreated willingly. Had he been alone, he would have stood his ground. Fought until he, or they, were dead in the sand. But the sad truth was that he had others to worry about. Others to care for and to ensure they reached safety.

Evie was walking at his side with her features drawn in an uncommon look of fear and worry. The sprite was usually so unflappable. Nothing seemed to touch her or weigh her down. Yet the ambush in the Acropolis seemed to do just that.

They had lost several good souls. The warlock's forces had known to cut them in two parts, to circle off Vjo and the highest-ranked of the House of Words. They were the weakest in open battle. It was not their strength. Even the House of Fate tangled better in battle than the scholars and doctors. Their value was elsewhere.

Lydia had been with Vjo when the chaos began, when their plan went so terribly wrong and in record time. Edu knew somebody had betrayed them. Who it was, he did not know. But as to the why, he could suspect. Someone laid down all their lives in exchange for something they cared about, for someone they loved. Information in exchange for protection. An age-old tale. One always doomed to fail in the end.

Whoever cut such a desperate bargain would suffer for it. Edu doubted he would have to raise his own hand in recompense to whomever had done the deed. Their fee would come due long before he had the chance to collect it. It was always the way.

"They knew we were there. Somebody ratted us out."

Evie's voice was never so dreary. It broke his heart to hear her so hurt and hopeless. He thought it was because of their rather spectacular failure. *No, she is simply smarter than perhaps I give her credit for.* He smiled behind his mask and looked down at her, meeting her yellow gaze that was tinged in betrayal and sadness. *She is upset because we were betrayed. Kinship is her weakness.*

Nodding, he wrapped an arm around her and hugged her to his side as they walked. He wouldn't lie to her. What would be the point?

"Who do you think it was?"

Edu shrugged. Someone in the House of Words, he guessed. Someone who would reason that a last-ditch bargain was their only choice. No one in his House, or the House of Moons, would ever stoop to such a thing. The House of Fate was too committed to avoiding such direct actions. They were always one to follow the path of the stream. Only Ini felt so inclined to throw rocks into the flow to divert the course.

"Probably somebody wearin' purple, stupid chickens," she grumbled. "They'll get theirs. Already probably have. I don't figure Aon keeps traitors around for fun."

Much smarter than I give her credit for. He scooped her up in his arms suddenly, hooking his arm beneath her knees and sweeping her up. She shrieked in laughter and threw her arms around his neck, her morose mood instantly forgotten.

There was a low growl, and he turned his head to see a

towering beast next to him. Kamira. The sunlight shone off the ruddy and rich tones of her fur. She was a massive thing in her preferred form, looming over him. It was rare that anyone or anything had such an opportunity.

The tigress was clearly angry and miserable. He also imagined the hot sand was hardly pleasant on her paws. The swish of a long tail behind her was another decent hint at her mood.

The shifters would be eager to take their animal forms to head to the mountains. Walking would take days, and it would be a waste of energy and time. Out here, they were also vulnerable to attack. Kamira was communicating without words that she was ready to go, now that they were clear enough from the city to know there would not be a second altercation just yet. They had not split up for that reason—all would be needed to stand their ground if they were pursued out of the city.

Why isn't he attacking us? Edu furrowed his brow behind his mask. *He is letting us go. He wishes us to escape. But for what purpose? Not out of the kindness of his heart. Either he desired Lydia and nothing else, or he is making a point that he does not see us as a threat.*

The dismissal bristled his nerves, but he would not look a gift horse in the mouth. Regardless of the reason, it was a momentary reprieve. Edu nodded to Kamira. The tigress's muscles moved in a wave of sinew and power as she instantly dug into the sand and took off for the mountains on the horizon. All those wearing marks of green shifted to their chosen forms and followed.

"They get to do that, but we have to walk?" Evie huffed. "That's not fair!"

Edu chuckled. *No, my little love, we will not have to walk.*

Clenching his fist, he flexed his power. Circles of fire appeared in the sand, out of which crawled the winged drakes he preferred to ride into battle, when he did so on a mount and not on foot. His warriors all followed suit. Many were taking those in blue with them, as the House of Fate would otherwise be stranded. The largest of the lizards strode up next to him, claws sinking into the sand, forked tongue flicking out of its mouth as it tasted the desert air.

"Oooohh!" Evie's face lit up in joy. She had yet to ride with him, and he found himself grinning at the idea. The girl would enjoy flying. He plopped her on the back of the drake and climbed up behind her. He placed her hands on one of the spines, instructing her to hang on. She did so obediently. In fact, she clung on a little too tightly for his dragon's comfort. The creature huffed back at him annoyedly.

He patted his drake's side, consoling the creature. It only grunted deep in its chest and spread its wings, eager to be done with any task that did not involve killing, eating, or mating. He sympathized.

As its powerful wings beat the air and lifted them up off the ground in a kick of sand, Evie screamed.

Edu couldn't help but laugh.

* * *

Lydia was too tired to summon anything to carry her to the mountain range. She was too tired do much of anything, except pick a direction and walk.

And so, that was what she did, headed toward the mountains as the sun beat down on her. It wasn't that she really minded the walk. She needed time to think anyway. It was the heat that was the bigger pain in the ass. The heat, her soreness, and the ache in her heart.

She had sat in the dust of the city square long after Aon had left her there in stunned silence. It wasn't long before the tears had come, and she had buried her head in her hands and wept. Too much had happened in too short of a time for her to just take it in stride right now.

When her tears had finally stilled, she stood, brushed herself off, and faced the choice in front of her. Walk toward the King of All's towering palace and temple in the center of the city or walk to the mountain range to join the others in a war against him.

Surrender or fight. There never really was an option.

At first, she had thought she needed to run from the others. Hide somewhere else to keep them safe.

But every time she thought she had a plan, this world worked hard to yank it away from her.

This plan was no different. He wasn't going to chase them —he *wanted* a war. He wanted her to join up with the others who wanted to fight. He said he wanted to see her in her full glory on the battlefield.

Glory. Right. Nothing was glorious about this.

She knew why he wanted to fight her a second time. Because it would take far more than one hysterically awful beatdown for her to learn that resistance was useless. This wasn't about defeating her. He'd won against her, no problem, and he could do it a second time quickly enough. This was about surrender. It always had been from the very beginning.

He wanted her to admit that she desired him. He wanted her to admit that she still yearned for him. Even if he was a stranger, a large part of her wanted to see if she could love him too. Life would be easier if she could. There was hope, if she could.

How she wanted Aon at her side—*her* Aon—right now. What she wouldn't give to sit there with him and listen to him crack his dark jokes. His scathing commentary. She missed him. The man she had tangled with in that city square was like the eldest brother to the warlock she knew. Someone in the same family, maybe, but not the same guy.

Fuck the Ancients. Fuck them for doing this to her. For

doing this to everybody. For picking up their ant farm and shaking it like the dicks they were.

She wasn't ready to give up yet.

That was why she hadn't begged for him when he had her pinned like she had wanted to. That was why she didn't turn around and walk straight for his palace.

Not because she hadn't wanted him—holy hell, she had—but because maybe, just maybe, there was a way to turn things back to the way things were.

Maybe, just maybe, there was hope.

Each version of Aon believed the other one was the lie. And she was stuck in the middle.

Does it count as a love triangle if it's literally the same person?

The thought was so stupid and sad it made her laugh.

She let herself. It was cathartic, even if the laughter was tired, beleaguered, and broken. Only her life would turn out like this. As she walked toward the mountain ranges on the horizon, the buildings slowly petered out until there was only sand. There were a few tracks left by the hundreds who had passed, but they were quickly being wiped away by the desert wind.

She shouldn't be surprised at this point how she reacted to this Aon's version of physical affection. He had always had that power over her. Even if there was an arguably different man behind the steering wheel, it seemed some things stayed the same.

Maybe she was the one who was insane. It wasn't right to feel the way she did, but it was inescapable. The danger and the darkness that came with him made for a thrilling and addicting mix. And the warlock was a drug to her. Even now, when he was near her, he robbed her of all reason. She was putty in his hands, and she loved every minute of it.

He was right. Some deep part of her enjoyed every second of the brutal fight and had relished in what followed. If he had kept going... she shivered. She knew that if he had wanted her then, he could have just taken her, and she never would have told him to stop. She wouldn't have wanted to. But he wanted her to ask for it.

Wasn't that always his game? Aon, or whoever he was now, was never about taking. He was about convincing her to *give*. From the first moment he met her, he could have overpowered her. He never did. And in that square, even when he had her pinned, he hadn't done anything that he knew she wouldn't secretly want.

Yet again, it came back to surrender.

He's not the same man. He wasn't the man she loved. She could see it in the coldness of his eyes—the age that seemed etched onto him like a stone and not the quickly shifting canvas she had known before.

Wasn't he? There was that smirk, that dark grin, that seductive game to him that she recognized. There might not be much of him left, he might not remember much of the past five thousand years of his life as he alluded to, but there was *something* of her Aon in there.

She'd fallen in love with part of a jigsaw puzzle. What if he was right, and if she took the time to learn the whole picture, she'd love the whole thing?

That made this worse, not better.

Around and around she went in her head. It was as tiring as the pounding overhead sun.

Rubbing her hand across the back of her neck, she sighed. She was sore, and she wanted to lie down and take a nap. She was weary. Physically, mentally, all of it. The Ancients wanted to break her. To see how far they could push her before she snapped. And they may just find out soon if they kept up this bullshit.

Without anything else to do, without any other option, she shoved her hands in her pockets and walked. Even if her thoughts were spinning around in circles, she was walking in a straight line.

Small favors.

* * *

Lyon was kneeling at the foot of the throne before his King. The chamber was cast in stark shadows. The sun outside would never reach this place, but an eerie red light glowed on the wall behind the jagged dais the man sat upon.

From massive sculptures on both sides of the throne poured a familiar substance into deep trenches that ran on either side of the path to the stairs that led to the throne.

It was meant to mimic the altar below. To worship the Ancients was to worship their only son, and vice versa.

His King sat, his human hand curled beneath his chin, as he looked off thoughtfully. There was a light smirk on his face, betraying his deep enjoyment of what had transpired between him and Lydia. Lyon had heard the highlights.

His expression hinted after more intimate details that Lyon would not wonder over.

Lyon's heart cinched in his chest at news of Aria's death, and he would mourn for Maverick's loss. How he had begged his King to spare the woman, to save the doctor such pain. Aria was merely terrified, betraying her people for her love. But his King's word was law. Traitors were not to be allowed to live, regardless of whose side they may be on. For a traitor could never be trusted to serve.

And so, Lyon would pray to the Ancients that Aria and the Elder of Words may both find peace.

His King was still smirking to himself, his gaze thoughtful and without focus as he looked off into the shadows of his throne room. Likely caught up still in the memory of his standoff with Lydia.

The man thought of himself as both a servant to the primordial creatures who gave him life and the King of All. He was a figurehead to the gods, and only when his mind wandered to his future queen did his expression change from one of foreboding harshness.

How foolish the masks had been, to wear them for so long. Lyon found himself contemplating the thought as he looked upon the face of a man he had called a friend but whose features he had never known. The ability to see the man's face made him easier to read, and for that he was glad. It was obvious the warlock was enjoying thoughts of not only what had happened —but what was to follow.

It was that topic over which he had come. "Forgive me my impertinence, my King."

"Always."

"Why did you let Lydia go?" His King could have taken her prisoner and instead had let her go to join the others in a fight against him. It was an odd strategy at best, to invite war to his doorstep.

"There are two reasons. I would greet Edu and the others in a battle, as that is what they desire. Edu would never slink into some dark corner and find a new way to live. Not once in the years before I descended into madness was he content to do such a thing, and certainly not now that he has lived the past five thousand years free of proper rule. I will force them to watch their defiance unravel before the week is out. To let it linger is to let the festering poison grow in strength."

It made sense, Lyon supposed. He would not anticipate facing his former friends and allies upon the battlefield with the same mild amusement as he saw upon his King's face. But it was better to destroy the notion of freedom from the new order of things before the rebellious may find purchase or devise plots.

"But to let Lydia go? Edu and the others would fight you

without her. Why let her free to join them?" Lyon asked, confused.

"That would be the second reason, old friend." His King leaned back in his chair, dark eyes flashing in mischief. "She will come to stand by my side of her own free will."

Lyon tilted his head curiously. "I do not believe we are acquainted with the same woman."

The warlock grinned. "Never steal that which you can convince someone to give you. She merely needs the right inspiration. And I plan to give it to her."

* * *

Walking sucked.

The sand sucked.

The sun sucked.

This world sucked.

Everything sucked.

The glare off the pale desert was blinding Lydia, and she was sick of squinting. It was all giving her a headache. For the first time since she had turned immortal, she was hungry. She was tired. She was miserable.

Not just because of the sand.

"I've said this before, and I'll say it again. This isn't goddamn fair." She was whining at nobody. The empty air didn't care about her problems. Or she didn't think so anyway.

But it seemed that someone, or something, had been listening.

Something moved beneath her. Something buried beneath the desert. She froze, her eyes widening as she realized the empty air might not have heard her... but the sand apparently did.

Something began to push up from underneath the surface of the desert, shifting and writhing. She took a step back as a shape began to emerge. Not from the sand, but as if it were made from the sand itself. Rising like a liquid, forming a shape that dripped the particles back down to the ground.

Claws. A giant hand, spindly and thin, reaching up from underneath and caging up over her. Lydia shrieked and jumped backward just as they came crashing down, merging back into the desert dunes as if they had never been there.

Another talon rose up to her left, grasping for her. She dodged again, staggering out of the way as a third appeared to try to catch her in their skeletal palms, each one made from impossibly animated sand.

The Ancients. Either that or Aon was to blame. She supposed, in truth, there was very little difference between the two now. The line was blurred, even to the man in question.

But why had they come calling? It was clear that they weren't trying terribly hard to catch her. Just to scare her and get her attention.

The sands shifted again, and their intentions became clear. A figure stood in front of her, sculpted from the desert like a perverse sandcastle. Aon. But this was *her* Aon. Dressed in his suit, his metal mask adorning his face. He stepped toward her and reached out his hand. Palm up, asking for her own. Like he had done so many times before. Asking her to join him.

It was just a facsimile. Just a puppet. But that didn't stop her heartache from inspiring her to raise her hand from her side to reach for him. How desperately she wished he was real. The living sand stepped toward her, and as her hand nearly touched his, the sand changed. Shifted and morphed to take the form of this *other* Aon. The King of All. She staggered away from him as he watched her in a cruel, blank expression. Somehow the coldness in him still came through.

She tripped and fell. Landed hard on her back as the sculpture of sand moved toward her. As he leaned down to grab her, the terrible marionette that seemed to dissolve and rise like liquid from the desert, something else grabbed his wrist to stop him.

Edu. Kind of. Edu, but made of sand. This was a puppet show, she realized. The Ancients were talking without words. The sculpture of Edu went to strike Aon, but his throat was torn out by the King of All. As Edu fell, he dissolved back into the desert from which he came.

Figures rose to strike against the King of All. Vjo, Dtu, Kamira, Maverick, faces she recognized. And one by one, he disposed of them all. Laid them all back to dust at his feet. It was a terrible dance of murder and mayhem, played out in specks of rocks that moved like viscous liquid at their command.

When the King of All was the only one left standing, the figure turned to face her and reached out for her once more, single hand outstretched. Pleading and demanding all at once. It held the pose for a moment before he dissolved into nothing as well, collapsed back into sand, and the horrible vignette was over.

The Ancients were showing her a warning, a threat, and a promise all at once.

Stand against him, and all will die.

Give in to him, and spare their lives.

"Fuck off!" she shouted at the empty desert around her as she picked herself back up to her feet. "Fuck you and your stupid mind games!"

This had to stop.

They might not have Ziza to commandeer, but they still found ways to talk to her. And their message hadn't improved. She needed to get away. From here, from the glaring desert sand, from the anxiety that jabbed at her like a bully behind her in math class with a sharp pencil.

Something in her itched to be cut free. Something inside her wriggled, wanting to be let out of its cage. She didn't know what it was, this desire that felt like an urge to bolt for the horizon. It was a nervous kind of excitement inspired by the need to run, like a horse clomping at a gate, wanting to be let out to gallop.

Not knowing really what she was doing, she pulled the pin and let it go. Like a dam crashing through a crack in the cement, it all rushed out at once. Before she could even second-guess her decision, she wasn't... herself anymore.

Her body changed. Just shifted. Just took a step to the left of where she had been and now was something else. Something both foreign and familiar. She had no arms anymore, but a massive pair of glowing turquoise wings. Her legs were a tail, ghastly and black and flickering in and out of the world like smoke. At the end was a tuft of the same odd, ghostly feathers. She was some hundred feet long.

Q had always just been part of her soul, given life.

He had never been gone—he had never been real. Just a piece of her with the volume turned up.

And now, she wasn't afraid of wearing that part of her. Letting it take literal wings.

She could fly.

That thought drove her forward and out of her stunned confusion. She could *fly*. She flapped the massive wings and felt the power of the air beating beneath them. She kicked up sand, but the cloud didn't bother her any as she struck up toward the sky.

The hot air kissed her face as she soared upward, circling and quickly catching an updraft. The air was cooler up here, with less reflection of the blinding sun off the sand. She could see the acropolis only a few miles away with its sprawling buildings and monuments. Now that she could see it from here, she recognized the magic circle it was built to mirror. Aon wore the same one on his back, taking up most of the space between his shoulder blades. She'd never thought anything of it. But now, it all made sense.

It was his city, after all.

She pushed the thoughts away as she played in the wind, testing her wings. She looped and dove, soaring up higher and reveling in the joy and freedom of the act. She was laughing like a child. She didn't care.

The joy of it chased away the foreboding message. For a brief moment, she found happiness even in the gloom of all that had happened and was transpiring around her.

This... this did *not* suck.

FIFTEEN

The sun had set while Lydia had flown over the desert. Well, "set" maybe wasn't the right word. Eclipsed. The mysterious disk just slid over the glowing orb to mute the glow, and it was much, much better than the unforgiving glare.

The mountain range was certainly easier to reach now that she knew she could fly. It felt so strange, to be in a different body. Or, more correctly, to have changed her body to this one. But she wasn't afraid. Instead, she felt oddly... free.

It certainly beat the hell out of walking.

All through her flight she hadn't seen anyone beneath her. If the others had made it to the mountains, they hadn't walked either. She was sure Edu, Dtu, and Vjo had tricks up their sleeves to get their people to the mountain faster than by foot. It was either that or they were already prisoners.

She shoved that thought from her mind as fast as she could. If that was the case, and she really was alone, she didn't know what she would do.

The mountain range was coming closer, and with it, the chance of finding solace in the presence of others. She never thought she would ever be happy to see Edu in her life, and the idea of the big man in his honest, cut-and-dry view on things would be very, very welcome right now.

As she drew over the mountain range, she circled around a few times, trying to get the lay of the land. It looked like it might be littered with cave openings, gaps in the hillside that were dark nooks. Maybe they were nothing—or maybe that was where everyone was hiding. There was only one way to find out.

Swooping down, she flapped her large, glowing, turquoise wings, and landed near one of the cave entrances. Shifting her body back to her normal, human form, she staggered and fell in a pile of limbs.

Coming back from that wasn't exactly graceful yet—but, hey, details. When she got up, she jumped up and down a bit in excitement, laughing at what she'd just done.

She had just *flown!* Goddamn sprouted wings and *flown!* Oh, how she wished Aon was with her. How she wanted to show him her new trick. The pang of loneliness and loss struck down her mood like a pin in a balloon, sending her reprieve from the sadness withering to the floor.

Sighing, she had to keep going. She had to push through what had happened and find a way to keep putting one foot in front of the other. That was the only way she had survived this insanity so far, and it was going to be the only thing that pulled her through.

Walking into the cave, she quickly realized that... well, caves were dark. She muttered to herself about how she was an utter idiot before raising her hand and summoning a torch for herself. The fire that burned from the wrapped fabric was, naturally, turquoise.

Q would be so proud.

She smiled at the thought. All Q had ever been was a teddy bear against the darkness. But oh, what she wouldn't give for that comfort right about now. She walked through the tight passages and wondered if she was alone in here. If she was even on the right track, or if the others had—

A knife pressed up against her throat.

Lydia froze and raised her free hand in a show of surrender. "Toots?"

Turning, Lydia bloomed into a grin and threw her free arm around the neck of the man behind her. He nearly dropped his knife in confusion but managed to hug her back, even if the sudden movement had almost sent him off balance and staggering into the wall.

"Tim!" She'd never been so happy to see the greaser as she was now. In fact, she couldn't think of a time she had ever been happy to see the man. That meant that Edu was here. That meant some people were safe for now. As safe as any of them could be from Aon. Lydia couldn't help but grin up at the man. "I could kiss you, I'm so happy to see you!"

Tim laughed and hugged her tighter as the surprise wore off, pressing her up against his chin in a far more familiar gesture than she expected. "Hey, now. I mean, judging by the looks of things, you might've finally settled in, but this may not be the time." He snorted. "What'm I saying? Okay, I won't say no. Let's do this."

Lydia snickered as she pulled away from him and slapped her hand on his chest in a playful rebuke. That hadn't been what she meant, and he knew it. "It's good to see you, Tim."

"You too. And..." Tim paused as he looked her over. She realized when she had changed back into a human, she had done so into a tank-top, revealing the writing on her arms and the visible line of ink that ran straight down her chest where it disappeared under her clothing. He followed the writing with his gaze pointedly. "I take it back. You're not a toots—you're a babe now."

She slapped her palm against his chest again in response. It was a stupid compliment, but it had been one, nonetheless. "Thanks. But eyes up."

He finally tore his gaze away from her cleavage and coughed. "Sorry, sorry. C'mon, Edu'll be thrilled to see you."

"Really?"

"He posted us to keep watch for you. He hoped you'd escape and catch up."

That was oddly flattering. That the big man had actually been concerned about her. It made her smile unexpectedly, and she was glad Tim was now leading her through the caves using his own torch and couldn't see her touched expression.

It was about twenty feet before Tim snapped his fingers as he remembered something. "You're not under Aon's control, are you?"

"No."

"Great."

"Wait. That was enough for you? What if I was lying?"

"Meh." Tim shrugged. "I don't figure you for a liar, even if you were brainwashed like Lyon."

Shaking her head, she couldn't keep the smile off her face. The man wasn't terribly bright, but he was endearing anyway. In spite of himself, she found herself enjoying his company. Maybe she was just getting desperate.

After a few minutes of walking, they entered a large cavern. It struck her that they had gone from hiding in tunnels beneath the city to hiding in caves. They were refugees on the run and had only changed one set of rock walls for another. They were too exposed above ground.

There was a pool of water to one side, a freshwater underground spring. It made perfect sense then why they would gather here. Stalactites and stalagmites dotted the space, calcium and mineral deposits that betrayed the reason for the oddly humid air in the cave, despite the arid landscape.

People in red, green, purple, and blue were scattered about

the room in groups, hunkering down together and quietly talking or sleeping. Unnatural lights were illuminating the vault, blue and orange balls stuck to the surfaces. Seeing as she no longer needed her torch, she vanished it back into the nothingness from where it had come. It would only add smoke, where the magical lighting didn't.

There were at least a hundred people here. Many she didn't recognize from before. So others *had* made it to the safety of the hills before they had managed to flee the city. A hesitant kind of hope nudged at her. These cave systems were huge. Maybe there were more survivors than she had guessed.

As Tim led her across the chamber, she saw Edu sitting on a rock close to one wall. Vjo and Dtu were there as well, both in their human forms. The cave was too small to support otherwise. As she approached, the three of them looked up to her. Vjo stood, clearly startled by the sight of her.

"Lydia, how did you escape?" the Queen of Words asked, shocked. To be fair, Lydia was just as confused by the whole situation.

She didn't respond but shot the woman a knowing glance, her jaw twinging as she walked up to the group and sat on a rock. The spider was too smart and too quick on the draw not to put it together.

"I see. He let you go," Vjo assumed correctly as she sat back down.

"Yeah. I'd like to say we fought." Really, she was just the ball of feathers on the end of a string, and he had been the house cat. "He kicked my ass. Then let me go." She shot a glare at Dtu. "And I don't want to fucking hear about it from you, Fido."

Dtu was silent, his masked face merely watching her. Edu sighed heavily and leaned back against the wall and folded his arms across his massive chest.

"Edu likely wonders why," Vjo presumed. Edu nodded. "As do I."

"It's simple. He's giving you all a choice, and I'm the messenger." She sighed. "You can stay away and be free—live in peace, away from the city, and he'll leave you alone. Or, you can rally your forces and fight him and he'll meet you in war."

"And what of you?" Vjo prompted.

"I don't get that choice. I either get to fight or to surrender. Running is…" They hadn't covered that option, but she knew exactly how it'd go. "Running wouldn't last long. He'd find me."

"Is that what you want?" Dtu snapped.

"I want the Ancients back in a pond where they belong, asshat. I want none of this to have ever happened!"

Dtu snorted in disbelief. "You're his *mare*. Now, he's taken the throne of the world. You will be the Queen of All. He just needs to snap his fingers, and you'll run to have him breed you just like the bitch you are, you—"

She slammed her fist into Dtu's face and had him pinned to the ground before she even realized she had done anything. He hadn't been expecting the attack, and now she had him on the ground with one of her obsidian daggers pressed against his throat and her other hand twisted in his matted hair. "Shut your goddamn face, you two-bit dimestore Halloween decoration! My relationship with him is my business, *not* yours."

Dtu went to move, and she lifted his head from the ground only to slam him back down with a heavy *thud*.

She had enough of being abused for one night—maybe a lifetime—and she was sick of Dtu's disgusting insults. "If you talk about my love life one more time, I swear to anybody who's listening that I will find a way to neuter you like a goddamn stray and make sure it doesn't grow back! *Do. You. Understand?*"

Dtu coughed. "I—"

She slammed his head into the ground again. "Do you *understand*?"

The shifter was silent for a pause. "Yes."

Edu was laughing, clapping his hands together, clearly amused by her angry rant.

Standing, she let Dtu go from where she left him sprawled on the ground. Stepping away from him, she glared down at the shifter king. "The situation is complicated. It's messy, and it's painful. I love the man he *was*, and the man I knew is not the one who's in control anymore. And now, I don't know who he is anymore. Do you think I want him to be like this?"

Dtu was silent.

"Well?" she shouted and kicked his leg hard. "Do you? Do you honestly think I wanted this to happen?"

"No." Came his quiet reply.

"Good. Then the next time you want to open your fat fucking mouth, Dtu? *Don't.*"

The wolf growled low in his throat but said nothing. Satisfied that the fight was over, she sat back down on a rock and let the other man pick himself up off the ground and retake his own seat.

She shook her head, turning her obsidian dagger over in her hands. They deserved to know the truth. All of them. "They've... told me to love him, or else they'll *make* me love him. Take my free will away. Like they did to Lyon. I can't give up. All this world has ever tried to do since the day I came here was to take *me* away from *me*. To change who I am, to twist me into what it's wanted. I want the man I love back. I don't want a lie."

The sound of someone shifting drew her to look up. Edu had stood and moved toward her. He gestured for her to stand. As she did, a little nervous of what he was going to do, she let out a startled squeak as he leaned down and hugged her. More correctly, he lifted her straight off her feet and held her just a little too tight. Her squeak turned into a grunt as she suddenly learned the meaning of the word "bearhug."

It was the only way he could communicate his sympathy without Ylena there. Or maybe it was also to say that he agreed with her. When he put her back down, he planted a heavy hand on top of her head and rocked it back and forth.

She laughed despite herself. "Thanks, Rambo."

Edu nodded and turned to sit back down. He leaned over to take a finger and write into the dirt of the cave. It was the best he could do.

"*We fight,*" he wrote.

"We should run to the horizons. The King of All is many things, but a liar he is not. If he is setting us free, we should take it. War against him is madness." Vjo sighed. "We cannot win. It is a doomed proposition."

"And you really want to live in this fucked-up sand hell for the rest of eternity?" Lydia gestured at the cave. "You want to hide from him for the next however-thousands of years? I don't. I say we stand and fight. Or we find a new way to win."

"What do you mean, a new way to win?" Vjo tilted her masked head slightly.

"I've had the unfortunate pleasure to talk to both the Ancients and the nameless King of All—he says he's the same man. The same person I knew as Aon, only cured of his madness. I'm not so sure. I think the corruption goes much deeper than that. But if he is in there somewhere, if there is any hint of the warlock, I might be able to get through to him. I might be able to get him to turn on the Ancients."

"Do you suggest we try to talk some sense into him?" Dtu snorted in laughter. "Now, it is your turn to speak madness."

"He barely remembers the past five thousand years. He called it a fever dream. He won't want to go back to that, but if I can convince him that life as a free man is better than this... slavery he's in, I have to try." Lydia slid to sit on the ground, leaning her back against the rock. She needed to stretch her spine. She was still working out the aches from getting her ass handed to her in a paper bag earlier in the day.

"He does not recall the years he spent as King of Shadows. Interesting." Vjo tapped her finger on the chin of her mask as she thought. The wheels in her head were likely spinning faster than Lydia could hope to track, so she let the woman do her thing.

"He said only flashes. All he could remember was me. That sounds fishy. I think the Ancients are to blame for that. If he thinks those times were abject misery, he won't willingly try to go back."

"Very likely a correct assumption," Vjo provided.

"Do you remember anything of the time before the Ancients were imprisoned?"

"Yes." The spider queen looked down to the ground and began to fidget with one of the silver chains that adorned her dress. "We all chose to forget. We no longer have the luxury. He gave himself the name Aon when he betrayed the Ancients. When he chose to reject them and to become like us. Perhaps it makes our distrust of him seem foolish in hindsight. It was by his hand that he came to join us as he did."

Edu shook his head, clearly disagreeing with her but being unable to voice any other more in-depth opinion than that. Poor man. She never really thought much about his inability to speak, since he always had his empath following at his side. Now, she saw how crippling it could be.

"He earned our distrust through his own selfish actions," Dtu grumbled. "He did himself no favors."

Edu pointed at Dtu, seconding the wolf's statement.

"I know how much of a douchebag he can be. Trust me. But he's complicated, always doing the wrong thing for the right reasons." Lydia folded her arms across her chest. "I'm not saying he didn't ever do anything wrong. I'm just saying that maybe you all should have tried to really ask him *why* he did something without making assumptions. Just once."

Dtu sat silently for a moment. As did Vjo. She supposed Edu had no choice. She figured that was one point for her. It was rare that she made a valid point around these freaks, so she took it as a matter of pride.

"Anyway," Lydia sighed, "my choices are this. I can either kill myself, which... I don't know if the Ancients would even allow to happen. I don't know how powerful they really are."

"Neither do we. I have read texts on the matter, but I do not think they hold a candle of truth in the face of where we are now," Vjo said. "I do not know their reach or the extent of their influence. But I will promise you that it is less significant than they will make it seem. They are manipulators. Not gods."

Lydia nodded. It was a good piece of advice to keep in mind. "So, I can either try to kill myself, which doesn't help any of you out at all. In fact, he'll probably go on a rampage because of it and kill everybody. I can surrender to the Ancients, which I won't do, and is a fate worse than death. I can run for the hills, which will only last so long before he finds me anyway. Or... I can go to him, and either talk him down from whatever tyrannical and insane plots he's hatching or try to convince him to betray the Ancients a second time. I don't see how I have any other choices in front of me."

Silence stretched on for a beat. It seemed no one, not even Vjo, had another option for her.

"Then why not march into his home this minute?" Dtu asked. "Why come here to fight with us?"

Lydia let out a long breath and looked across the stretch of cave to Edu where he sat some ten feet away. "Because I might not have been here very long, but I know that man"—she pointed at Edu—"would rather die than live like this. I know he's planning on falling in a blaze of glory on the battlefield."

Edu nodded once solemnly.

She rolled her eyes. "If, or when, we fail, I'm hoping I can stop that from happening. I'm hoping I can keep the 'King of All' from killing you all."

"You think you can convince him not to kill his oldest foe?" Dtu huffed again. "You aren't insane. You're an idiot."

"Use your own brain for once, wolf," Vjo snapped irritably at Dtu. "She means she will bargain with him for our own safety."

Lydia smiled faintly to the spider. "I'm your insurance policy. He wants me. I'm the only thing he's ever wanted in all his life. He thinks he can convince me I still love him in return."

"Do you?" the wolf asked.

"I don't know him."

"You aren't curious to find out?" Dtu leaned toward her. The viciousness had left his voice and was far calmer. "If Qta returned this moment from the grave with the personality of a different man, I do not know if I would be able to resist trying."

"I won't lie. Sure. I'm curious. And I... I'm tempted. But I have more people to worry about than just me. If he's a tyrant —if he's going to hurt people I care about? It doesn't matter if I love him."

He leaned his elbow on his knee. "You do not care for us."

"No. But Vjo seems nice enough. Edu and I are just starting to get along. You? You're an asshole and can go hump a cactus, for all I care. But Kamira, Maverick, Evie, and all the rest? I care about them. They've been friends to me. If I'm going to wind up as his prisoner—again—I might as well make it count for something."

Another long silence before Dtu nodded. "Noble. I will give you that." He stood. "I need to piss and then sleep if we're marching to war tomorrow." He walked away with no more pomp or circumstance than that.

Lydia couldn't help but laugh at how crass the man was. She supposed animals had no filters. It made sense.

"We should all rest. While the wolf's choice of words is questionable, I cannot disagree. We will have a long stretch ahead of us." Vjo stood and gathered her skirt with its myriad of buckles and chains around her legs. She jangled like a wind chime when she moved. "You came to us out of concern for a people who have only ever done you ill. For that... I thank you. I may only pray that the Ancients take mercy upon you and repay you for your generosity of spirit." She began to walk away. "But I fear this world is not known to give, but only to take. Good night, both."

Unsure as to what to say to the other queen, Lydia only smiled again and raised her hand to bid her good night as well. Standing, she popped her back and groaned in pain. "Ow. Fucker..."

Edu huffed a quiet laugh.

"I don't think he went easy on me. Then again, if he tangles with you, and I still have all my ribs in their usual places, maybe he did." She cracked her neck with another grunt.

Edu was standing as well. He beckoned her over with the wave of a hand. When she walked up to him, she found herself craning her neck to look up at him. He tapped a finger over his heart and then planted into the middle of her chest.

She wasn't sure what he was trying to say. Not exactly. But it felt like a compliment. Perhaps he was saying that she had a heart of a warrior. Or that he sympathized with her feelings. But either way, it felt like a deep confession. She smiled up at him. "If there's one good thing to come out of all this stupidity, Edu... I think I'd like to call you a friend, if that's okay."

He hugged her again. This time it was gentler. It wasn't the brash hug of a fellow fighter in a war hall, it was the embrace of a companion. There was sadness in it. She knew he didn't expect—or didn't want—to live in this world for long.

The idea of Edu being gone hurt her. She was surprised. The man had been her tormenter and her murderer. But to think of this world without him felt wrong. It would feel... emptier. It would feel sorely lacking. She hoped she had a chance to get to know him better.

"Don't go looking for death, Edu. It'll come for you on its own. Besides, you'd break Evie's heart." She looked up at the man as he stepped back to put his hands on her shoulders. She felt like she had a brick on each side with how heavy they were. "People would miss you." That was as close as she was going to get to confessing that she was suddenly, and unexpectedly, on that list.

Edu nodded wearily, and his shoulders slumped. He suddenly looked very tired, as though his age was quite literally weighing on him.

"I know. I know you're sick of this shit. Sick of always trying to keep the world safe. I'm sick of this shit enough as it is, and I've only been here for six months."

Edu laughed and nodded once more. He looked up over her head—which admittedly wasn't that hard, as she didn't even reach his shoulder—at the group of people behind them, at everyone gathered around in the caves, afraid. When he nodded a second time, it was in acceptance. He looked back down to her and patted her heavily on the shoulder. It was another "thank you," she could tell. He then flicked his head, gesturing her to go on.

Lydia chuckled. "Sleep well, Rambo." And with that, she wandered off. She needed to go find some dark place to shove herself. Somewhere quiet to get some sleep and pray the King of All and the Ancients left her alone for a night.

It was two caverns over that she caught sight of someone. He was sitting on a rock, his elbows on his knees, his head in his hands. A picture of perfect misery. She recognized the cut of the man's suit and his long brown hair pulled back in a ponytail, if nothing else.

Maverick.

Walking up to the man, she stood next to him silently. She didn't want to intrude, and yet... she didn't want to leave him alone either. He lifted his head and looked up at her, and his visible yellow eye was ringed in red. The man had recently been crying. His mask caught the unnatural light of the orb glowing on the wall nearby.

She didn't say anything. If he put his head back down, she'd walk away. She assumed the doctor was an exceedingly private man. She'd leave him alone if that was what he wanted. She'd completely understand.

He didn't speak but merely slid over on the rock, making room for her. She sat next to him, and when he just sat there silently, she leaned on his arm. There were no words she could say that would make what happened okay. There were no platitudes that wouldn't come off as trite or insulting.

She didn't understand what it was like to watch your significant other burn to death because they were trying to save your life.

Besides, she hated statements of sympathy. Hated hearing "I'm so sorry for your loss." It always fell flat. Always felt useless. And so, she stayed silent and just leaned on the doctor, leaned on her friend and let him know she was there. To her surprise, he wrapped an arm around her and hugged her to his side.

They stayed like that in silence for a long time. Minutes dragged on as they both thought over their respective woes. They had both lost someone they loved. Just in very different ways.

He was clearly thinking the same thing when he finally broke the silence. "We share an affliction."

"Not exactly." She leaned her head on his shoulder. "I still have hope. Hope that somewhere, buried in that madman, is the *other* madman I love. It's useless, and it's poison, but it's there."

"Then yours is a fate worse than mine."

That got a sad, quiet laugh out of her. There was that same, horribly dry sense of morbid humor she loved from him. After a long pause, she looked up at him. "I hate saying this, because it's stupid. But I really, really am sorry."

"Thank you."

Maverick leaned his head down and rested it atop hers. It was a shockingly personal gesture from the doctor, and she smiled and found his hand, squeezing it tightly and doing her best to comfort him.

"Ah, good. The pity party is over here," said a familiar female voice. Looking up, she saw Kamira walk over to them. She was carrying a bottle of what looked like wine in each hand. She sat on the floor at Maverick's feet and scooted lower to lie on the ground. "If I have to explain to *one* more person what has happened or if they ask me how I feel, I will scream and tear them to shreds."

Kamira let out a small, inhuman growl in her throat and shut her green eyes. She plonked both bottles of wine down at Maverick's feet. "No, Maverick. You do not share Lydia's affliction. *I do.*" She tucked her arms beneath her head, clearly planning on napping right there, lying nearly on top of her and Maverick's feet. "Our loves may yet live to taunt us."

"Fair point." Maverick pulled his arm back from around Lydia and tried his best to resume his normal air of dignity. He reached down to take one of the bottles of alcohol and take a swig.

"I have a plan, though," Kamira said with a smirk.

"That being?" Maverick's solitude was now entirely destroyed by the appearance of the two of them. For better or worse, maybe. He didn't seem upset by the distraction.

The tigress's smirk bloomed into a full grin. "I'm going to beat the *stupid* out of him."

"Ah. Yes. Of course," the doctor responded dryly. To his credit, he didn't roll his eyes.

"It's worked before. It'll work again."

"Under entirely different conditions," Maverick dutifully reminded the woman. "I am sure that will be terribly effective against the power of the Ancients."

"Then I'll just keep beating him up until it does."

"Mmhm."

The banter was making Lydia laugh. It made her feel unquestionably better as their argument continued. Honestly, she stopped paying attention to the details and just smiled at the two of them and how different they were. One a passionate, overemotional and primal creature, and the other a cold and calculating professor.

And now, they were both attempting to get drunk.

They were both suffering the loss of a loved one and finding comfort in the familiarity of their oddly affable yet combative friendship. Now that she could see it for what it was—as a bizarre form of companionship—it was charming.

It merely confirmed her decision to come here and do what she could to keep Aon from destroying them all. To keep that vision in the sand from coming true. Even if it meant that she was a bargaining chip, she would give up her freedom for their safety in a heartbeat. These people were worth fighting for.

Lydia leaned her head on Mav's shoulder again as the two kept bickering. He looked down at her with a faint smile. She smiled back and let her eyes drift shut a moment later. Holy hell, she was tired.

"I am glad you have survived all your trials and tribulations, Ms. Lydia," Maverick said to her after his argument with Kamira had died down. "Even if you have brought utter doom upon our world."

She snickered and lifted her head. There was that sense of

humor of his again. "Thanks, doc." She yawned and covered her mouth. "Sorry. Excuse me. It's been... a long day."

"Get some rest, friend," Kamira said with a sad smile. Clearly, the shifter had been enjoying a distraction from her own grief and loneliness. "There will be enough strife on the morrow when we go to war with your lover."

"Thanks for the reminder." She nudged Kamira's leg with her foot, and the tigress grinned toothily. Lydia walked out and only made it halfway before Kamira called after her.

"If you get lonely, you know where I am. You're a far better bed warmer than my husband!"

Some things could not be shaken, even by the end of the world.

SIXTEEN

Lydia really should have known better.

She shouldn't have expected to be left alone in her dreams. She found herself standing in... well, she figured a room like this could only be described as a throne room.

It was enormous. It stretched on for a hundred feet in either direction up a long stone path. Red, glowing liquid ran in pools on either side. The familiar liquid came pouring from statues that framed both sides of a large, looming, twisted chair carved of black stone.

Every square inch was decorated with art and symbols, lauding and celebrating the creatures the statues were meant to represent.

The Ancients.

And the man who sat upon the throne, his head leaning on his fist, elbow on the arm of the imposing piece of furniture.

The King of All.

His eyes were shut, and he made no move to acknowledge she was there.

Drawn like a moth to a flame, she walked toward him. She couldn't help it. Even after their last meeting had ended with him beating the snot out of her and leaving her in the dust, confused and torn, she still felt that pull. The one she had always felt, ever since the very beginning.

Since the night she first saw him in a dream very much like this one, asleep in his crypt, it'd been hopeless. She'd been trapped by him, whether he'd meant to do it or not.

The fear she felt for him now was very similar to the fear she felt then, if for very different reasons. Walking up the dais his throne was on, she stopped only a pace away from where he sat.

His face had looked placid from so far away. Etched in stone, cold and unfeeling. So very unlike the Aon that she had known.

But now, as she saw him closer, there was a crease in his brow. One of unhappiness. One of... doubt, maybe.

Of *sadness.*

"Now, she comes to haunt my dreams."

His voice broke the silence, although he did not speak much louder than a whisper. Neither did he open his eyes or move.

"I didn't do this."

"Nor did I. The Ancients are at work this time." Still, he didn't move or look at her. "You trouble enough of my thoughts. I hardly would seek out more."

"I'm troubling *your* thoughts?" She tried not to laugh. "That's pretty rich."

"I love you. I have never loved another soul in all my years. I do not know what to do." Finally, his dark eyes opened and lifted to meet her gaze. She was right. That was doubt she saw. Doubt. Grief. And loneliness. "For you do not feel the same. Worse yet, you wish me *gone.*"

"I—I don't want you gone." She swallowed the rock in her throat. She kind of did. Didn't she? But faced with that heartbreak, the cruelty of the statement was worse than the punches he'd given her a few hours earlier.

"You wish me to be a broken part of myself. You wish me ill."

"I... I'm sorry, I—" She trailed off. His pain hurt her as though it were her own.

"I suppose it is to be expected." He winced. "But it still pains me, all the same. I wonder... will you try? Honestly *try* to look at me as you did before?" His dark eyes slid shut once again. "Or if you will commit yourself to despising me for only that I am not precisely as you knew me."

Part of her wanted to turn and run. She preferred fighting him. It hurt less than this, somehow. "I miss him. I miss who you were."

"I know." He reached out his hand for her, his flesh-and-blood one, asking her to come to him. His face creased in pain. "I can be just as good to you. Better. I was a madman, a broken thing... cruel and uncaring. Am I not as worthy of your compassion as him?"

It was a plea. He was begging her, and her heart shattered. How the hell could she turn away? Slipping her hand into his, she heard him let out a sigh of relief. He had been holding his breath.

Straightening in the throne, he looked up at her as he drew her close, pulling her onto his lap, straddling his thighs. She went tense as he wrapped an arm around her lower back, tugging her closer.

Seeing her concern, he shushed her gently, nuzzling his head into the crook of her neck as he wrapped his arms around her, holding her close. He was begging her with every motion not to resist. Not to fight him.

When he kissed her throat, lips hot against her skin, she let out the breath she hadn't realized *she* had been holding. He trailed his kisses up the line of her neck to her ear to whisper to her.

"I thought perhaps I wished to hunt you. But I wake in the

night and find myself alone with memories of what it was like to have you there beside me. I find myself reaching for you, and when you are not there... I feel torn asunder. The hole I have borne in my soul ached for that it had never been filled. But now that it knows what it was to be full, it burns with your absence. Whomever observed that it was better to love and lose was an abject fool."

Yeah, she wished he was beating her up. It really did hurt less.

"I'm scared," she admitted in a whisper.

"Be not so, my love. You are in no danger. You are safer now than you ever were." Slowly, his flesh-and-blood hand began to wander up and down her back, stroking her skin, soothing her. Strong, unstoppable—but not forceful.

"I am. We both know what they'll do to me if I say no to you." Her eyes slid half-shut as his lips began to trail slow, sensual kisses along her jawline.

When he feathered a kiss over her lips, ghosting over hers, she almost melted against him. "But it has not yet come to that."

Lips finally devoured hers in a searing embrace. She moaned against him, unable to stop herself as he pulled her closer, all tension gone from her as she gave in to the strength in his grasp.

Deftly, he stripped her of her top, tossing the clothing aside without a care.

This was wrong. She should stop him. The King of All was her enemy. She was going to face him on the battlefield in war. She was supposed to *fight* him. Fight *this*.

"My starlight, my beautiful love..." He kissed his way down her throat again, following the trail of one of the lines of turquoise ink that decorated her skin. With his metal claw in the center of her back, supporting her weight, he tilted her backward.

She could lean forward. Grab hold of him.

Or... she could trust him. Let him hold her. Let him, in this dream, have the comfort that he needed. That they *both* needed. "This isn't surrender."

"Of course not." He kissed one of the marks emblazoned in the center of her chest. "An armistice, nothing more."

Armistice. Sure. Letting out a wavering breath, she rested her hands on his arms as he tilted her just a little farther back, arching her so he could reach his destination.

She moaned as he captured one of her pert nipples between his teeth, instantly sending a slight sting coursing through her. The pain didn't do anything to change her mind.

Anything but.

His human hand grasped her other breast, kneading it mercilessly as he pinched and teased, tormented and soothed her. Soon, her hand was tangled in his hair, fisting the dark locks, shuddering at the combination of pleasure and pain that he wove through her like the master artisan he was.

Tilting her back up straight, he brought his clawed hand around to trail the pointed tips of his claws over her collarbone, just enough to leave goosebumps in his wake.

"A pale shadow of the real world. But for now... enough." He murmured the words against her skin as he kissed her where her shoulder met her throat. Her skirt had long since ridden up over her thighs. And he was wearing those dark robes wrapped around his waist.

It made it easy, if nothing else, to pull her underwear aside, grasp her hips, and pull her down onto him—impaling her on his length to the hilt without warning or mercy.

Arching her back, she cried out at the sudden overwhelming sensation.

His arms wrapped around her, clawed hand hooked over her shoulder from behind, pinning her to him like a vise. But he tipped her back far enough that he could watch her face, studying her reaction, drinking in her expression.

"Beautiful..."

She might be on top. But he was setting the pace. She was no more in control of what was happening than a puppet on strings. He pulled her away from him only to bring her back down, slowly—but with all the force of a piston in a machine. Unstoppable. Inhuman.

It was *amazing*.

Aon had always been a wild animal with her. Even when he was restrained, it was always a creature at the end of his leash, ready to snap—but this? This felt like he could keep her like this for centuries and never tire of it.

"Only shattered memories linger at the edges of my mind, flashes of you, of how you taste." He leaned down to run his tongue along the line of her lower lip. "It does not do it justice."

She felt like she was at his mercy. Truly and utterly. But she knew this wasn't even half of what he was capable of. This was an unexpected tryst in a dream.

"I—" She couldn't form words. She couldn't think straight. She could only feel him. The strength in his arms. The power of his presence. The way he filled her meticulously—slowly— *claiming her*.

She was his.

It didn't matter whose name he used or didn't use. It didn't matter what he remembered or didn't remember. And in the worst possible way, it didn't even matter if she loved him or not.

In this way, unquestionably, she was *his*.

And always would be.

"I cannot wait until we can dance like this in the waking world. What a joy it will be to hear you beg and mewl and whimper... I want to hear all these little noises of yours where I can truly enjoy them." He jerked her down onto him with an abrupt violence that made her see stars as pleasure ripped through her unexpectedly, cresting as the ecstasy dragged her over that cliff.

"Yes, my starlight." He chuckled. "My queen."

"Please—" She didn't even know what she was begging for. More? Mercy? Yes?

A second harsh impact ensured neither of them would ever find out as words were robbed from her. She cried out, her head reeling. He never picked up his pace. He never needed to.

This was about *power*.

A third and she was unraveling again in quick succession, clinging to him weakly for dear life.

A fourth and she was sobbing, overwrought. This felt like the fight again. He wasn't going easy on her. He was making a point. And he was enjoying it.

And he was proving to her that deep down inside... so was she.

A fifth and he finally took pity on her. He held her close to him as he buried his head into the crook of her neck, roaring in his own release, as she felt the heat of him flood her. Still, he kept himself buried in her to the point of that blissful ache she had come to need from him.

Only when he had calmed after several moments did he separate them, but kept her on his lap, her head collapsed against his shoulder. They were both panting, though she was in a far worse shape than he was.

He was stroking her back with his human hand, cradling her in his arms, like she was some precious thing to him.

She was.

He loved her.

He loved her more than anything in the world. She didn't doubt that.

After a long few moments of silence, he spoke. "Tomorrow you will march against me. Tomorrow we shall meet on the battlefield. Are you ready?"

"As I'll ever be. That is to say... no. You?"

He chuckled at her honesty. "Why would I not be? I will win."

She paused. "I know you will."

"Then why fight?"

"It's all I have left to do. I can't... just roll over." She shut her eyes and suddenly felt very weary of this whole thing. It would be so easier to just lie down and let it all happen. To just give in. "I have to try. Who knows, maybe you're right—and you're secretly the good guy. Or, maybe everything is messed up. But I saw what they did to Lyon. I don't have high hopes."

"We are not 'messed up.'"

"They're threatening to change me." She cringed at the thought but saw her first line of possible attack with him. "And if they do, how do you know you would still love me? I wouldn't be the same."

He smiled sadly and cupped her cheek in his palm. "For I always will. There is nothing they could do to you to change that."

It wasn't meant as a backhanded comment, but it felt like one. He said he would always love her, no matter what the Ancients did to her mind. She clearly couldn't say the same.

She watched his jaw twitch as he looked away, clearly kicking himself after seeing the hurt on her face. "I did not mean to upset you."

"You're not quite sure what to do with people, are you?" She let out a small chuckle. "I guess you have that in common with your other self."

He grunted and narrowed his eyes. Opening his mouth to seemingly argue the point, he paused, sighed in surrender, and leaned his head back against the chair once more and shut his eyes. "No. I do not. I am accustomed to being the King of All. Voice and will of the Ancients. I never tarried in the affairs of those my creators brought to me for amusement. They were my toys to wage against each other to pass the time, nothing more."

"And you wonder why nobody liked you?"

"Shush." He smirked, revealing he was not as angry as he tried to pretend. "It is hard to explain."

"I get it. You're a big deal, we're not. We merely adopted the dark, you were born in it." Lydia grinned to herself. Nick would have been very proud of her at the quote.

"Pardon?"

"Never mind."

There was such an empty sadness on his face—such a forlorn confusion and doubt painted across his features—that she had to try to stop it. She put her palm to his cheek, and he let out a breath of relief, leaning into her. She let her thumb trace back and forth against him slowly, and his expression soothed into one of quiet bliss. "I don't know who you are."

"You are about to have the time to learn. Tomorrow you will fall in battle, and you will be at my side."

"And then what?"

"Then I will show you that you love me. And you will agree to wed me as my Queen."

"And if I don't...?"

"Then you will be broken before the Ancients. I will have you as my bride, one way or another. But that outcome I deeply wish to avoid." His voice was quiet, clearly distracted by her touch. After a long pause, his dark eyes opened to capture her gaze. "Tell me there is hope, my love."

Could she love him? Could she come to feel the same way about *this* version of the man she had cared for so strongly? She didn't know the answer. But that meant it wasn't a no. "Yeah. There's hope."

He smiled thinly. "The same kind of hope that inspires you, Edu, and the rest to march against me? The one that tells you there must be some secret way to turn back the clock?"

"The one and the same. Hope's a poison that's impossible to cure."

"Indeed. Even when it is nonsensical, it is pervasive." His arms wrapped around her and pulled her against him. "Beyond all reason, Edu tries to destroy me. You wish to convince me to betray the Ancients and return to my madness. And I, committing to that same foolishness, cling to the chance you may come to love me once more." The touch of a hand on her chin turned her face to his. His lips ghosted over hers. "I will drink this poison gladly, if it means one day I may have your heart once more. No matter the cost."

It was a dark promise. One that meant he would never give up pursuing her. Never give up trying to convince her to love him. She was trapped in his web, and no matter how hard she struggled, he wouldn't ever let her go.

She wanted to ask him what would happen to her mind if she couldn't love him—if there was no hope. If it was just as futile as their war tomorrow. But she never got the chance. Partially because she honestly didn't want to know. The future behind that door was not a pleasant one, and she would be happier not knowing the outcome.

Also, because he never gave her the chance. His lips descended on hers, and he overtook her like an oncoming tidal wave. His hand wove into her hair, tangling his fingers into her strands and holding tightly, leaving her no room to argue as his metal talon pulled her hips tighter to him.

When he finally broke the embrace, she was breathless. She felt bowled over by a truck on the freeway, left sitting there wondering what the hell had just hit her. "This part of you still belongs to me..." he said in a dusky rumble. "It is far better than nothing."

"I hate you sometimes." She narrowed her eyes at him, frustrated that he could twist her around his fingers like that. "I really do."

"Mm, you only complain after the fact," he observed with a smirk. "You are only annoyed that I am right." When she tucked her head against his chest in silent frustration, he chuck-led. "Rest, my love. I will see you on the morrow. And before long, you may shoot me such indignant glares in person."

Caught between her dread of him and the lure of his touch, the dream began to fade.

SEVENTEEN

It was just before dawn as they gathered outside the caves. Edu, Dtu, Vjo, and Lydia all stood assembled. The commanders of the battle.

Lydia tried very hard not to laugh at the idea of being a commander of literally anything.

Kamira and Maverick stood close to one side, listening. Kamira would play a substantial lead in the fight, and Maverick would be left behind with those who couldn't, or weren't willing, to go to war.

Someone had to survive if the rest of them fell. And Maverick, by his own admission, wouldn't last long.

Edu was the Warrior King. But without Ylena there to translate for him, he had to get creative. The big man knelt in the sand and picked up seven rocks from the dirt. He tossed one to Dtu, Vjo, and one to Lydia. Each of the stones was to represent one of the kings or queens of Under, apparently. He picked up an eighth stone and waved Kamira over. The shifter shrugged and took it in her palm.

Edu drew a circle in the sand. Pressing his finger into the center, it became apparent that it was the Acropolis—Aon's city that they were about to attack. He placed two of the rocks inside the ring.

"Those two stones represent Aon and Lyon, respectively," Vjo said. Edu nodded as she presumed correctly.

Edu drew lines in the sand in groupings, like legions outside the city in three parts. From what she could gather, a few thousand masked souls had made it safely to the mountains. Maybe five or six in total.

He took his pebble and placed it at the head of the central group. He took Vjo's and put it down next to his. Gesturing for Dtu's, he put it at the front of the leftmost set of lines. Then taking Kamira's, he mirrored it on the other side of the main army. He placed Ini's down next to Dtu's.

"The Houses of Flames and Moons will lead the main forces straight against Aon's," Vjo provided. "Dtu and Kamira will take smaller groups to the side to avoid being outflanked by the warlock. The House of Words shall join alongside Flames, and Fate alongside Moons."

Edu nodded and then took one of the two stones inside the city and placed it at Kamira's.

Vjo let out a thoughtful hum. "Yes, you're right, Edu. Lyon will likely seek Kamira out on the battlefield."

"Good," Kamira said with a flash of teeth. "If he does not find me, then I will do the same instead, I promise you that. It's best if we fight during the sunlight hours. He and the rest of the House of Blood will be weaker then."

Edu nodded. They would attack during the day.

"What about me?" Lydia asked as she watched the scene unfold. She felt entirely out of place standing here with them. They had all been through wars before. She very much hadn't. It wasn't that she was afraid. Not of the fight, anyway. Fearful of the King of All? Yes. But she still felt like she had no business being in a real war.

Edu picked up the last stone—the one representing Aon—and placed it opposite Edu and Vjo's at the main army.

"Aon will not enter until later in the fight, very likely. He will let his undead and those in his House do the first part of the battle for him," Vjo said for Edu, who nodded.

He then took Lydia's stone away from her and put it down opposite the King of All's. "You must save your strength for when that happens," Vjo continued for him.

Edu moved his own marker close in toward Lydia's and the King of All's. "If he is distracted with you and your creatures, it may create the opportunity Edu will need to take the warlock down. It is the only hope of felling him."

Lydia nodded. It was a good plan. It might work.

Gee, hadn't she just said that to herself recently?

"Looks like I'm the bait again," Lydia grumbled.

* * *

The sunlight would be beautiful if it did not sting his eyes so terribly. Lyon stood behind his King on the balcony of his throne room. It overlooked the city and its winding streets of rock and monuments, peppered with palm trees and grassy reeds. The river sprawled out before them in the near distance, shining and reflecting the light as the eclipse ended. The eerie darkness slipped away as the disk moved out from obscuring it.

The King of All held out his arms as if to greet the light as it washed over him. Lyon felt no such impulse and instead turned his head away and winced in the sun.

"I do not know how much benefit I will be in this fight, my lord," Lyon said to the other man.

"Do not trouble over it. The light will play no factor in today's glory," the warlock responded. He was not surprised that his King had a scheme in mind. Lyon let out a small breath through his nose as the heat of the sun washed against him. He was forced to take another step into the shadows to retreat from the pain.

"You seem... quite pleased this morning, my lord," Lyon observed.

"Indeed I am. And why should I not be? Today, I will finally rid this world of Edu and the others. By the morrow, my queen will have come home."

"You plan to destroy Edu, Vjo, and Dtu?" Lyon's eyes went wide. At his sound of surprise and dismay, the warlock turned around to shoot him a dark glare. It was not his place to question. "Forgive me." Lyon put his hand across his chest and bowed. "It is your right to do as you wish."

"You would counsel against it."

"I will mourn to see them gone from this world. They have been here so very long."

His King let out a small sigh.

The Priest could not help but wince as the King of All placed a hand on his shoulder. Lyon had expected a blow.

"I should not judge you so harshly. To them, you were a friend for eons. You do not know how young they really are. To me, they are nary much older than you. I walked these sands for countless thousands of years with no one else. Tens of thousands, my friend, I walked alone before the Ancients saw fit to fetch Edu and the others."

Lyon could not truly understand the depths of what his King was saying. Even he in his advanced years could not really wrap his mind around all that time spent with no one else. No wonder he was so desperate for a companion. He had spent more time in solitude than his own original people of Earth had even known what it meant to have language and words of their own. When they were little more than scattered apes who feared the skies.

"I will destroy Edu and the others who stand against me this day. They will not tolerate my rule, no matter how succinctly I display to them that they have no hope of overturning me. Others will be gifted the mantle of their required stations, just as you took over for that idiot child Rxa."

Lyon nodded and said no more on the subject. He would accept the will of his King as law. Still, it broke his heart to think of the deaths of those he once served. The world would be somehow lesser in the others' absences, but the necessary change of this new world did not come without loss.

His own heart twisted for what he may need to do when he faced down Kamira on the battlefield. She could not understand the peace he felt in his soul for his service to the Ancients and the rightful King who stood before him now. Lyon hoped he could convince her. Prayed he could make her understand and join him.

There was a higher chance of convincing a fire not to burn. If his wife could not be persuaded... his instructions were quite clear. She was to die. His King offered to do the deed to spare him the torment of ending Kamira's life if it came to that, but Lyon had politely refused.

If Kamira were to die, it would be by his hand. He would have it no other way.

Even if it may destroy what was left of his aching heart to do so.

* * *

Lydia stood at the back of the legions upon a dune, watching the rows of men, women, and shifters in every form march forward. It had taken them the better part of two days to get from the caves back to the city. Moving small numbers of people quickly was easy—larger numbers like the thousands they marched with? Much harder.

The sun was bright, and it was shortly after the eclipse had ended that they decided to approach the edge of the city the

King of All called home. His forces were already there... and in much higher numbers than theirs.

She tried not to let the hopelessness tug at her. Five thousand versus what looked like fifteen or twenty. She didn't really know. She always lost when she had to guess how many pieces of candy were in the jar. But she knew for certain that her "enemy" had far—*far*—more soldiers than they did.

Their only hope was that they had the two Houses that were most accustomed to battle—Edu's and Dtu's. Those two men alone would rip through hundreds of Aon's undead and shuffling creatures without breaking a sweat. The fight might be more even than it looked.

They fought in broad daylight to weaken those men and women who had inspired so much of the vampire mythology of her own world.

She herself had landed in her enormous snake form. Shifting in and out of being a giant winged snake was still bizarre, and she had become a human again by winding up in a pile of limbs on the sand. Kamira had howled in laughter and tried to give her pointers on how to make it look more graceful next time.

Now, she stood on her own, looking down at the crowd. She wasn't supposed to approach the fight until Aon showed up and entered the fray. The warlock hadn't been a front lines kind of fighter. Nobody knew what to expect from him now that he was... whatever he was now. Slave to the gods. King of All. *Whatever.*

Edu stood at the head of the main body of their forces, and he wasn't easy to miss even from a distance. He was a tank in his battle armor, looking like a beetle with his giant horns against the sand.

Lydia remembered how terrified she had been of him the first time she saw him. So much had happened since she ran away from Edu that first night—since she put a bullet in his brain in a sad attempt to escape. And like all her escape plans, it had been futile. This world just tugged her along by the wrist, no matter how much she fussed or fought.

Why did she think this was any different?

Who'd have ever guessed she'd be standing here like this, about to join Edu in a battle against the man she loved?

Screw this world sometimes, seriously.

Lydia let out a long, dreary sigh.

"What is the matter?"

Lydia squeaked in surprise and whirled. Someone was standing too close to her, and as she turned to lash out and attack the source of the familiar voice, he caught her wrists easily in his hands.

The King of All stood there watching her with a faint smile on his face.

She froze, unsure of what to do. He wasn't supposed to be here! This wasn't part of the plan!

Seeing her wide-eyed moment of terror, he chuckled and raised her palm to his face and placed a kiss against it, warm and slow. "You are so beautiful when you are afraid," he said in a rumble and stepped closer. He kept her wrists in his hands but lowered them to her sides. "I came to wish you the best of luck. I came to tell you how eager I am to face you on the field of battle, once and for all."

"I—I—" she stammered uselessly.

He let go of her wrists and raised his hands to cup her face. She flinched away at first, but he shushed her. His touch, even with the metal gauntlet, was soft and unaggressive. He didn't seem here to hurt her.

She couldn't help but hold her breath as he leaned in and placed a kiss against her lips. It was a far cry from the way he had kissed her when they last met in the waking world. This one was tender, and she felt echoed within it a kind of aching loneliness that cracked her heart.

Even in his kindness, he was cruel. When he broke the kiss, he placed another against her forehead. "I also came to say that I love you."

"Damn you," she hissed as she pushed back from him. He was watching her with a mild smirk at her reaction. Tears stung her eyes, and she barely willed them not to fall. "To come here, to do that to me? Do you think I'm going to betray them now?"

"That was not my intention." He simply shrugged. "Quite the opposite, indeed. I simply did come for a kiss and to wish you good luck."

"Go away, *Aon*." She snapped his name at him pointedly. He chuckled again and sighed resolutely as if dealing with an angry child. "Don't you have a war to fight? You'll be down the vampires, after all."

"Hm?" The King of All turned and looked over at the armies below them. They were hundreds of feet away and all utterly oblivious to his presence on the wrong side of the battlefield. "Ah, yes. Oh, and a clever plan, fighting me in broad daylight to weaken Lyon and his House. A shame, really..." The warlock trailed off as he reached his black metal prosthetic up toward the sun. He closed his fist, and all at once—like someone clicking off a light switch—the light was gone. "It was so utterly futile."

She gasped and drew back, staring up at the sky in horror and awe. The disk that blotted out the sun in an eclipse every night was back.

But this time it had merely appeared there, fully formed.

He smiled at her, and when he reached out to touch his fingers against her cheek, she staggered away from him. "You really are so stunning like this..."

She heard a roar from below. It was the sound of thousands of people shouting. She turned her gaze away from the eclipsed sun and down to the battlefield. The armies were now charging at each other with his side leading in the confusion of the sudden disappearance of daylight.

"I should go." His smile turned into a faint, triumphant grin. "As you pointed out, I do have a war I must attend to. I believe I will start by finally burning the marks from that cretin Edu and sending him to the void."

"*What?*" She went wide-eyed. He couldn't be serious.

"You march in a war against me. Edu would not allow me to live if he succeeded in felling me. You know this." When she flinched, he smiled sadly. "Ah, yes. You will ask me to spare them, won't you? Even though they would not pay me the same courtesy?"

Yeah. She was going to do exactly that. "Don't kill them. Please."

"You already know the fee. You have planned this all out already. But not until I have beaten them—and you—and shown you all the futility in your actions." The King of All took a step back from her and bowed at the waist. "I will see you shortly, my love." And with that, he disappeared in a swirl of black smoke.

There was only one word for this, she decided.

"*Fuck.*"

EIGHTEEN

When the sun blotted out from the sky, Kamira couldn't honestly say she was shocked. The warlock was a trickster and would use every ounce of his strength to upend the playing field. He knew that in a war of tooth and claw, he would undoubtedly lose. The warlock would have to play dirty to win.

Kamira let out a roar, her form that of the tiger-esque beast she preferred. The creatures of rotted flesh and bone posed no threat to her. She tore through them like paper and returned them to the chaff that they were. The men and women in black and white bore more of a challenge, if but barely. The soldiers who stood behind her were tearing through them all with little resistance.

That was until the figure in white appeared with his own commanders at his back. Kamira let out another roar at the man she knew so very well, challenging him to a battle.

Lyon.

Her beloved.

And once more her prey.

He gestured, his arms growing over with the gold armor she had seen him wear so infrequently in years past.

Lyon was not an aggressive man by trade, but he was a vicious competitor when it came to it. It would not matter. Kamira *would* win. She took two steps toward her husband and let her form shift back to her humanoid one.

It was clear he had instructed his people to leave her to him, as the men and women in white garb tore after her own army. She did not dare watch to see how the fight was going without her. She had to drown out the chaos around her as she kept her eyes locked on the challenge at hand.

"Stand down, lover," she shouted at him over the fray of the fight.

"Would that I could," he responded coldly. "Surrender, I beg you. Spare us both this pain. You have no chance of winning this fight."

"It isn't about victory, you idiot." She laughed as she stepped toward the Priest. "It's about knocking some sense into you." The markings on his face had changed. Lydia had spoken the truth—he was indeed the King of Blood now. She felt some pride in his new stature. He had always deserved to rule. She wished she could celebrate his ascension. Now, it might mean her downfall.

In their sparring matches—sexual or otherwise—she had always been able to best him. He was always reserved, always resigned. For a vampire, he rarely let his bloodlust get the better of him.

But now? With those marks of white adorning his pale features? The ones she wished to kiss, not claw?

She wasn't so sure.

He sighed and shook his head. "Please. Come with me. Take my hand and let me take you to see the altar of those gods we serve. Let me set you free of all this." He held out the gold talons of his hand toward her.

"It's not that I am not enticed, husband," she said with a fiendish grin. "But the smell of your blood tempts me more!"

Leaping at him, she was fully ready to tear him to pieces, her form changing in mid-air back to the enormous tiger. The fight was fast, it was brutal, and both bled.

It was chaos in the battlefield, several others in their duels staggering into the way.

At one point, she hurled him through the crowd, paving a trough in the carnage with the man's body. He had grown stronger in the fifteen hundred years since they had last dueled in earnest. Either by the benefit of time or his newfound kingship, it did not matter.

She had her work cut out for her.

Each time they faced off, he asked once more for her surrender.

Each time, she refused.

Time and time again, for what may have been half an hour or more, they dueled to a stalemate.

This last time, he pushed himself up from the ground, his clothing bloody, torn and dirty from their fight. She was as equally scuffed, and she had several matching gashes cut into her flesh from his golden talons.

"Enough of this." He sighed darkly. He gestured his hand, and chains, gold and shining, shot up from the ground. Startled, she jumped back, but it was too late. She was trapped. The chains cinched around her, dragging her to the ground. The golden links bound her power. She knew this trick well.

It seemed as Lydia had gained Qta's gifts, so Lyon had learned Rxa's.

"I am sorry, my love," he said as he walked up to her. "I did not wish to resort to this. I hoped I could convince you to surrender."

Shifting her form to her human one, she tried to escape before the chains could catch back up to her as her body shrank. But she only made it a few feet before more tangled her up in their grasp and she fell hard to the ground.

"I will never surrender to you or the Ancients!" She snarled, baring her teeth at the vampire. At the man she loved so very much, now left warped and twisted with strange loyalties.

"Then you must die."

Now, that made her laugh. Not at that she did not believe he meant his words—but for precisely the opposite reason. She believed he meant to do it! And it was for that reason she found herself darkly amused at the way this world had played itself out. *Lyon*, her sympathetic, bleeding-hearted sap, turned cold executioner.

"Oh, what they have made of you, my love—" Still, she laughed. "I wish you could see it."

Damn the Ancients to the pits of any hell for what they had wrought.

He rolled her onto her back and peeled the mask from her face, tossing it aside. He lifted his golden claw, as though he meant to tear off the marks on her face and render her unto the void.

"Surrender. Please, my love."

"Never." She smiled up at him.

"Then you bring this on yourself."

Never would she beg for pity. If she died, she would be happy to greet oblivion by Lyon's hand. "Do it." Still, she smiled, grinning up at her pale executioner. The man she loved more than anything. "Do it!"

* * *

It was not long before the King of All arrived at the battlefield. Good. Edu was impatient, tearing through his useless army and spawnlings. It was not a valuable or enjoyable fight, merely a waste of time. He cut through them like weeds and found it just as entertaining.

When the sun had blinked from the sky, hidden behind the

disk that eclipsed it, he was irritated but not surprised. Aon would not fight on the open field without an advantage, and this granted Lyon and his kin a reprieve from the light.

Finally, his foe appeared in the chaos, standing across from him.

Edu recognized the man, if but from his memories of the old days. Dressed like an ancient god, dark and unmasked eyes flashing in a hungry superiority. No mask obscured his face. And for the first time in five thousand years, Edu saw the face of the man he despised and feared more than any other in this or any other world.

It had not been Aon.

It had been *him*.

Edu could feel the chains that had kept him bound as a slave, whispering at him as though he wore them once more. Turning to face him, he hefted his sword to point the tip of it at the warlock, challenging him to a fight. If the King of All accepted, Edu would win. Not a single soul—*not once*—had ever bested him in fair single combat.

There was little hope of the King of All ever fighting fair. He never had, not even then. The faint, amused smile on his face belied this time would be no different.

"Hello, Edu," the warlock greeted him, ignoring the warrior's challenge. "I would ask you how you are, but... you cannot respond, can you? The Priest told me that I took your tongue one day, long ago." He looked down at the gauntlet on his hand, turning it over, debating the metal and clawed prosthetic that replaced his own flesh. "I must admit I do not remember doing so. It suits you, though. You were so irritating when you could speak."

Edu snarled in response and took a step toward the King of All, who did not seem to care.

"Always so immature. So childish. I see you have not grown much in the past five thousand years that I spent as a shattered and broken shell of a man." The King of All simply sighed.

Impatiently, Edu stormed toward him and swung his blade, but it passed through empty air.

"Petulant once more," his foe said from where he reappeared, some ten feet away.

Edu growled as he lunged toward the man only to have him disappear and reappear again.

"Oh, will you take a moment to converse with me? I am trying to catch up with an old *friend,* after all." The King of All laughed. "Ah! Yes, forgive me. Once more, I forget you cannot speak on your own. Allow me to help you."

Once more, he disappeared and reappeared farther from Edu, and this time he was not alone.

Ylena was on her knees before him, arms bound behind her back.

Edu hitched in his steps as he had already been intending to attack the warlock.

But now, the King of All had a hostage.

Edu felt his jaw clench tight, and he balled his fist up at his side.

No, his foe would *never* fight fair.

"Let her go!" Ylena shouted, her sense of singularity gone in his overwhelming emotion.

The King of All chuckled, looking down at the woman at his feet. She was bruised but seemed otherwise unharmed. Her mask was removed, revealing the red ink that decorated the woman's beautiful features. "*Fascinating.* It seems she can hear your thoughts and emotions just as the Priest claimed. I wonder, does it go both ways?" He dug his claws deep into Ylena's shoulder, sinking in up to the first knuckle of each finger. "Do you feel her pain?"

Edu grunted and could not help but spasm as he felt the cuts as if they were his own. No, worse than that, he knew the pain as Ylena felt it. If the injury were genuinely painted on his skin, he would not feel the agony that made her cry out as she did. Edu was no stranger to pain. Ylena, on the other hand, did not have his resolve. She was no warrior. Her pain tore at Edu as though he were a young boy.

Ylena was still crying out in pain as the King of All sank his claws in deeper, ripping into her flesh. Edu twitched, and the overwhelming stabbing feeling almost brought him down to one knee.

"What a revelation..." The King of All let out a breath, his intrigue showing clearly. "You do not just feel her pain. You feel it as *she* experiences it. And here, when I thought I could never find a new way to teach you pain." He laughed as he ripped his claws out of Ylena's shoulder and with a foot against her back kicked her forward to fall face down, unable to stop herself with her arms behind her back. Blood poured from her wounds and pooled beneath her into the sand.

The King of All put a knee on her back and sank his claws into her rib cage, tearing through flesh and bone like it was nothing. He grabbed one of her ribs in his hand and yanked, snapping and tearing it free from her body.

Ylena was screaming, and the sensation of her agony in Edu's mind brought him down, collapsing to his knees in a cold sweat. *Was this what it was like to feel pain as others do?*

The King of All did not laugh. Did not gloat. Did not mock their agony. He simply directed Ylena as though he were cleaning a fish. As though this were some task that were required of him.

Edu tried to push himself up to standing, but the King of All lifted his hand, and Edu felt something sharp pierce through his chest.

A spike of black metal had risen from the ground and gone through him like a javelin. When he did not fall, his foe sent ten more to join it. Now, Edu knew he would die as he felt the metal split through him. The pain of his own mixed in with that from his suffering empath, and it was too much. Edu sank to his knees once more.

"Stay put now, if you would be so kind." The King of All reached down and twisted his human hand into Ylena's hair, fisting it and yanking her bloody and broken body up to her knees. The woman was barely conscious, her grasp of it threadbare at best. "If you feel her pain as she does, I wonder how you will experience her death?"

Edu let out a scream as black claws tore through Ylena's face. Ripped the soulmarks from her flesh and painted her face in a different kind of crimson than the mask she had worn for so long.

Without them, she could not survive her wounds.

Without them, she was mortal.

"I have suffered your insolence for far too long. Your stubborn adherence to this childlike need to *spite* me. It ends here, Edu. I tolerated your games when I had nothing to lose. But you took her from me once before—I will *never* let you take her from me again!" The King of All finally showed real emotion. And it was *rage*.

Edu's head spun, and he felt weak. He felt as though something had sundered him in half. As if his heart had been torn out of his chest, or perhaps as though half his soul were shredded from him.

The King of All dropped Ylena's lifeless form to the sand that hungrily swallowed the blood that pooled upon its surface. Edu felt as though he would join her. He slumped against the spears that kept him pinned, his strength sapped. His soul empty.

The warlock approached him with a disgusted grimace upon his features. He reached out his gauntleted hand and unlatched Edu's helm from his armor. Uncaring for the pain it brought him to do so improperly, he tore Edu's mask from his face and tossed it and his horned helm away. It rolled in the sand, discarded and useless.

Edu knew what he meant by doing this. He knew now he would die. Ylena had merely gone a few moments before him.

The King of All's metal prosthetic burst into black flame. "You burned her heart from her chest. And now, I shall do the same to you."

There was the sound of large wings flapping from over Edu. "Hey, *asshole!*"

The King of All's face twisted in disappointment for a brief second before a gigantic, ghastly snake with turquoise wings crashed down upon the warlock. Giant jaws snapped around his midsection, and with a toss of its head, it hurled the man in black as far as it could.

Unconsciousness was coming for him quickly. He could not help the girl in her plight. But some small part of him was disappointed he would not join Ylena on the other side.

She would have to wait a few more moments.

* * *

Lydia had picked up the King of All in her mouth and chucked him as far as she could—which was weird and, honestly, kind of hysterical at the same time. Nick had tried very hard once to explain to her what "yeet" meant, and she thought she might have just figured it out.

The King of All had hurtled into a sea of battle and disappeared into the mess of limbs and weapons. She had a few seconds to try to understand what she'd just interrupted.

Edu was out. He was trapped in the fake-death that happened to them all, and she had no idea how long it might take him to come back. Ylena, though, was another matter. There would be no coming back for her.

Lydia hadn't arrived in time to save the empath, and her

heart wrenched at her death. She hadn't realized that something was going poorly in the fight with the King of All until it had been too late. He must have used the empath against Edu.

Dirty trick. *Remember who he is. Remember who you're up against.* Neither version of the warlock would have hesitated to use a weakness like Ylena to his advantage, to be fair.

Huh. The King of All had ripped off Edu's mask. *So that's what he looks like.* He was handsome in his own right, if burly and broad, and looked very much like the Vikings she suspected he inspired. Square jaw, stubble, scars, and covered in big red marks instead of tons of delicate small black ones like Aon.

She had stopped the King of All before he could rip off the crimson marks that decorated most of Edu's face. She had arrived in time to stop him, but not to help Edu. That also meant... she was on her own.

Well, shit.

She swung her long tail and cleared a large section of the undead and those in black who were coming too close for comfort. She knocked them back like rubble. It was bizarre, to be so... big. Someday she'd get used to being able to do this. If she lived that long.

Curling herself around Edu's fallen form, she took in a long breath, held it, and... then... breathed turquoise lightning down at the King of All's army. They screamed. Those who didn't fall to the ground, unconscious or dead, ran terrified from her.

Lydia laughed. *Way* too hard.

That was fucking *amazing.*

The sound of clapping caught her attention, and she turned to see the King of All standing a dozen feet away with a proud smile on his face. "Well done, my love! Quite the entrance."

"I'm learning." Her voice was still her own. She knew her jaw hadn't moved when she talked, the same way that Q's hadn't.

Lydia didn't want to tangle with Aon as a giant snake. She

was still too unwieldy, and it still felt so weird. She took Kamira's advice as best she could and tried to predict where her limbs would reappear when she changed back. This time she only staggered a few feet and managed to keep herself upright.

When she looked back to him, his head tilted to the side slightly. It was clear he thought the fact that her bumbling around was immensely adorable. He let her catch her balance, after all. He could have taken the moment of vulnerability and used it against her, but he didn't.

He wanted to fight her, one on one, fair and square.

She couldn't forget what he had just done. What he had been about to do. "You killed Ylena."

"Was that her name? She served a purpose." Seeing the look of disgust on her face, he sighed and shook his head. "You forget how very old I am, my love. You forget how many ants I have seen come and go in my time."

"Is that what we are to you? Ants?"

"That is what they are to me. You are very much more." He took a step toward her. She held her ground, and it inspired him to take a second. He was calling her bluff and seeing where the proverbial line in the sand might be.

"Because I'm a queen?"

"No, because you are Lydia. Because I *love* you. You were worse than an ant, not but a blink of an eye in the past. You were mortal. I sheltered your little life as best I could—but I was too weak, too foolish to succeed." Hands clenching at his sides, she watched as his anger climbed. "I wished to pretend I was a child like them, and I nearly destroyed you for it. I remember holding your corpse, holding your lifeless body—one *he* made real—" He pointed a finger at Edu where he lay in the sand. "—One he sought to make real again!"

"Edu was just trying to protect Under, he didn't understand. I've forgiven him."

"I have not." The King of All snarled.

She took a step back from his anger. She didn't like him enraged. It was scarier than when he was cold and impassive. "I —but the other you—"

"This is the only me! *We are the same man!* And *I* failed you!"

She flinched. "The part of you I met first had nothing to do with what happened. Edu killed me. Rxa tried to destroy me. You did your best."

"I did nothing of the sort!" The King of All was lost to his fury. Not at her, but seemingly at himself and at everyone else. "I was lured into the sense of hope that those puerile cretins would pay me a moment of reprieve. That I may be allowed some shred of happiness. No. They took you from me. *Twice!* I will never allow them, or anyone else, to do it a third time."

"They were manipulated by the Ancients. They're to blame for all this. They rejected me from the pool as a mortal so I could fall in love with you. They told Ziza I had to die. They brought me back like this."

"Edu wanted your death even before you were my mortal. When you were merely a mystery. And what of Rxa? What hand did the Ancients play in his betrayal? The Angel was mortified you kept your power separate from your body. He was aghast you did not serve our Ancients. What hand did they play in that sequence of events?"

"They're controlling everyone and everything. All of this is by their design. It's—it's all scripted." She waved her hands at the world around them. "This is all them!"

"The Ancients did not plant thoughts inside their minds. They cannot do such things." He took a step toward her. "If those worms were as righteous as you now claim, they would have fought against the manipulations of our creators as you do now."

She cringed. Damn it all, she hated when he was right.

"You see?" The King of All finally got close enough to her

that she had to take a step back. He smiled at her admission that she was afraid of him, and he stopped his approach. "You were a threat to them. A threat to their wish to see me miserable. How long before Dtu made an attempt on your life, even if Rxa had not?"

"This isn't right. Please, we can set things straight. We can try to put things back the way they were."

He laughed and looked up at the eclipsed sun that hung overhead. "My love, don't you see? That version of me sacrificed all he held dear to protect you. The man you want to bring back destroyed the world so he could ensure you would never be harmed again. Even through the madness that consumed me, I knew what I had to do to save you, once and for all. Why would I ever go back?"

"Because it's wrong. Because you aren't the real you anymore."

The King of All vanished in the blink of an eye. She whirled, positive he was going to appear behind her. But he predicted even that, and as she turned, he still managed to catch her, wrapping one arm around her throat and the other over her waist, pulling her back flush against his bare chest.

"The *real* me? By whose measure? I walked this world for tens of thousands of years as the man you now behold. The fever dream you knew was only a month's stretch of time in comparison. You claim the illness was preferable? Why is he *real* and I am *false*?"

She fought the urge to squirm in his grasp but lost. She tried to twist away from him, but he only growled low in his throat and tightened his grasp. Not threateningly, but because he clearly enjoyed the sensation. "Because he wasn't being mind-controlled by a bunch of angry puddle monsters."

"You think I am their puppet."

"You said you were their slave."

"We all serve them. Even you. You argue against the tides of the ocean, of the movements of the sky itself."

"I won't give in. I won't surrender."

"You will in time. Everyone does."

He nuzzled her head, smelling her hair. Her stomach twisted into a knot, and she felt a sudden warmth seep through her. Damn him for always being able to pull her strings. "I won't lose hope."

"Hope of what?"

"That I might get through to you."

"You fight, for you think you can still win a freedom that cannot be found. You will never be free. Not of this place—not of the Ancients—and certainly not of me." He leaned his head in toward her ear and kissed the spot where it joined her cheek. "Look at the war around us. Do you hear the cost of your supposed freedom? My world is simpler. My world is honest. There will be no deceit to haunt you, no traitors lurking in the wings."

"That doesn't make it *right*."

"Righteousness. Peh. I had the desire to kill them all, you know. I wished to wipe this whole world away and leave only you and I to dwell within it. Friends and foe alike, I wished to send them all back to the void." He kissed her cheek again, holding her tighter against him.

Cold fear ran down her spine at his words. "Why? Why would you do that?"

"I need only you. You make me whole. They are but distractions, rabble, and noise."

She struggled in earnest now, trying to break free of his grasp. "You can't!"

He laughed, and his arms tightened, now pinning her painfully against him. "Have I done the deed?"

"What?"

"Did I make good on my desire?" He sounded as though he

were trying to talk a child into eating their spinach. "Do we live upon this world as the only two souls?"

"No." It was stating the obvious.

"Why? Why do you think I let them all live?"

"I'd hate you if you did."

"You would forgive me in time. Perhaps it may take a year, a hundred, or a hundred thousand, I do not know. But you forgave me for the death of your friend in a matter of weeks. You would forgive me for this deed as well."

She elbowed him as hard as she could in the side. "That's different! You didn't kill Nick because you were annoyed by him."

Her blow only made him laugh louder. "I might as well have, so weak were my reasons. But do not change the subject. Your hatred is not the reason they all still live. What could it be?"

"I don't know!"

"You know me, though. Think."

"I don't *know* you. That's the problem. I don't know who you are anymore!"

Sighing heavily, he whirled her around in his arms, twisting her to face him without letting her go. The hand that had been around her throat now grasped her chin, keeping her face turned up to his. "*I am the same man.* That which you knew was but my shadow. Now, you see the whole. You know me, Lydia. Why would I let them all live?"

There was a horrible kind of desperation in his eyes, a pleading need for her to believe him. To *see* him. She was trying. But the coldness, the darkness that loomed in his eyes was scaring her. "I... don't know."

He sighed, defeated. "Because their presence makes *you* happy. Because you care for Lyon, and Evelyn, and all the others. I let them all live for that it *pleases* you to have their company."

He was still a madman. Just a different kind of one. "That's... that's too much power for anyone to have."

"I am the *King of All!*" Letting her go, he half shoved her away from him, his face twisted into a mask of anger before schooling his expression back to one of stone-like calm. "I could beat you down, pin you to the sand, and stake my rightful claim to you this moment. I could destroy them all. I could wipe every miserable life off this sand, but I do not. I let this farce continue—all for *you*. For love of *you*."

She summoned her spear to her hands. "I won't let you hurt them."

"You will try, I am sure."

Narrowing her eyes at him, she relied on her anger to push her fear away. This was going to be a pointless fight. It always had been, from the very start. From the moment she woke up with that thing on her arm, it had always been useless. But it had never stopped her from trying. "You said you wanted to fight me. I'm sick of talking. Shall we?"

"Yes, please," he answered, holding his arms out to his sides, inviting her to start the dance. "I would love little more."

This time, she felt far more prepared. Far more ready for what she was going to face against the warlock. This time, she could predict him just a little bit better. As the fight went on, she was surprised she kept her ground. It was fast, it was brutal, and he was landing hits, but so was she. Not to mention, she had creatures of her own to wield against him. Each time she created monsters from nothingness, he was forced to take them on instead of her, leaving her able to get in close to attack him.

Bats, snakes, her weird shadow-monsters, lizards—hell, even giant undead goats—she pulled from the well of her mind everything she could throw against the man. He, to his credit, did not use anything but his own magic against her.

She had to retreat quickly as the ground exploded in black spikes, each one lancing out toward her. She was learning how fast she could move and how easy it was for her to jump over them or off them. It was amazing what adrenaline could inspire you to do.

It was a dizzying flurry of wings, of nails, of black fire and iron spikes. Of tendrils of dark power that tried to catch her or rip her to pieces. She felt like she might be gaining some ground on the warlock. As he tangled with one of her shadow creatures, she took the opportunity to dig the blade of her spear through his midsection.

The King of All grunted and looked down at the object buried in his body and gripped the wooden shaft with both hands.

She froze, unsure if she had just... won the fight. *Did I actually just kill him?*

The hope was short-lived.

The smile that he paid her was one of almost explicit pleasure. "Good girl." He disappeared, leaving her spear behind, bloody but with nothing else to show for her success.

He reappeared behind her, and she felt the rake of his claws against her back. She hissed in pain and swung her spear, and he caught it in his human hand. He was breathing heavily, and so was she. The fight had been abject chaos and hard for even her to track, and now that she took stock, they were both battered and bleeding.

This time she had managed to *actually* hurt him. The wound in his side was healing but slower than she had seen from him in the past. She had tired him out, maybe even just a little.

"I think I have seen enough." His voice was cold. Her spear exploded into black flame, and she had to toss it away from her to keep from going up in flames with it. The fire had burned her, and she hissed in pain and staggered backward.

In her distraction, she had not seen him blink away. Suddenly, he was at her back. He banded an arm around her waist and yanked her flush against his chest. His metal claws were around her neck, holding her still. One move and he could tear her whole throat out.

"As diverting as that was, we are now once more back to where we began. Now. Be still." When she began to summon the power to teleport away, he tightened his grip dangerously. "Ah-ah. None of that. It is over. You were glorious. Absolutely *astounding*. Such a quick study. Were it but us on this field... I would have done this with you for *hours*. But we are not alone, are we? I fear while we raged on, your revolt has ended."

He was directing her to look out at the battle, and as she did, her heart sank into the sand at her feet. She had been so caught up in her fight with the warlock, she hadn't even looked to see what had happened.

It was utter desolation. All of those in red, in green, in purple and blue were either lying dead on the ground or gathered together in clumps on their knees.

She knew it had been inevitable. But faced with the reality of it, it still hurt and twisted in her gut like a knife.

They had lost.

"Edu has fallen. Dtu and Vjo are my prisoners. Lyon has defeated Kamira. Without your leaders, your paltry army has crumbled. The survivors beg for quarter and mercy. It is over," he whispered to her, his face close to her ear. His breath was warm against her, and she shifted in his grasp. He chuckled at her response to him, even now.

She tried to turn her head away from the view, but he shifted his grip from her throat to her chin and forced her to look at the bloody sight. "You didn't fight fair," she ground out. "Edu could have taken you down."

"Oh, yes, most certainly, if I was foolish enough to face him one on one." The King of All placed a kiss against her temple. "There is no such thing as fairness upon the field of war. Only victory and defeat. Now... you have a bargain to make, don't you?"

Cringing, she felt like he'd just knocked the wind out of her. She knew this was inevitable. She knew they were going to lose, deep down inside. But how she had *hoped* that they might have pulled off an underdog win.

Fuck *hope*.

He turned her around in his arms until she faced him, pulling her flush against his body. There was no escaping him. He caught her chin in his clawed hand and tilted it to face him, clearly wanting to watch her expression.

The feeling of his body against hers was enough to make her swallow a lump in her throat. Damn it all, he really was like a drug to her. Just being close to him made her want to melt against him and beg him to never stop. But she had a job to do. "Let them go. All of them. Ini, Vjo, Edu, and all the rest. Let them walk away from here. Let them go to the horizon and find somewhere quiet and far away from here. Somewhere they can find a new way to live in this world."

He smiled, thin and triumphant. "That is quite the request. What do you bargain in return?"

"You know what."

"I would still have you say it."

Unable to meet his gaze, she focused on one of the marks by his neck. "Me."

"I already have you." He chuckled. "You will not leave the city now unless I allow it. You are my prisoner in chains, if I wish it."

Shaking her head, she prayed she had read this whole situation right. There was a chance that he pulled the rug out from under her and told her "too bad, you're my prisoner *and* they all die." She could only *hope* that he hadn't been lying to her.

Swallowing down the lump in her throat, she put her cards

on the table. "I'd be your willing prisoner. I would—I would be here to... try to love you, my—my King."

He tipped her chin up to look at him, then let his hand trail back to her shoulder. She shivered at his touch. At the hunger and the darkness in his eyes. "You will stand willingly at my side. You will open your heart to me. You will not seek to escape or conspire against me."

She nodded.

"I will not ask you to be my bride just yet. I will not ask for your heart or your mind to be mine. It would be a lie. But in so much as you would promise to *try*..." He looked over her to the battlefield and to the bodies that were strewn about. He took a step back from her, and for a moment she was terrified he would say no.

"Very well," he said with a shrug. "I have shown them how pointless their resistance truly is. Let them scatter to the winds and make their paltry homes and live their meaningless lives. Besides... I have what I came here for."

She really wanted to punch him in his smug face. She had proposed this. Even if he had predicted it, it had been her idea. And it meant that he would spare everyone else. "They all go free. All of them. Swear it."

"You have my word. Well, save for one." The King of All looked off thoughtfully. "I fear Lyon and Kamira have had a charming reversal of fate."

It took a moment to realize what he was saying. Then she remembered the story that Kamira had told her about how she and Lyon had met on the battlefield when she had taken Lyon as a prisoner.

"That's... fine." She ran a shaking hand through her hair. Kamira could take care of herself, and she wasn't worried about the two of them. Lyon would never hurt her, mind-controlled or not.

Or at least, she really didn't think so.

"Good. Now, take my hand, my sweet starlight. I tire of this place." It was a command. He held his hand to her, metal palm up. It was clear he was used to giving missives.

This had been the deal. She reached out and put her hand in his clawed metal gauntlet. He closed it around hers and drew her in. It was a gentle pull, making her step forward of her own volition.

She moved close to him, and he wrapped his arm around her once more, zeroing the distance and pressing her up against his chest.

He hovered his face close to hers, threatening to claim her lips with his but hesitating. "You belong to me, Lydia. You always have, since the moment the Ancients chose you. Since the very night I laid eyes on you, I knew I had to have you. Tell me once more that I am your King. Tell me you wish for me to take that which is rightfully mine. Even, if for now, it is a lie..."

One of his arms banded around behind her, drawing her flush against him. Her heart was racing as desire welled in her. He might not have her heart, but it was so easy for him to prove what parts of her mind and body were well and truly his.

Her words were breathless when she gave him what he wanted. Maybe what they both wanted. "Take what's yours, my King of All."

As his lips descended upon hers, the world around her melted away.

And she knew the last real fight of her life would truly begin.

A LETTER FROM KATHRYN

Dear reader,

I want to say a huge thank you for choosing to read The Masks of Under series. This was my first series I ever officially published out into the world—and the tale of Lydia, Aon, and all the rest will forever be near and dear to my heart.

If you'd like to stay in the loop for all my future series and releases, just sign up at the following link. Your email address will never be shared and you can unsubscribe at any time.

www.secondskybooks.com/kathryn-ann-kingsley

There are several kinds of writers out there in the world—those who are happy to tell their story to a blank page, and those who thrive on hearing about how their readers engage with their tales.

I'm the latter.

I absolutely love hearing from my readers – you can get in touch through social media, my website, or even join my Discord (the link to join is on my website) to interact with both me and other fans.

Stay Spooky and Happy Nightmares,

Kathryn Ann Kingsley

KEEP IN TOUCH WITH KATHRYN

www.kathrynkingsley.com

𝕏 x.com/vodriel

instagram.com/kathrynannkingsley

PUBLISHING TEAM

Turning a manuscript into a book requires the efforts of many people. The publishing team at Bookouture would like to acknowledge everyone who contributed to this publication.

Commercial
Lauren Morrissette
Hannah Richmond
Imogen Allport

Cover design
BRoseDesignz

Data and analysis
Mark Alder
Mohamed Bussuri

Editorial
Jack Renninson
Melissa Tran

Proofreader
Catherine Lenderi

Marketing
Alex Crow

Melanie Price
Occy Carr
Cíara Rosney
Martyna Młynarska

Operations and distribution
Marina Valles
Stephanie Straub
Joe Morris

Production
Hannah Snetsinger
Mandy Kullar
Jen Shannon
Ria Clare

Publicity
Kim Nash
Noelle Holten
Jess Readett
Sarah Hardy

Rights and contracts
Peta Nightingale
Richard King
Saidah Graham